DIVIDE AND RULE

BOOK TWO IN THE DIVISION BELL TRILOGY

RACHEL MCLEAN

Catawampus Press

catawampus-press.com

Rita turned towards the write screen, her eye deliberately avoiding the camera high in the corner. She pushed back a yawn and laid her fingers on the screen. It sprang to life.

She spun back to the class, forcing a smile.

Twenty nine children – Darius Williams was late, again – sat to attention at four rows of desks. Every one of them was neatly dressed, striped blue tie tucked into the regulation grey shirt. The boys' trousers were grey and neatly fitting, with no scuffed knees or frayed hems. The girls had scrubbed knees lined up under the desks, regulation pleated skirts, all exactly one inch above the knee. Every knee was pink, every neck stretching out from a starched collar was alabaster. This was a model class, an all white class. She, the teacher, didn't count.

"Morning everyone," she breezed. "Welcome to this beautiful sunny Wednesday morning."

The children said nothing. A few coughs. The sound of a pencil case being unzipped.

She pushed at the smile again, willing her face to hide

the longing to be back in bed. She shouldn't have gone to the pub last night. Shouldn't have let Ash stay over.

"So," she said. "Maths books out."

The class did nothing.

"Please."

A hand crept up in the front row.

"Yes, Saskia," she asked, steeling herself.

"Um, Miss Gurumurthy, haven't you – haven't we missed something?"

Rita blinked, holding onto the smile.

"No, Saskia. It's definitely Maths first." She looked up. "Every day, in fact."

There were a couple of polite laughs. Half of the class were looking up at the camera, trying not to let their gaze stay on it for too long. They knew better than to break the fourth wall.

Saskia's hand was still raised, although not as high as it had been. "But the oath, Miss?"

"Now, Saskia. Miss Gurumurthy is my name."

"Sorry, Miss Gurumurthy. But surely—"

Rita took a deep breath. "Don't worry, Saskia. We're going straight into Maths today."

The girl blushed and lowered her hand. Rita heard a muttered *again*.

She lifted her head and frowned. "Who was that?"

Silence. The rows of eyes were off the camera now and directed at the desks.

She turned back to the screen and gave it a swipe. She loved the way it responded to her touch, quick and lively like a lover.

There was a knock at the door. Rita looked up to see the headteacher, Mrs Toft, peering in through the glass. Two dark figures lurked behind her. *Not another school governor visit*, Rita thought.

Rita turned back to the class, knowing she was expected to carry on as normal.

The class lifted books out of desks. The door squeaked open. Rita felt the hairs on the back of her neck rise but didn't turn. She willed herself to relax, her stomach to be calm.

"Good morning, Miss Gurumurthy."

The head's voice was heavier than usual. Rita waited for the habitual *don't mind us* to follow, but there was nothing. She felt her heart accelerate.

Rita turned, plastering her smile on again. It disintegrated as she took in the two men in dark suits standing behind Mrs Toft.

Rita raced through the possibilities. Citizenship classes? Security checks? Darius Williams?

She swallowed. "Good morning, Mrs Toft."

The children behind her were silent. She could picture their open mouths.

The head looked at her hands, which twisted together in front of her. The knuckles were pale and the skin rough.

Rita waited.

"These gentlemen need you to come with them, Miss Gurumurthy."

The headteacher retreated as the policemen stepped forward. One of them unclipped handcuffs from his belt.

A wave rose through Rita's chest. She felt cold sweat break out on her face. Behind her, the children were silent as the grave.

One of the men grabbed her hand. She tensed, pulling away, but he was stronger than her. She looked at the class. Best not to protest, for their sakes.

She felt her bones turn from steel to jelly as the man clamped the handcuff shut and pulled her towards the door.

"Miss Gurumurthy!" a boy shouted. She blinked and turned, her eyes pricking. Gavin McLeish was standing up at the back, leaning over his desk. He looked like he might cry. He opened his mouth to speak again but was silenced by a look from Mrs Toft.

Rita turned to the headteacher.

"Why is this— Did you—?"

But the Head stared up at the wall behind Rita, standing to attention like a good citizen. She stayed there, blinking, as the men led Rita out of the classroom.

CHAPTER TWO

THE PRISON GOVERNOR WAS PLUMP WITH SOFT PINK features and wispy blonde hair that was grey at the roots. She was holding a file, which Jennifer presumed to be hers.

She smiled. "Hello again."

Jennifer closed her eyes. She'd met this woman before. She remembered the hurried trip to the prison, the anxious meeting in the governor's office. An inmate – Hayley Price – had committed suicide, and there had been an outcry. Jennifer's job as prisons minister had been on the line, and so had that of the woman opposite her. Jennifer had saved them both.

She looked at the woman's name badge on the lapel of her pale grey jacket. The jacket needed dry cleaning.

Ms Phipps, it said. *Prison Governor.*

Call me Sandra, she'd said on their first meeting, to which Jennifer had replied *call me Jennifer*. She hadn't though. It was *Minister* all the way.

Things would be different now.

Jennifer considered for a moment.

"Sandra," she said. "Good to see you again."

The governor frowned, her eyes hooded, her cheeks darkening. "Ms Phipps, I think."

Jennifer sighed. "Ms Phipps."

Philips, the guard who'd brought Jennifer here from her cell, stood behind her, hovering at the door. The governor nodded at her.

"Thank you, Philips. You can leave us now."

Jennifer heard Philips mutter agreement then pull the door closed behind her. For once she didn't slam it.

The governor gestured towards the chairs in front of her desk. "Please, sit down."

Four chairs were lined up against the wall behind Jennifer. She hesitated and chose one of the middle two. Sitting on it made her feel low and distant from the governor, shielded behind her desk. She stood again, pulled it closer to the desk and sat down. She wasn't playing any power games.

Ms Phipps placed the file on the desk. "We'll dispense with the pleasantries, I think. You were convicted of harbouring a suspected terrorist." It wasn't a question. But there was still the word *suspected*, at least.

"Yes."

"And you are aware of the current law in this area?"

Jennifer nodded.

The governor smiled again. "Don't worry, Jennifer. This is a good thing, for you."

Jennifer said nothing, unable to imagine how this could be good. She thought of Cindy, waiting for her; would she be back at their cell, or waiting on the landing?

"You may be interested in a development that results from the new laws."

Jennifer pulled herself upright. "Please. Tell me what's happened to my son."

"Why would I tell you that?"

Jennifer frowned.

"Your solicitor is the person you should be asking about that."

"Exactly. I've been promised a visit—"

The governor raised her hand to stop her. "I've got a message to relay to you. I need you to listen."

"What sort of message?"

"That's better. So, going back to the anti-terror laws. They've been very effective. But it's had an impact on the prison population, as you may have noticed. We were already overstretched and this is more than we can cope with."

Jennifer stared at her. What did this have to do with her? "Look, I don't care about prison overcrowding. I'm not exactly prisons minister anymore." Jennifer cocked her head. The governor blushed again and looked down at Jennifer's file. She licked her lips then looked up again.

"I believe you should care even more now you're a prisoner. Anyway, back to what I was saying. A new type of institution has been set up. One which, shall we say, provides a punishment to fit the crime. While also being of benefit to society at large."

Jennifer knew nothing of any new institutions, or of what they might have to do with her. The governor was lying. She'd been an MP only two weeks ago, for heaven's sake. Shadow Home Secretary. She would know about this.

Then she realised. "Please. Let me know when I'm going to see my lawyer. And I still don't know the outcome of my son's trial."

The governor sighed. "Oh, do stop worrying about your son and listen to me."

Jennifer pursed her lips.

"How are you finding it here? On the other side?"

Jennifer shrugged.

"Women accepting you? See you as one of them?"

Jennifer said nothing. For many of her fellow inmates, the last time they'd seen her would have been on a ministerial visit. Many of them would have known Hayley.

The governor didn't need to know about the welcome she'd had. The bruises she could feel on the backs of her legs. The invitation by Cindy, her cellmate, to be her *pet*.

Ms Phipps looked down at another file on her desk. "The legislation allows for people convicted of crimes like yours to be detained in a new facility. No cells, all the latest technology. Almost a hotel, in fact." She looked up, smiling.

"I have no idea what you're talking about."

"No, of course you don't. This hasn't exactly been publicised. Am I not making myself clear?"

The governor leaned forwards. Her tiny eyes were like grey pinpricks in her cushiony face. "What I'm trying to tell you is that you've got a choice. You can be transferred to one of these centres. If you choose."

"I have a choice?"

"Yes. You can either stay here, or be transferred to the new centre. No cells, beautiful grounds, very low security, all high tech." She laughed. "Sounds wonderful to me. You may want to consider it."

"Tell me what's happened to my family."

"You need to make a decision, Jennifer. Do you want this transfer, or not?"

This made no sense. Jennifer had never in all her career heard of a prisoner being given the choice of where they were to be incarcerated. In the US she knew that some states gave death row convicts the choice of how they would be executed, but a choice of prison? In the UK? Never.

"Why do you need me to decide? Surely you can just put me wherever you want."

"I wish it were that simple. A technicality. You were arrested in the Palace of Westminster. It's exempt from the new laws, so we can't just send you there. But you can choose."

Jennifer heard a movement outside, in the corridor. Philips was back. Or she'd been out there all along. She'd seen Philips with Cindy at breakfast, whispering.

"You're wrong," she said. "I'd know about any new law."

"There was no new law. This is covered by existing legislation."

Jennifer shook her head. "I have to speak to my solicitor first."

The governor rounded her desk. "There isn't time."

"Sorry?"

"We're making you this offer now. You won't get it again. There's a van heading to the centre tonight, and you could be on it. If you want."

"So when do I get to speak to Edward?"

"Edward?"

"My solicitor."

The governor waved a hand. "You can worry about that tomorrow." She paused. "You'll like this place. All the creature comforts you're used to. Big old house. In the Oxfordshire countryside. Burcot Park, it used to be called."

Jennifer had visited Burcot Park, attended a function there as a minister. It was beautiful. Why was it being used as a prison?

The governor looked at her watch. "Of course we could just send you back to your cell. It's early still, time for you to catch up with your fellow inmates. A reunion with your friends down there on the landing." She looked up.

Jennifer shuddered, remembering Cindy's voice in her ear. *Come back here, when she's done with you.*

The governor was heading for the door, her tights rustling beneath her skirt. Philips would be outside, waiting. This choice wasn't going to be presented again.

She swallowed.

"Yes. I'll go."

CHAPTER THREE

The city had long since flown past and they were on country roads, hedges blurring outside the window. Rita squirmed in her seat, the policemen chatting in low voices in front. They'd said nothing to her since pushing her into the car outside the school, and she'd said nothing in return.

Why hadn't they taken her to the Rose Road station, just half a mile away from school? She'd had to go there once after a fight between parents in the playground. That had been before the changes, when children – and parents – were expected to mix. When they'd only just started to decide that they preferred not to.

She thought about asking where they were taking her, but decided against it. She'd managed not to speak so far and she wasn't about to start. She knew enough about her situation to understand that there was little she could say that wouldn't incriminate her. Somebody had told the authorities that she'd transgressed, so that was that.

She wondered who it was. One of the children? Even Saskia wasn't that zealous. Maybe a colleague? She was the only teacher who wasn't white, but that didn't seem to bother them. Only a year ago she'd been one of three; the other two women had been encouraged to transfer to the new Muslim school in Perry Barr, the other side of the city. The school felt uncomfortable about her presence but couldn't do much about it. It wasn't as if the Muslim school would offer her a job, not with her Hindu parents.

She pictured the headteacher, standing by the door as she was led out, refusing to look her in the eye. Had *she* said something? They'd had words a month or so ago, a *friendly chat* Mrs Toft had called it. A threat more like. Start reciting the oath every morning with the children, or else. The *else* was never articulated. She couldn't think which law it was that she'd broken, but she knew that specifics weren't always necessary. If they wanted to pin something on you, they would. Bastards. Today they were hounding Muslims and demanding unthinking loyalty, but yesterday it had been gays, or lefties like her, or whoever else was the current scapegoat.

The car slowed but didn't stop. The man in the passenger seat pulled out a map – old-fashioned, she thought – and placed a finger on it. He looked out of the windscreen and pointed at a sign as they passed it. *Burcot Park*. It meant nothing to her.

She pulled herself upright and peered out of the window as they turned a bend. An imposing house appeared ahead of them, at the end of a winding gravel drive. *Nice*, she thought. Someone's country pile. Or maybe not, given that she was being brought here. Some sort of police station, she figured. A lot of them had been moved from small buildings in the city centres to larger premises out of harm's way. She never expected them to look like this.

She stretched her neck and readied herself for the solid

hand that would soon be pulling her from the car. The car stopped at the end of the gravel drive, in front of a pair of ornate double doors. They were in need of a coat of paint, but their stained-glass panes looked antique.

The driver pocketed his keys and turned to her.

"Don't move."

She stared back at him. As if she were going to make a run for it, out here in the middle of nowhere.

He grunted and turned back to his colleague, who was gazing out at their surroundings.

"Nice place."

So this wasn't their normal place of work.

The driver coughed. "Yeah. We haven't got time to goggle though, Bill."

His colleague shrugged and elbowed his door open. Rita stiffened, waiting for him to open her door. Instead he headed away from the car and towards those double doors. He raised a fist as if to knock on them and then thought better of it, using the palm of his hand to push at the heavy wood. The door opened and he looked back at his colleague, grinning. Then he slipped inside.

Rita sighed and chewed a fingernail. These coppers were the most unprofessional pair she'd ever had the pleasure to meet. But their unfamiliarity with the house and its grounds made her nervous. If this wasn't a police station, what was it?

The man emerged through the doors, blushing. He scuttled to the car and yanked his door open, throwing himself into the passenger seat.

"Wrong entrance."

"What?"

"You heard. Got a right grilling. We're to go round the back."

The driver muttered under his breath then turned the ignition. Rita resisted an urge to snigger. The car pulled away.

"Which way?"

The man – Bill, she thought, wondering if he had a family and if they knew what his job involved – pointed in front of them. His face was damp with sweat. "That opening, there. In the hedge."

"How are we bloody well supposed to see that?"

"Shush." He glanced round at Rita. She stared back, blinking. She wasn't about to show how scared she was.

Finally they found the entrance and eased the car around the side of the building. The driveway was narrow here, clearly not designed for guests, and the car brushed against the greenery on either side, each scrape accompanied by a wince in the front.

They stopped in a courtyard at the back of the building. High brick walls surrounded them, empty flower beds at one end, the house obscured by bushes and an elderly oak tree.

The driver jumped out and was opening Rita's door before she managed to compose herself. He reached in and grabbed her arm. His fingers were warm and fat. She grimaced.

"Come on then," he snapped.

She shrugged off his fingers and got out of the car, pulling herself up to her full height of five foot one. The air was cold and thin, missing the familiar tang of pollution. From the grounds away from the house she could hear birdsong and the bray of a horse. Surely the police didn't keep their horses all the way out here?

"Follow me."

She licked her lips and followed. Her hands were still

cuffed and the metal chafed against her skin. She tried to shift her arms in front of her to relieve the pressure but that just made it worse. She looked down to see a red weal forming on her right wrist.

"These cuffs are too tight."

The two policemen stopped and turned to stare at her. She pursed her lips.

"It's inappropriate force. You need to fix it."

The junior one, Bill, raised an eyebrow at his colleague. His colleague let out a heavy sigh and looked around them. There was no-one in sight. They were closer to the building now; high windows glinted in the sunshine. She wondered who was in there. How long they were planning to keep her here.

"Alright." He looked around again, seeming to calculate the distance to the edge of the grounds. It was considerable. He pulled Rita towards him and unlocked the cuffs.

"No running off though."

She shrugged and rubbed her sore wrist. The skin was dented, a long ridge that reminded her of the scar on her leg from when she'd broken it as a teenager. She hoped this would heal quicker.

The man grabbed her other wrist. His colleague went on ahead, disappearing down some steps at the back of the house.

They followed to find an open door leading to a basement or a cellar. She shivered. She didn't like the dark.

She looked at the man next to her again. They'd shown ID, but she'd barely looked at it, she'd been so focused on Mrs Toft's expression and on leaving the children behind.

Were they really police at all?

CHAPTER FOUR

Jennifer sat on the plastic chair, staring at the door ahead of her. It was chilly in this corridor, and sounds echoed towards her from what seemed like miles away. Somewhere out of sight, a conversation was going on between two women. Whether they worked here or were inmates like her, she couldn't tell. She only caught brief snippets – *group, women, drugs*. The drugs bit didn't surprise her – if this place was anything like Bronzefield, there would be plenty being smuggled in.

But this place wasn't like Bronzefield. It wasn't the Burcot Park she remembered, the one with easy chairs, fine food and doors flung open to the gardens. Her welcome, instead of being from a friendly, besuited receptionist, had been from an orderly in a white coat. Roy Dukes, his name badge said.

It lacked the cold, echoing feel of a prison like Bronzefield. Instead of metal and sweat, it smelled of damp and old wood. And it was quiet. There were no radios here, no shouted conversations across landings or through walls. She'd spent one night in a room with two roommates. They were nothing like Cindy. Paula and Mandy, both in their twenties, had whispered nervously between themselves in the night, heads together where their beds met.

Thin, with grey faces and prominent cheekbones, both seemed jumpy, flinching when she'd dropped her shoes on the floor before going to bed. Paula was the dominant one; Jennifer could sense Mandy looking to her for reassurance and calm. In fact, she wasn't sure about Mandy's state of mind. She cried out a few times in her sleep and whimpered for at least ten minutes after waking up. Paula had slid out of bed and held her, rocking her like a frightened child.

The voices along the corridor stopped. A door slammed. It was followed by the hum of a boiler somewhere and the occasional scrape of furniture or feet from the floor above. She wondered what was up there. Whether it still masqueraded as a grand house.

The door in front of her opened and she straightened in her chair. A woman emerged, giving Jennifer a startled look before pushing a lock of greasy hair behind her ear and hurrying away. Her footsteps were quiet as she retreated along the empty corridor.

Jennifer stared at the door, waiting. Finally it opened and a man appeared. He wore a suit – somewhere between expensive and cheap – but no tie. His hair was unkempt, curling around his ears. His eyes were a deep brown, almost black, framed by long eyelashes.

He smiled at her. "Jennifer?"

She nodded.

"Come in."

He stood back and held the door open for her to pass. Inside was a nondescript office. It had a single window high in the opposite wall, at ground level outside, and the walls showed signs of damp. They were mainly bare except for a couple of certificates she couldn't read at this distance and two small photographs of a toddler, blu-tacked to the wall near the desk. The desk itself sat against the side wall, with two chairs arranged diagonally, one next to it and the other facing the wall. An arrangement designed for collaboration, not confrontation.

Without being asked she sat in the chair closest to her, facing the wall. From here she could read those certificates – *Mark Clarke, Psychiatrist* – and see the photos better. They both depicted a small boy with shiny blond hair and blue eyes. In one he was riding a balance bike, grinning at the camera with his legs splayed out wide. In the other he was building a snowman, bundled up in bright yellow snow gear that made her think of Hassan. There was another person in the picture, a hand wrapped around his and the edge of a pink coat. The photograph had been torn to eliminate this person – a woman, she assumed. An ex.

The man took the other chair and smoothed his hands on his trousers. He held out his hand. She shook it, surprised at the gesture.

"Pleased to meet you, Jennifer," he said. "My name's Dr Clarke. But you can call me Mark."

She eyed him, wary that the familiarity could be designed to put her off guard.

"Hello," she replied.

"So," he said. "My job today is to orientate you to the centre. You've already been given your clothes, I see."

She nodded. She was wearing jeans and a t-shirt, clothes she'd been handed in exchange for her prison sweats when she'd arrived. She wondered what had happened to her suit. Was it still in that plastic box, back at Bronzefield?

His eyes crinkled. Trying to be friendly. Maybe it was for real, maybe not. She noticed a scar under his right eye, faded with time. His eye looked alright though – he'd had a lucky escape there.

He noticed her looking and put a finger to the scar, then shook himself out. She flicked her eyes away from it and to the desk. It was littered with dirty mugs and pieces of paper. She glanced at them; memos, scrawled notes. Nothing about her.

"So," he continued. "Let me tell you about the programme."

She put up a hand. "Stop."

He leaned back, watching her.

"I've been promised a meeting with my solicitor."

"Ah. Yes. Well, let me make a note of that and see what I can do."

"I have a right to see my solicitor."

He stiffened. Was she going to see Edward here? Did he even know where she was?

"As I said, I'll see what we can do." He pulled one of the sheets of paper towards him and added another scrawl to it. She wondered if it would get any further.

"And I want to know where my son is. Samir Hussain. No-one's told me when his trial is. Will I be called as a witness?"

His face clouded. "They haven't?"

"No." She dug her fingernails into her palm. *Cooperate,* she told herself. *Don't make a fuss.* People were relying on her.

"I would have thought that the governor at Bronzefield would have—"

"No. She didn't say anything."

"OK. Well in that case I have to tell you that it's already happened. Your son was convicted." He tilted his head.

"What? But how can they—"

He shrugged. "It was fast tracked. All terrorist cases are."

"My son is not a terrorist."

"Terrorist sympathiser. Same thing, as far as the authorities are concerned."

She looked down at her hands. They were trembling.

"I don't imagine it's a surprise to you," he said. "You must be familiar with the legislation."

She was. She'd been a backbencher when it was passed, one of the first of Trask's hardline measures to combat terrorism after he came to power. After defeating her party. A defeat that she, and her stupid bloody principles, had brought about.

The truth was, she'd known since receiving that note from her friend Catherine – *he's under suspicion, a group –* that Samir's trial would be a foregone conclusion.

She felt her insides loosen. She scrabbled through memories of the law, her understanding of what would happen to Samir now.

"Will he be deported?"

"I think you know I can't tell you that."

"Why not?"

"The nature of your son's crimes, and the security implications, means that certain aspects can't be made public." He licked his lips; they were full, with broken skin as if he chewed them regularly. He glanced over her head. She frowned and followed his gaze; there was a camera watching. "I don't know where your son is myself," he muttered. I can't tell you. I'm sorry."

She watched his face, wondering if he was lying. She'd watched so many men lie to her in recent months that she'd lost the ability to tell deceptions from truth. She ran over her memories again, trying to work out what this place was, who this Mark was.

"What is this place?"

He visibly relaxed. "Ah, now that I *can* answer. This is a British Values Centre. Established last September. I expect you know all about it, given your past."

September. She'd still been on the Opposition backbenches, licking her wounds and facing the reality that her colleagues despised her for what she'd done. She'd missed a few votes, dealing with problems at home, hardly caring if the Whips chastised her for it.

"Not really," she said. "Tell me."

"Alright."

He walked to a filing cabinet under the window and pulled out a plain white booklet. He put it on the desk in front of her. The British Values Programme. This was the legislation she'd fallen out with Catherine over. Before the Milan bomb had changed everything.

"I know about this. It's about loyalty to the state. Schools, civil servants. There's a mantra. An oath."

He leaned against the wall, nodding.

"I voted against it," she said.

He laughed. "Of course you did. Jennifer Sinclair, the rebel. Woman of impeccable principles. Brought down your own government."

"It wasn't as simple as that."

"No?"

"No."

This was irrelevant.

"If you can speak to someone and arrange for me to speak to my solicitor I'd be grateful."

"Like I say, I've already noted it. But I need you to read

that leaflet in front of you. It's the British Values Programme, as it applies to you. To everyone in this place."

She picked up the leaflet and opened the first page. *Step 1: admitting that you've been disloyal to your country*. She snorted. There were plenty she'd been disloyal to, but her country wasn't one of them.

"So what do I have to do?" she asked.

"Read that. All six steps. I'll be taking you through them. One at a time. When you get to the third step, your group will support you."

"My group?"

"Other women. Who've committed similar crimes to yours. We work together here, to support each other. To help each other get through the programme, and understand how to atone for our crimes."

"Atone?"

"You'll see."

"And if I cooperate, what will happen?"

He smiled. "You'll pass the programme, of course."

"What does that mean?"

"It means you're released."

Her eyes widened. She flicked through the leaflet. Six steps. And all she had to do was work through each of them and say what they wanted her to. This was easy. Six lies, and she'd be free.

"Does everyone go through this?"

"How do you mean, everyone?"

"Everyone who's been convicted under the anti-terrorism laws."

"You're thinking of your son."

She said nothing.

He sighed. "I think I've made it clear by now that I'm not about to answer that question."

"No." But it gave her hope. If Samir was given this chance too, then he could lie, he could get out. If he was sensible. She'd believed him to be a sensible boy, no trouble, always quietly getting on with his schoolwork. But then there'd been the racist taunts, and the fighting. The truancy. The girlfriend, in the photo Edward had shown her. Meena. Who was she, and how had he met her?

She imagined Samir in a meeting like this, talking to a man like Mark.

She squeezed her eyes shut. She'd have to trust that her son valued his freedom over his anger.

"OK," she said. "I want to do it."

"Of course you do."

"How do I start? What do you need me to say to you?"

"It's not as easy as that."

Her shoulders fell. Of course it wasn't.

"Take that with you," he said, gesturing at the leaflet. "Study it. I'll see you tomorrow, and we can start the process."

CHAPTER FIVE

RITA PEERED DOWN THE STEPS. AT THE BOTTOM, AN open door led to darkness. A vague smell of bleach. The dull tang of stewed vegetables. Not a police station.

Next to her, the policeman checked his watch. "I think you need to go down there."

He pulled his shoulders back and put a hand on her shoulder. She shrugged it off.

"I can do it myself."

"Go on then."

She picked her way down. The steps were bare concrete. To one side was an iron railing running up to ground level. On the other was the red brick of the house. As she descended, the doorway became brighter but the sky above receded. She suppressed a shiver.

When she was halfway down, a man appeared in the doorway. He was tall and gangly, wearing a white coat, like a doctor or a lab technician. Not police. Or maybe forensics? Why did they need forensics?

What might a man in a lab coat do to a person in the basement of a place like this? She stopped walking. The policeman behind crashed into her and cursed under his breath.

The man smiled. On his lapel was a badge. *Roy Dukes, Orderly*. No logo. No sign of what this place was. But at least he was no doctor, no butcher.

"Where am I?" she asked. "Why have you brought me here?"

"Not my job to tell you. Come on."

He turned and started walking, footsteps echoing along what sounded like a long corridor. Curiosity overcoming dread, she went as far as the bottom of the steps, letting her eyes adjust to the gloom.

There was a sound behind her and she turned to see the two policemen above her. One of them raised a hand.

"Bye."

They were leaving her here?

She turned. The orderly was further away now. He'd stopped at the far end of the corridor and was beckoning her to follow. His smile didn't do anything to alleviate an air of menace about the way he held his body. She backed up, almost tripping over the bottom step.

The policeman – the passenger, the one who hadn't been here before – was behind her, grabbing her arm to keep her upright.

"You'll be OK," he breathed. "Don't worry."

She looked at him, eyes wide. She wanted to throw herself on his mercy, beg to be taken away. But he was police.

She nodded and drew in her breath. She turned and walked towards the orderly.

The corridor was flanked by high windows on one side, almost at ceiling height here but at ground level outside. It wasn't as gloomy as she'd thought, but instead was pierced by shafts of light from each of these windows. On the other side were doors, all of which had peeling blue paint.

She picked up her pace and was soon with the orderly. He said nothing but turned to open one of the doors. A ring of keys rattled in his hand.

He stood back to usher her in. She felt a moment's dread – was she about to be locked in here? – but stepped inside anyway. She'd been arrested in plain sight after all, and the due process of the law would apply. This was an interview room or something, somewhere she would be questioned before being released on bail or maybe held overnight if she was unlucky.

She imagined the questions they'd ask. How did it work now, with the new laws? Was she entitled to a solicitor? Or did the speedy process take away that right too?

Either way, she wouldn't let them get the better of her.

Inside the room was a desk. It wasn't the bare table of an anonymous interview room but the desk of a regular occupant. There was even a potted plant. She wondered how it survived in here, then realised it was plastic. Next to it was a pot of pens and a neat pile of notebooks. And in the middle of the desk was a name plate. *Counsellor*, it said. No name. Surely if she was allowed to know the name of the orderly, she would be told the name of her interviewer?

"Take a seat, please," the orderly muttered.

Between her and the desk was a single chair, one of those institutional orange plastic ones with black metal legs that they used at school sometimes. It felt incongruous next to the desk, which was large, wooden and battered, and the chair opposite, which was leather. It too was old, with scuffed arms and pockmarks in the seat back.

She eased herself into the plastic chair, controlling her breathing. She didn't want them to know about her claustrophobia. Maybe they already did; that could be why she'd been brought here.

The orderly left, closing the door behind him. She went to check it. It wasn't locked. She eased it open, peering into the corridor outside. It was empty.

Should she make a run for it? The outside door would be locked. She would never find her way to the front of the building without being caught. A weight fell over her as she closed the door and sat down again. *Good girl*, she muttered to herself.

The room was shifting now, floating as if in a hallucination. She placed her hands on the desk, gripping the worn wood. She closed her eyes and pulled a breath in through her nose, panting it out again. Lion's breath, a yoga technique that always brought her senses back.

The door opened behind her. She turned to see a petite woman in a hijab enter, her face expressionless. She flicked her eyes towards Rita, looking as uneasy as Rita felt.

Rita frowned. Arrested for not reciting the oath and she had a Muslim woman questioning her? Maybe this was a test, a double bluff designed to trick her into saying things she might not to some middle-aged white man. Be careful, she told herself.

The woman rounded the desk and sat down, all but disappearing behind it. She pulled her chair in and placed her elbows on the table, straightening her back to lean her chin on her fingertips.

"Hello, Rita," she said. Her voice was friendly, but that meant nothing.

Rita said nothing.

The woman opened a drawer and brought out a laptop. Bulky and black, it took a while to boot up. Public sector, thought Rita. That was some consolation. The two of them sat in silence while the woman watched the screen, the reflected light on her face brightening as the computer came to life.

She tapped at the keyboard and then closed the lid.

"You might be wondering where you are," she said.

Rita almost laughed. Of course she was bloody well wondering where she was. But she wasn't about to reveal her fear. "Is this some sort of police station?"

The woman's mouth broke into a small smile. "It hardly looks like one, does it?" Her voice was soft and low. Rita wondered how old she was: mid twenties? Young enough to be her daughter, at a push.

Rita leaned forwards. "When do I get a lawyer?"

The woman shook her head. "I'm sorry. You don't."

This may not be a police station, but she'd been arrested by the police, and she knew her rights.

"Who were those men who brought me here?"

"Police officers. Of course."

"So why aren't I in a police station right now?"

The woman licked her lips. "Have you heard of the British Values Act?"

"Yes." It was all they ever talked about in staff training these days. Her job wasn't to teach anymore; it was to brainwash a generation.

"Are you aware of the provisions for people arrested under it?"

Rita frowned. That hadn't been covered in teacher training. She said nothing but felt sweat break out on her upper lip.

The woman continued. "Under the Act, they – we – can keep you here instead of a police station. You'll get a trial, of course." She paused. "Things aren't that bad, yet. But it won't be the kind of trial you expect."

"Why not?"

"There's a process. Appropriate to the nature of your crime."

The woman's eyes flicked around the room again. Rita looked up and realised that there was a camera in the corner, watching her. She craned her neck; there was one facing her interviewer, too.

"You've been accused of disloyalty to the state," the woman continued. "Under the British Values Act. You'll be kept here until your trial, and then – well, then we'll see."

The woman gave her a wary look.

"But what exactly am I accused of?"

"We'll come to that in due course, as part of your rehabilitation."

"Rehabilitation?"

The woman nodded. "There's a programme. Six steps."

"Six steps?"

"Yes. Get through those, demonstrate that you've reformed, and you'll be released."

"But what about my trial?"

The woman's eyes narrowed. "That's a part of it. You'll have to demonstrate that you've reformed."

"What's this programme?"

"You'll find out. We'll be working through it together."

"We? You and me?"

"And your group. When you're ready."

Group. So there were others here. She wondered where they were; there'd been no sign of life when they'd driven through the grounds. Were they all teachers like her, or something else? She shuddered.

This was wrong. She was just a teacher who'd omitted to recite some words with her class. She was no traitor. She stood up.

"You've got it wrong. I shouldn't be here."

The woman raised an eyebrow. "Why not?"

"Because I'm no traitor. If you think someone like me is a traitor to the state, then you've got a seriously skewed idea of what's important."

"Have you looked at this place?"

Rita shrugged.

"It's nice, isn't it?"

Another shrug.

"This is a low security institution. Be glad you're not in a high security one. I've heard it's not very nice."

"I don't care. Call those police. Tell them to take me to a police station. I'm not the person you think I am."

"Rita, please sit down." The woman glanced up at the camera again. She licked her lips. Was she sweating?

"Have you noticed anything about me?" the woman asked.

Rita stared at her. Was this a trick question? She looked the woman up and down. "No."

The woman gave her a look that said *really?* She put her hand to her hijab. "I'm Muslim," she said.

"Well, yes."

"Admit it, you were surprised to see a Muslim woman in a place like this."

"OK."

The woman smiled. "I'm a graduate. Of the programme."

"A *what?*"

"A graduate. I was like you. Rebellious, difficult. But then I came here and went through the programme." She took her hand off her headscarf and put it back on the desk. "I changed. I'm not like that anymore."

"And they still let you wear that?"

Rita waited for the woman to register shock; she knew she was being disrespectful.

She didn't. "Of course. It's not Muslims the state has a problem with. It's dissenters. Rebels. People who don't understand that there's something bigger than themselves, and that they'll be better off if they conform."

Rita considered. This was bullshit, she thought. A trick. "You don't really think that."

Again the hand went to the hijab. "Because of this, you think I can't be loyal to the state. Well, you'll find out the truth. In time."

"No I won't. Because you're going to let me go."

The woman stood up and crossed to the door. "I'm afraid I can't do that." She opened the door and leaned out for a moment. Then she turned back to Rita.

"So, we'll see each other again tomorrow. For your first one-to-one. Roy will take you to your room. In the meantime you'll have a chance to reflect. To prepare yourself."

"I'm not going through any programme."

"You will. You'll understand the error of your ways, and you will."

CHAPTER SIX

"Good morning everybody."

The counsellor looked around the group, smiling broadly. Jennifer wondered what was going on behind that smile; did he enjoy this?

She sat in a circle of seven chairs, two along from Mark. Between them was a slight black woman with curly grey hair and hollow cheeks. Her skin had a grey tinge to it and her lips were thin and in constant motion. She muttered something beneath her breath; a pattern of sounds within which Jennifer couldn't distinguish any actual words. When she wasn't muttering she was clasping her knees, pulling them up to her chin and clattering her feet on the chair. She wore thin brown sandals that looked as if they might disintegrate at any moment, and her bony feet poked out from them; they were at least two sizes too small.

Jennifer eased her chair away from the woman, wondering if she'd been like this when she arrived here or this place had made her this way. She shuddered.

Mark looked around the group, his eyes glistening. His

cheeks were flushed and he was breathing hard; he'd been running.

He poked his tongue between his teeth and examined each woman in turn, finally alighting on the woman opposite him, two seats away from Jennifer. She was young, almost young enough to be Jennifer's daughter, and plump with rosy cheeks. She had thin blonde hair and was sitting very still, watching Mark intently. As his gaze fell on her she stiffened and straightened her back. She blinked back at him, her mouth slightly open. Her teeth were yellowing.

"Sally." Mark smiled at the woman. She sniffed in return and drew herself up further, her feet scraping against the legs of her chair. As Jennifer had arrived, the women had been pulling these chairs to the centre of the room to form a circle. They'd done it in silence then taken their places without discussion, not making eye contact as they sat. They'd left an empty seat; who was missing?

The room itself was large and echoing, decorated with rectangular patches where pictures had once adorned the walls. The floor was polished wood, like the corridors on this level, pitted with scrapes and dents. The only real hint of what the house had once been were the curtains that hung over the window at one end. They were thick and heavy, made of an expensive looking blue fabric. The walls were a pale blue, a few shades lighter. She wondered what this room had been; a sitting room, maybe? It would have been a pleasant place to sit at this time of day, with the sun coming in through the tall window.

She was jolted back to the present by Mark's voice.

"Why don't you show Jennifer how it's done?"

Jennifer felt her face grow hot. The other women turned as one to look at her, then averted their eyes. Only the woman next to her, knees up to her chin, hadn't looked at her. She was gazing into space, hissing something under her breath.

Mark leaned towards her and waved his hand to gain her attention.

"Bel. Shh."

She widened her eyes and fell silent.

"Put your feet on the floor please."

She obeyed, sliding her feet down to the wood as if wary of something that might bite her.

Mark turned to the blonde woman again. Sally smiled at him, blinking. She cocked her head to one side and rubbed an invisible spot under her lip.

"Step Six?" she asked. The counsellor shook his head.

"No. Step One, for now."

This was met with a scowl, quickly replaced by that smile. "I'm ready for Step Six."

Mark gave her a look. "Step One please. For Jennifer."

Sally glanced at Jennifer, her eyes narrowing. Then she looked back at Mark and widened them again.

"Not a problem."

Mark nodded and Sally stood up, positioning her body square on to the psychiatrist.

Jennifer watched, heart quickening. She thought she'd prepared herself, reading over the booklet Mark had given her till she had it all by heart. But she hadn't been expecting a public performance.

This is what you do, she told herself. Standing up and lying in front of a group of people. Selecting which parts of the truth to include. It was her bread and butter. She still had it, and she was going to use it to get out of here.

She leaned back to watch Sally, eager to learn anything that would help her. The words she knew, but there might be something else; a gesture, a way of holding yourself.

Maybe a salute. She shuddered. It hadn't gone that far, surely.

Sally cleared her throat. "I confess that I have been disloyal to the British state."

She pulled her shoulders back and looked ahead, like a child expecting a reward.

"Go on," Mark said.

A nod. "I disseminated information which undermined the authority of the state and could have bred dissent or division." Her voice was bright, rehearsed. Jennifer wondered how many times she'd practised this. How long all of them had been here.

Mark motioned for her to sit. "Thank you Sally. I knew I could rely on you." He looked around the group, deciding who to pick next.

Sally put her hand up. Mark frowned. "We're not in school. You can speak."

She smiled at him. "Sorry. Can I practise the rest of my stages? I want to prepare."

"No. Not just yet. We need to get our newcomer started."

Sally's shoulders slumped. She looked at Jennifer again, her lip curling.

The woman next to Jennifer started humming. Her head was down now, her eyes closed.

"Will we all have to do this?" Jennifer asked, surprised to hear the faintness in her voice. She cleared her throat.

Mark looked at her. "Yes. Today is special, as we have you new to the group. Today each of us will do Step One."

The woman on Jennifer's other side groaned.

"Maryam?" Mark looked annoyed.

Maryam pulled back her long dark hair, wrapping it around her neck. Then she smoothed her hands over it, working through her scalp. "I'm ready for Step Three," she said. "I'd rather not start again." Her voice was low, with a light Manchester accent.

"You won't have to start again," Mark said. "It's just this morning we're all doing Step One. I want you to show Jennifer how it's done." He gave her an insincere smile.

She tugged at her hair again, unwrapping it and twisting it around her neck in the opposite direction.

"OK?" Mark asked, his tone that of an adult addressing a difficult child.

Maryam nodded. "Yes."

"Take your hands off your hair, please."

She frowned and pulled her hands away from her head, slowly as if resisting some unseen force. She looked at them and placed them in her lap, twisting them together. They were blotched with red weals and the fingernails were ragged.

"Why don't you go next?" Mark asked her.

She inhaled. "Alright."

Mark waited for a moment. Jennifer's eyes flitted between him and her neighbour, wondering how long it had taken Maryam to get to this stage. She imagined Samir, doing this. Surrounded by petulant teenagers. Or worse.

Maryam stood slowly, her chair toppling as she pushed it back. Annoyance passed over Mark's face.

She took a deep breath, closing her eyes. "I admit that I have been disloyal to the British state."

Jennifer watched her, waiting for the next part.

"I hid a suspected terrorist. I put my neighbours and the wider community in danger."

Jennifer's fists clenched in her lap. Her eyes shot to Mark. Was this what she would be expected to say?

But Mark was looking at Maryam, his gaze harder than it had been for Sally.

"Thank you Maryam. Very good, this time. Sit down."

His attention moved on. The next chair was still empty. Maryam kept glancing nervously at it, as if expecting someone to take it and not wanting them to.

Finally, next to Mark on the other side, was her roommate Paula. This was the first time in the two days that Jennifer had seen her without Mandy. Already it seemed wrong. The two of them always arrived at the room together and left together. She'd seen them sharing a table at every meal. She herself had sat alone, wary of making friends until she'd worked out the power structures. If prison had taught her anything, it was to keep her eyes and ears open.

Mark twisted in his chair. "Paula," he said. "Your turn."

She lifted her head to look at him, her eyes dull. This was a different woman from the one she'd seen with Mandy, whispering conspiratorially.

Next to her, Sally shifted in her seat. She was smiling at Paula, encouraging her with her eyes. Paula looked back at her, twisting her face into a look of disgust. She looked at Bel, who was tapping her ear repeatedly. Mark was ignoring it, but his face twitched with each repetition.

Paula sighed loudly. "Do I have to?"

"Yes."

"Go on," said Sally. "It's easy."

This was met by a scowl. Jennifer wondered what had happened between these two women, whether she would be dragged into it. But if Sally was at Step Six, maybe she would be gone soon.

Paula stood up, pulling at each of her fingers in turn.

"I confess that I have been disloyal to the British state," she intoned.

"Come on Paula, put some feeling into it," Mark snapped.

Paula gave him a look of revulsion.

"I confess that I have been disloyal to the British state," she repeated, all but barking out the words. She closed her eyes. "I co-ordinated safe houses for suspected dissidents."

Mark shook his head. "Uh-uh. We've talked about this before."

She tightened her mouth. "I co-ordinated hiding places for suspected terrorists." She stressed the last word, glaring at Sally as she did so.

"From the top," muttered Mark.

"Really?"

He turned to her, his eyes flashing. "Yes. Really. Do you want to earn your way out of the centre, or not?"

She pouted. "Alright then. I confess that I have been disloyal to the British state." Her voice was mocking. It reminded Jennifer of the way the Prime Minister Leonard Trask spoke to her. And to Catherine, sometimes.

Mark stood and approached Paula. "Try again."

Paula shrank back, almost tripping over the chair behind her. "Alright, alright," she said, her tone still sarcastic.

There was a pause. Jennifer couldn't see Mark's face but she could see Paula's eyes widening. The other women watched in silence except Bel, humming under her breath. Outside in the corridor she heard voices; someone shouting.

Mark sat down. He looked around the group and smoothed his hands on his trousers. They were turning threadbare at the knees. "Again," he said, not looking at Paula. His voice was hard.

Paula looked ahead and upwards. Jennifer put her tongue between her lips, nervous for this woman who had given her no reason to feel any sympathy up to now. She wondered where Mandy was, whether they had shared this experience. Maybe the empty chair belonged to Mandy?

Paula cleared her throat. "I confess that I have been disloyal to the British state. I co-ordinated a network of hiding places for suspected terrorists."

She sat down again. The words had been flat and expressionless. Garbled.

"That'll do," said Mark. He looked at Bel, then shook his head. He switched his gaze to Jennifer.

"So, Jennifer," he said. "Think you can do it?"

CHAPTER SEVEN

This time the woman was already in her office, waiting. Rita let the orderly guide her inside and took the hard plastic chair again.

The office had changed, a few items added to the desk – a half-drunk mug of coffee next to the potted plant; two framed photos, turned away from Rita. There were some photos on a cork-board which had been hung on the wall, and a postcard from Naples. A name had been added to the empty badge.

Meena Ashgar, Counsellor.

The woman spotted Rita looking at it. "Now you know my name," she said. "Call me Miss Ashgar."

"If you say so."

"Yes. Please." The woman cleared her throat. "Anyway, you need to know the drill. You'll come here at 10am every day for your first two weeks. Hopefully we can get you through this quickly. Roy won't bring you next time, you'll be expected to find your own way."

Rita ran through her route here. Her room was in the eaves, three floors up. Two separate flights of stairs and two empty corridors. She'd heard voices on the ground floor, coming from the front of the building. But the building itself was bare and soulless. There were pale patches on the walls where pictures had once hung, and on the polished wooden boards of the ground floor where rugs had lain. Once again she wondered how many people were here, and if she would meet any of them.

"Do you have other prisoners here?"

Miss Ashgar flinched. "We don't like to use the word prisoner."

"So what word do you use then?"

"Patient."

"*Patient?* But I'm not sick."

"Under the law, you are. The programme is designed to cure you."

Rita laughed. "This is ridiculous. I'm not sick, I'm not doing any programme, and I want to know my rights."

The counsellor closed her eyes for a moment, then forced a smile. She rounded the desk, crouching to bring her face level with Rita's. She sniffed and wiped her nose with the back of her hand. When she spoke, her voice was low.

"Look. I know what you're going through. It happened to me too. But I went through the programme, and now I understand. I was sick. Not physically, but in my head."

Rita scowled. *Bullshit*, she thought. She looked ahead, not meeting the counsellor's eye.

The counsellor pursed her lips. "I want to help you. If you cooperate, then you'll get out sooner." She stood and scratched her neck under the fabric of her headscarf. It was warm down here. "We got off on the wrong foot yesterday. Let's try again." She licked her lips. "Yes?"

Rita continued to stare straight ahead. The counsellor sighed and glanced at the camera behind Rita.

"OK, if that's how you're going to be." She went back to her chair and opened a drawer. She pulled out a white leaflet. She looked at the camera again, then back at Rita. "Do you know what this is?"

Rita shook her head, looking at it out of the corner of her eye.

"It's the British Values Programme. Normally you get a copy of this when you arrive, but I think we need to approach it differently. I'm going to read you the first page."

Rita didn't want to listen to this. She had no intention of submitting to any kind of programme, at least not until she'd had a fair trial. She hadn't even been formally charged yet.

The counsellor looked up with another nervous smile. Rita flicked her gaze away.

"Right," she said, tweaking her hijab where it had come loose over her ear. "I'll read you the introduction."

Rita shrugged.

"'Welcome to the British Values Programme. This programme is designed to help you understand that the British state is not your enemy. Far from it; it has your best interests at heart. This is a country with a long tradition of tolerance and openness; the programme is designed to help you understand that and accept its benefits for you and society at large.

"'You'll go through six simple steps as you progress through the programme, with the help of your counsellor. If you embrace it, you can work through the steps in as little as six sessions with your counsellor. If you refuse to engage with the programme, it will take longer. It's your choice.'"

Miss Ashgar looked up. "Making sense so far?"

Rita grunted.

"OK." The counsellor folded the leaflet shut and placed it on her desk. She sniffed and scratched her chin. "Let's start by examining your thoughts, before I introduce the first step to you."

She waited for Rita to speak, then nodded, glanced at the camera then back at Rita.

"Do you know why you're here?"

Rita turned to her, her face hot. "No. You won't tell me. You should have charged me, and told me my rights by now. You can't hold me pris—"

The counsellor put up a hand to stop her. "You're frustrated. I was too. In fact, you've got nothing on the way I felt when I got here."

Rita eyed her.

"You don't believe me. You will. I'm going to help you go through the same process I did. You'll come to thank me."

"Never."

She smiled. "I'm going to put you out of your misery, tell you why you're here. It's because you failed to instil the proper values in the children in your care."

Rita snorted. What utter crap. The kids didn't need brainwashing. But who was it who informed on her?

"You do know that all schools are required to recite the Values Oath every morning?"

Rita didn't respond. Of course she knew.

"And that in your school, this was supposed to take place in the classroom?"

There was a pause while the counsellor waited for her to speak, then gave up.

"You're not helping, Rita. If you help me, I can help you. Do you know the oath?"

Rita felt a cloud of recognition pass over her face. Her anger at the thing had made her memorise it, so many times had she railed privately against its words. She resisted the urge to nod.

"Stand up, Rita."

Rita frowned.

"Please."

She heaved herself into a standing position.

"Let's recite it together."

Rita felt her insides recoil. She'd only recited it aloud once, in the pub. She had friends who were as angry as she was, and together they'd mocked it. Their parody had attracted quizzical glances from the other customers that had made them giggle and then turn quiet for fear of being informed on. You couldn't trust anyone. Not since Leonard Trask, the Prime Minister she hadn't voted for, had introduced his system of rewards for information. She knew people who'd been arrested purely because their neighbours wanted the recognition, although most of those cases hadn't got anywhere.

She sat down again. This wasn't 1930s Germany.

"Stand up, Rita. Please." Another glance at the camera. Rita resisted looking at it, and wondered who was watching. She pursed her lips and pulled her legs together, planting her feet on the floor.

The counsellor sighed and put a hand on her arm. Rita flinched.

"It will be easier for you if you work with me."

"I don't doubt it."

"Good. And so you'll help me?"

Rita looked at her. "I can help you alright. Help you see that they've brainwashed you."

Miss Ashgar smiled. "No-one's brainwashed me. I went through the programme and came to my own understanding of where I'd gone wrong." She coughed. "We can't force you to think a certain way, Rita. We don't want to. It only works if you embrace it."

"*Embrace it?* What's this, a religious cult or something?"

"Don't be silly."

Rita put her hands together and planted them between her thighs like a knife blade. She looked at her legs; the grey jogging bottoms they'd given her to wear made them look fat. What would Mrs Toft think if she could see where they'd sent her? Would she regret her act of loyalty to the state?

"OK," said the counsellor, her voice catching. "If you won't recite the oath with me, I'll do it on my own."

Rita shrugged, her eyes on the floor. The counsellor's shoes poked from beneath her long green skirt. They were bright blue and shiny.

She took a breath. "I promise to uphold the values of this great country. The rule of law, individual liberty and the tradition of tolerance."

Rita looked up through her eyelashes to see that her counsellor was staring ahead of her with her eyes closed. *No-one's watching you*, she thought. Then she remembered the cameras. She lifted her head to look properly at the woman. Was she putting it on, for their audience? And how the hell did she end up here, given the job of brainwashing people?

"I will encourage others to do the same," she continued. "If I witness activity contrary to these values or which puts Britain in danger, I will alert the authorities."

The counsellor took in a deep breath and paused for a moment, her eyes still closed. Rita wondered if she was considering her performance, assessing whether it had been good enough. Or maybe she was praying? Nothing would surprise Rita today.

Miss Ashgar opened her eyes. Rita quickly looked back at the floor.

"There, that wasn't so bad was it?"

Rita shrugged again.

"Have you ever said it?"

Rita looked up. "Yes."

She was rewarded with a smile. "Good. So you can do it again."

Rita felt her body grow heavy. She was hungry; breakfast had been a bowl of broken up cornflakes and a cup of orange tea so strong you could stand your spoon up in it. Her stomach felt hollow and her head ached.

"You're not leaving this room until we recite the oath together."

"What?"

"I have to get you to at least say it."

"I thought you said you couldn't force me to do anything?"

"I can't force you through the six steps. This bit I can do what I want with."

There was a steel to the counsellor's voice that didn't fit with her petite build and soft features. What had this woman – not much more than a girl – done to find herself here? Was there more to her than met the eye?

Rita considered. She was hungry and she needed the toilet.

"Can I have a break?"

"A break?"

"I need to go to the toilet."

The counsellor laughed. "That'll motivate you then. I guess."

"Really? You're not going to let me go to the toilet?"

"Sorry."

"What if I pee all over your chair?"

"You're not going to do that."

"Why shouldn't I?"

"Because you're not that kind of person."

Rita pursed her lips. She heard a voice from outside the door; someone outside in the corridor, calling. Were they calling her? Or her counsellor? Or was there someone else along here, in another office?

The voice went silent. She wondered when she would get out of here.

"Alright. I'll say it. Then you'll let me out, right?"

"Of course. You can come back tomorrow and we'll move on to Step One. Do the oath with me then I'll read it to you. You can prepare overnight."

"Prepare?"

"It helps if you can think about what you've done, consider where you went wrong. Step One is a breeze when you've done that."

Rita glared at her. "Was it for you? A breeze?"

The counsellor blushed. "That's not relevant."

It wasn't then. Rita wasn't sure why this gave her a small sense of satisfaction.

"But I think you'll find it easier than me."

"Why?"

Another blush. "I've said too much. Stand up and we'll do the oath."

Rita looked back down at her hands. If she did this, had they won? No-one would know.

She looked up at the camera. A steady red light shone to its left. Who was watching? She scowled at it, then stuck her tongue out.

"That was silly." Miss Ashgar was standing to attention

opposite her. "Come on then. Oath, I'll go over Step One, then you can go."

Rita looked into her eyes. They were steady and unblinking. A clump of hair had strayed from the hijab; it was dark and wavy, with an orange-red streak. The counsellor spotted her looking and shoved it back under the fabric, screwing up her nose.

"Yeah. I've changed my mind."

The counsellor's shoulders slumped. This was almost fun to watch.

"Seriously?"

"Uh-huh. I can hold it in."

A buzzer sounded from somewhere, making Rita jump and almost empty her bladder despite herself. Miss Ashgar frowned and looked at the door. She walked – glided almost – past Rita, who turned in her seat.

On the wall next to the door was a silver grille. Rita had assumed it was a ventilation plate, but realised now that it was a speaker. Beneath it was a small black button, so tiny that it looked like nothing more than a screw holding the whole thing in place.

The counsellor bent towards the grille and muttered into it. A distorted voice responded. Rita couldn't make out the words.

"Are you sure?" Miss Ashgar said.

A crackled response; it sounded like *absolutely*.

"Very well."

The counsellor turned towards Rita and looked at her as if coming to a decision. Then she put her hand on the door and pushed it open. Rita took in a breath, expecting to be released. But instead, Miss Ashgar opened the door and left her alone without a word.

CHAPTER EIGHT

The eyes of the whole group were on Jennifer.
Even Bel had quietened and turned to face her. Jennifer
wondered if she really had lost her mind or whether it was
an act, a way of hiding from Mark and what he expected
them to do.

She felt a hand on her knee; Sally, to her right, was
leaning in, a smile on her face.

"This is what you need," she whispered. "You're one
of us."

Jennifer pulled back; what did she mean, *one of us?*
What sort of information had this woman 'disseminated',
anyway? She returned the smile but said nothing.

Mark stood and stepped towards her. The women
looked between them, like spectators at a tennis match.

He held out his hands. "Stand up."

She pulled herself up to standing, jabbing her fingernails into her palms. The pain was reassuring, reminding
her that this was real, and she was still Jennifer Sinclair, the
woman who could take on anything.

Mark was smiling into her face now, encouraging. "Have you read the booklet? Step One?"

She nodded. Step One was easy. Step One was just facts.

"Normally you'd do this with me first," he continued. "In your one-to-one." His eyes darkened. "But I think you're ready to do this with the support of the group."

She cleared her throat, wondering about the women surrounding her. How had they got here? Could she trust them? And what did they know about her? Mark knew about her past, that was clear, but did they recognise her?

Sally stood up next to her. "Would you like me to help her, Mark?"

Sally's fingers touched Jennifer's and she shrank back. *Creep*.

"Thank you," said Mark. "But that won't be necessary. Jennifer will need your help for Step Three. We can wait until then."

"OK." Sally sounded disappointed. She sat down. Jennifer let her hands fall, the echo of Sally's touch sharp on her fingers.

The room had gone quiet. Bel's humming had been replaced by slow, steady nose breathing. Beyond Mark she could see Paula, her head cocked. There was a look of recognition in her eyes, and mockery.

Mark took a step back. "Can you give us the first part of Step One please." It wasn't a question.

Jennifer coughed and pushed her nails deeper into her palms. This was true, she reminded herself. But not in the way he thought.

"I confess that I have been disloyal to the British State."

She closed her eyes, memories flooding over her. The face of her boss, the then Home Secretary John Hunter, accosting her in the division lobby at the height of their animosity; Michael Stuart, former Prime Minister, glaring at her from the front bench. Maggie Reilly, fellow rebel, grinning at her as they'd won the vote, eyes full of triumph.

She'd been disloyal to the state, no doubt of it. If it hadn't been for her, none of this would be happening.

She looked around at the women, her eyes prickling. Did they know what she'd done? Did they blame her?

Mark put a hand on her shoulder. She stiffened.

"Good," he said. "Well done."

She narrowed her eyes. If he only knew.

He let his hand fall. "Now for the next part," he said. "I know I haven't taken you through this yet, so I understand it could be tricky. Just tell us in your own words."

She blinked at him. There was so much to tell. Bringing down her own government. Betraying her friends and colleagues. Catherine's betrayal of her in turn. Without her, Trask wouldn't be Prime Minister. The British Values Programme wouldn't exist. None of them would be here. And – she stifled a moan – her family would be safe, and together.

He pulled at his lower lip. Did he know what she was thinking? Was he worried she'd tell the truth?

No. She had to get through this. The priority was to find a way out of here, and back to Yusuf. To get Samir released. And to see her baby boy Hassan again.

She narrowed her eyes at him. *I do this*, she thought, *and in my next one-to-one you tell me where he is.*

She lifted her chin and closed her eyes. Bel had stared muttering again; out of the corner of her eye, Jennifer could see her rocking. Sally was shuffling in her seat, impatient.

She had to ignore them. To tell him what he wanted

to hear.

"I harboured a suspected terrorist."

Around her there was rustling, and a couple of relieved coughs. Paula and Maryam were possibly recognising a kindred spirit.

She waited for Mark to congratulate her, to tell her to sit down.

"Good," he said.

She glanced at the chair behind her, preparing to sit. The clock on the wall opposite ticked loudly.

Mark coughed. "Not just yet."

She looked back at him. She'd done what the others had. What else did he need?

He was pale, the crows' feet around his eyes visible against his skin. Did he enjoy this?

"Well done, Jennifer."

Mark's eyes flicked to Sally, who had just spoken. "Shh," he said, frowning. She shuffled in her chair and muttered an apology.

"Do we get to congratulate her?" asked Paula.

"Not yet," replied Mark. "Be quiet, everybody."

Bel stopped rocking and shoved a knuckle into her mouth. Jennifer stared at Mark, challenging him. *Get on with it*, she thought.

He had a copy of the booklet in his hand. He held it out to her. "Turn to page six."

She took it from him and did as she was told. The opening pages were preamble: the oath first, the one recited in schools and workplaces now. She was surprised she hadn't been asked to recite it. Maybe that came later. Or maybe they didn't want to push their luck.

Page six was devoted to the first step in the programme; the easiest step as far as she was concerned.

"Read the second section," he said.

She folded the page back and brought the page up closer to her face, aware of the women listening.

"'This is your opportunity to understand what you did wrong,'" she read. She looked up at him.

"Go on."

"'By describing your transgressions in a way that is personal to you, you can begin to accept why you need to change, and how you can atone.'"

"Thank you." Mark took the booklet from her. He looked around the women. "What does this mean?"

Silence. Sally was fidgeting in her seat, trying to come up with the perfect answer, no doubt.

"What one word did I give you to help you with this step?" Mark asked, his voice rough.

"Oh! I know." Sally sprang up and Paula rolled her eyes. "*Specific.*"

Mark smiled at her, a smile that didn't reach his eyes. "Good. Specificity. Sit down."

She grinned nervously and fell back into her chair.

Mark stepped away from Jennifer and started to pace. He circled the chairs, pausing to place a hand on the back of each one as he passed it. His voice echoed in the bare space.

"Specificity. You need to understand the specifics of what you did. For example, Paula here. She ran a network of locations where dissidents and terrorists were allowed to hide. A kind of underground railroad, to give it a romantic name."

Paula flinched and looked ahead of her, past Jennifer's shoulder. Jennifer thought of the constituents that she and Yusuf had directed to networks like hers. Had people she knew passed through Paula's hands? Were they safe, because of her?

Mark moved on, stopping behind Bel.

"Bel was a lawyer. She defended people like the rest of you. But that isn't all she did. She had fake papers created for her clients so they could flee the country. We caught up with her in Scotland, in hiding. Her husband had taken a gun with him, and we had to use force. It wasn't pretty."

Jennifer's eyes widened. *Wasn't pretty*, what did that mean? And did it explain Bel's state of mind?

Then she stopped up short. If Samir had access to a forged passport, he would never have stopped in London, never have taken refuge in her flat. Would he have been better off?

Mark passed Jennifer and approached Sally. She straightened her back, as if relishing this opportunity to hear what she had done. Mark pursed his lips as he looked at her.

"And Sally," he said, not taking his eyes off her, "used social media to spread hate speech. She shared and retweeted racist and homophobic messages."

Jennifer wasn't expecting this. It hadn't occurred to her that people would be in here because of far right activity. How long would hate speech remain a crime, when it was being spouted by government ministers?

Sally was returning Mark's gaze, her cheeks flushed. She nodded. Jennifer wondered how the others could bear to be in a group with her.

She waited for Mark to move on to Maryam, but instead he continued to Jennifer. She heard the chair behind her scrape on the floor as he put his hand on its back.

"So," he said. "Your turn, Jennifer. Tell the group what you did, specifically. Not what the courts told you you did. What you actually did."

She licked her lips. Could she lie? Was there any point?

Best to be honest.

"My son was suspected of involvement with a proscribed organisation. He ran away from home. I let him hide in my flat. In London."

Her heart was thudding against her rib cage. This shouldn't be hard, certainly no tougher than facing down Michael Stuart and Leonard Trask. Two Prime Ministers. She'd picked the wrong one to ruin.

"More specific," said Mark, his voice clipped.

"I don't know any more," she said. She thought of Samir's arrest, when she'd been busy pursuing her political agenda in the House of Commons. She should have stayed with him, stopped him from running.

"You do, Jennifer. Was it your idea to hide your son?"

She shook her head. His arrival in her flat had been a surprise. But she'd bought supplies, kept the fridge stocked for the times he sneaked in, while she was out. She'd encouraged him. What mother wouldn't, when the alternative was arrest?

"It wasn't entirely my idea."

Mark smiled. "Go on."

"My son, Sa—"

He nodded. "Go on. Tell me about your son. Samir Hussain."

Sally sniffed and Maryam looked up. Suddenly she was a different person in their eyes.

She looked at Mark. She imagined him as a TV interviewer, shrouded by spotlights.

He sighed. "Your husband. Was it his idea?"

"No. It was Samir's. But I bought food for him, in the hope he'd come back. When I was there."

"Alright," he said. "So tell me about your son. How much did you know about his activities?"

She felt hollow. She'd suspected nothing, had barely

pressed him when he'd played truant from school. Or when he'd got into a fight about racist language. Why hadn't she seen the signs? Then she remembered that photo.

"I don't know what my son is accused of. No-one has told me."

"No?"

She shook her head.

"Surely you had your suspicions? Surely as a good mother you should have taken action, nipped it in the bud?"

She frowned. She thought of the photos on Mark's wall. He knew nothing about teenagers. "No," she replied. She took a deep breath, pinching her nose to regain control of her breathing. "I don't understand. What do you want me to say?"

"Very well," he said. She stared at him, unsure whether she'd passed this test. Sally pulled away from her, her chair leg scraping against the polished floor. Bel was still again, her face buried in her hands. Opposite, Maryam smiled at Jennifer through her hair, which she'd wrapped around her jaw.

Mark turned and made for his own chair. He put his booklet on the floor then sat down.

"Well done, Jennifer," he said. "You've done well, considering. Now, let's congratulate Jennifer."

She felt her muscles tighten as the other women approached her.

CHAPTER NINE

Rita stood outside Miss Ashgar's office, shifting from foot to foot. She could hear voices from upstairs, and had spotted two orderlies passing as she'd made her way here. They were the only signs of life in this place since her counsellor had abandoned her the previous day.

Roy had appeared almost immediately, beckoning her to come with him.

"Where has she gone?" Rita had asked.

But Roy had told her nothing, leading her up to her room in silence and locking the door after her. He'd appeared twice more, to bring food. She wondered if there were other orderlies in the place, other counsellors. Other inmates. Her corridor was quiet, no sounds coming from the surrounding rooms. She'd wondered if at night she was the only person left in the building. The madwoman in the attic.

She glanced up and down the corridor, wondering if she was early or her counsellor was late. As she was about to give up and go in search of her, Roy appeared.

"This is getting to be a habit," she said. "Where are you taking me today?"

His face was impassive. "Follow me."

He set off along the corridor, turned a bend and opened a door, identical to Miss Ashgar's. Rita gave him a questioning look that was ignored, and went in. She turned to see Roy nod and head back where he had come from.

This office was larger, with a ceiling level window on one wall. Instead of being in the middle of the space, the desk here was to one side, with two chairs arranged diagonally. She wondered why Miss Ashgar had been moved here. A promotion, maybe? She didn't seem experienced enough for that.

The waiting around in this place was driving her crazy. She was used to days full of activity and noise; too much to cram into the school day for her feet to touch the floor, followed by a frantic commute home, marking, TV if she was lucky and then bed. On weekends she saw Ash, went to the cinema, the pub. When she wasn't doing more marking. Her body had begun to develop a life of its own, twitching with boredom and irritation whenever she had to sit or stand in the same place without doing anything for more than a few minutes. Here, she was directionless and alone. Not to mention confused.

Maybe they knew that, and were using it to break her down.

She saw feet passing above, clad in heavy black boots and blue trousers that looked like part of a uniform. She wondered what their owner knew about this place, and the people held in it. Would they hear her, if she called out?

She blasted out a series of short, sharp breaths, finding a whispered tune to fill the silence, then ventured towards the window. She put her hands against it. But the feet had gone, and what little she could see of the driveway outside was empty.

She decided that she may as well get comfortable. She took the chair closest to her and leaned back, trying to relax. Her back was aching and her limbs felt heavy and tired. She forced her eyes open, blinking a few times, and looked at the desk's contents.

If this was Miss Ashgar's desk, she hadn't brought anything with her. There was a pile of psychology books, a notepad – closed, unfortunately – and a small army of gonks on the corner furthest from the other chair. She picked one up; an ugly little thing, with staring, wobbling eyes and a shock of bright purple hair. Its webbed feet were thin, made of felt. She shrugged and put it back down.

Behind her the door opened. She stood hurriedly, checking that she'd left the gonk as she found it. Then she stopped herself. Who cared if she rearranged the desk? She shouldn't have been left waiting.

"Morning."

She spun round. Standing in the doorway, frowning at her, was a man. Tall with dark hair that curled around his ears. He was gangly, with a pale face blotched with pink. He looked like he could do with a few hearty meals.

"Who are you?" she blurted.

He passed her and pulled out the other chair.

"My name's Dr Clarke," he said. "I see you've made yourself at home."

He leaned past her and fingered the toy she had picked up, shifting it into its correct place. She could feel her heart picking up pace.

"Where's my counsellor?"

"Hmm?" He surveyed his desk, checking what else she

had disturbed. He patted the pile of books into place, making the spines align, and pulled the notepad to him. She watched him open it and turn to a blank page. She could smell his aftershave; he wore too much.

Finally he looked up. "I'm your counsellor."

She slumped back. "Oh." She wondered what had happened to Miss Ashgar. She was intrigued by her, a woman in a hijab counselling people who'd refused to recite an oath of allegiance to an Islamophobic state. This man, on the other hand, looked as if he had nothing interesting to reveal.

Maybe they'd got rid of her, decided that she wasn't the right person to lead Rita through the programme. Maybe she'd been too lenient.

"Where's Miss Ashgar?"

He leaned back, satisfied with the state of his desk. "I'm sorry. Who?"

She stiffened. "Miss Ashgar. My counsellor."

"I just told you. I'm your counsellor. Surely you remember that."

"No. Miss Ashgar is my counsellor." Her shoulders slumped. "Or at least she was. So you're my counsellor now?"

He shook his head, looking at her in the way Mrs Toft sometimes looked at the less able members of her class. "I don't know what you're talking about, Rita."

She crossed and uncrossed her ankles. The seat back was digging into her shoulder blades. She wasn't going to let him lie to her.

"I saw her just yesterday. And the day before. She told me she was going to work through some sort of programme with me. She wanted me to—"

She stopped herself. No point in telling him what had

happened, in case he decided to repeat it. She clamped her mouth shut and slumped back in her chair, going over the previous two days in her head. Everything from arriving here with those two policemen, to being escorted to the office by Roy, through to arriving here.

"Roy will be able to tell you. He took me to her office, the day I got here. He brought me from there just now. He saw me with her."

The man shook his head. "I think you'll find that's wrong, Rita."

She made to stand up. He gave her a warning look and she sat down again. "It's not," she said. "Ask him."

He sighed. "If you insist."

He stood and strolled to the door, giving her a disparaging glance as he passed. She shivered. Was he right? Had she had another counsellor, or not? No, of course she had.

He opened the door and poked his head out, calling to someone outside. He drew his head back in, shutting the door.

"He's on his way," he said, moving back to his chair. "Now, while we wait, shall we continue with your programme?"

She frowned. Was he taking over from Miss Ashgar? She thought about the way she'd resisted her counsellor, how she'd said she could *hold it in* rather than do as she was told and be allowed to go to the toilet. She blushed; she was behaving like a Year Two child.

"Whatever," she said.

"Now come on, Rita. You can do better than that."

She met his gaze, saying nothing. He was about to speak when there was a knock at the door.

"Come in," he barked. Roy came in, his shoulders

hunched. He gave the counsellor a wary look.

"Roy, thanks for coming in. Tell me, have you met Rita here before?"

The orderly looked at her. "Yes."

"Can you tell me when?"

"I was here when she arrived."

"Yes. And where did you take her, when she arrived?"

Confusion crossed the orderly's face. "Here." He blushed.

You're lying, thought Rita.

"Here? To my office?"

A nod.

"And did you bring her here yesterday, too?"

Another nod.

"Thanks." The counsellor smiled. "You can go now."

He turned to Rita. "It seems I've been your counsellor all along. You must be imagining this Miss Ashgar you talk about."

She clenched her fists. "I'm not." She dug into her memory. "I saw her yesterday, and the day before. She had an office, along from here. She's short, with a quiet voice. She wears a black hijab. Yesterday she had a long green dress on, and a blue cardigan over it. Her name is Meena Ashgar. She used to be a – a – a patient here, but she got through the programme and now she's a counsellor."

He shook his head. "Well, that's impossible."

"It's not." She willed herself not to lose her temper. "It's the truth."

He walked to her chair, standing behind it with his hand on its back. She leaned forwards, avoiding contact.

"Stand up please, Rita."

She stood, pushing the chair back so it would hit him. He stepped back to avoid it.

"Come with me," he said.

He opened the door and held it for her. She passed through, scowling at him.

The corridor was empty. Thin grey light filtered through the windows opposite the counsellor's office door. She could hear the wind outside, buffeting the old building. Finding its way through cracks in the brickwork. She wished she'd paid more attention when they brought her here, looked for an escape route.

"Which office was she in?" he asked, his tone light.

She walked to the bend in the corridor then pointed to the third door along. "That one."

"Come on then."

He started walking towards the door. She watched him for a moment. She knew Miss Ashgar wouldn't be there.

He turned to her. "I told you to come with me."

She shook her head. "There's no point."

He sighed. "Come with me. I want to see this Miss Ashgar you say you met."

"No. She won't be there. I'm not stupid."

He raised his eyebrows. There was a mole on his chin, with a hair growing from it. *Obnoxious bastard*, she thought.

"Come. Now."

She gritted her teeth and followed him, dragging her feet on the floor. Down here the floor was concrete, not the polished wood she'd seen upstairs. Her feet slapped along the hard surface, echoing in the blank corridor. She heard an engine start up outside and a door slam.

When they arrived at the door he gestured to it. "Open it."

"There's no point."

"Open it."

Her whole body felt tense. She clenched her fist as she

put the other palm up to the door. She wondered what would happen if she raised that fist, if she let it slam into his face.

She pushed the door open. It was unlocked. The room, of course, was empty. The desk was there, and the two chairs, but other than that it was bare. No pens, no pile of notebooks. No plastic potted plant. And no name badge.

"Is this where you believe you saw this other counsellor?"

"This is where I saw her."

He grunted. "Could you be imagining it, perhaps?"

She frowned. Could he be right? Could she be hallucinating? Had she dreamed the other woman, or imagined her? Maybe there were drugs in the food.

She looked at him. She hadn't seen him before today. She knew it.

"No," she said. "I'm not imagining things."

"In that case you must be lying."

"No. You're lying."

He grabbed her arm. His fingers were thicker than she would expect from his wiry frame. They dug into her flesh. "No, Rita. You don't accuse your counsellor of lying." He brought his head down so his mouth was level with her ear, just centimetres away. "You accept the help of your counsellor, or you will be punished."

CHAPTER TEN

THE SITTING ROOM HAD SEEN BETTER DAYS. JENNIFER
was sure she had been in here before, had looked out on that
view from the large bay window. In front of it there had
been a pair of blue sofas, the perfect spot to take a break and
chat to colleagues. She hadn't paid much attention to the
view then, so absorbed had she been by her work.

Now the window was fronted by a row of mismatched
armchairs that made her think of an old people's home. Two
of them were soft and threadbare, with floral covers pock-
marked by patches of dirt that could be years old. Three
more were high backed with wooden arms. And between
those were two of the orange plastic and metal chairs, their
seats floating incongruously above those of their neighbours.

Jennifer paused at the door to the room and took it in.
Outside the window, the sun shone on the vast lawns that
led downhill from the back of the house. Frost had formed
overnight and the ground glistened invitingly. She walked
to the window and looked out. Two women strolled across
the grass. Another was making her way along a path, an

orderly holding her arm. It felt more like a clinic or a convalescent home than a prison.

Behind her someone coughed. She span round to see two occupants in the chairs against the wall; Paula and Mandy. Paula glared at her, as if warning her to get out. Mandy looked down at her knees, whispering something.

Jennifer put on her brightest smile. "Mind if I sit here?"

Paula scowled. There was a moment's silence while she decided on a response. Two orderlies passed in the corridor outside, chatting. Mandy let out a squeal and then closed her eyes, slumping into sleep.

Paula looked at her friend, her eyes full of a tenderness Jennifer certainly hadn't seen in the group session. "Alright," she whispered. "But keep quiet."

Jennifer nodded. She was desperate to talk to someone. She turned back to the window and chose one of the brown high-backed chairs. She sat and shuffled into place, wincing as the scratchy fabric attacked her skin.

She had a book in her hand, something Mark had given her at the end of her group session. A reward. It was battered and some of the pages were missing, and it was a romance, not her usual choice. But it would fill the time. She picked it up and licked her finger, turning over the first page.

"It's not as easy as you think, you know."

Paula was kneeling on the floor between them. Behind her, Mandy was still asleep.

Jennifer put her book down, glad of the interruption. Romances still weren't her thing.

"Sorry?"

Paula gave her a condescending look. "The programme. You think you'll pass with flying colours, don't you?"

"I don't know." She didn't want to reveal her plan to

this woman, to prompt a conversation about why she was so desperate to get out. But then, she supposed, they all were.

Paula raised an eyebrow. "You're lying to him. It won't work."

"I don't know what you're talking about."

"OK. Let's say you're not lying. So you're going to repent everything that you did? Become a good little girl? Just like that, no questions asked."

Jennifer dug her fingernail into her palm. "Yes. I did some stupid things. I want to put them behind me."

A barked laugh. "We know that."

"Do you?"

She was answered with an unfriendly smile. "Everyone here knows about the disgraced MP whose son got her sent here."

"It's not like—"

Paula waved a hand. "Spare me. Your son's innocent, of course he is. He's your son."

"I thought you'd be sympathetic. It was people like you who helped us."

Paula glanced at Mandy, snoring loudly now, and pushed herself up from the floor. "Yes, but one of the *people like you* gave me away. Nice little Muslim woman, wouldn't say boo to a goose. I let her and her husband hide in my cellar. Just two nights. Then a week later I got the knock on my door."

"I'm sorry."

"Don't be."

Jennifer didn't know what she was supposed to say. Surely Paula didn't blame her for her arrest? She decided not to address it.

"So," she sniffed, pulling her shoulders back in an

attempt at bravado. "How do I get out of here? What *is* the best way to get through the programme?"

"Well done. You're thinking now."

Jennifer nodded.

"But I don't think I can help you."

"Oh." Jennifer was disappointed, but not surprised. "Why not?"

"You've got to work it out for yourself. The words have got to come from in here." She thumped her chest. "Otherwise you'll never get through Celebration."

"Celebration? What's that?"

A smile. "You'll find out."

"Tell me, please. There's nothing about any celebration in the—"

"Sinclair!"

She turned to see an orderly glaring at her from the doorway.

"You're late. Dr Clarke's office. Now."

She looked at the old-fashioned clock on the wall, then realised it wasn't working. They'd taken her watch off her in prison. How was she supposed to know when it was time for her session?

Best not to argue, she thought.

"Sorry."

She shot Paula a look to tell her the conversation wasn't over, then darted out of the room and towards the end of the corridor and the stairs to the basement. It made no sense for the offices to be hidden down there, when all these grand rooms were available upstairs. But nothing made sense about this place.

She ran along the dim corridor and skidded to a halt outside Mark's door. She paused to rearrange herself –

sweater smooth, hair tucked behind her ears – and raised a hand to knock.

"Come in."

She hadn't touched the door. She looked around. A red light winked at her from high on the wall; more cameras. She shrugged, making a mental note to check the sitting room for them later, and pushed the door open.

Inside, Mark was perched on his desk, arms folded in front of him. "Where have you been?"

She held his gaze. "Sorry. The clock was—"

"Never mind that." He pushed the empty chair out with his foot. "Sit down."

She approached the chair, uncomfortable that he was so close to it. But as she sat, he moved away, pacing the room.

"Have you been reading the booklet?" he asked.

"Yes."

"Good. You did well in Group."

"Thanks."

"I did make it easy for you though."

She frowned; how had *specificity*, and *not good enough* made it easier for her?

He pushed his tongue between his lips. "Don't think so? This bit is easy, Jennifer. You can do Step One, and you know it."

"Yes."

He smiled. "So. Let's take it one more time, you and me. From the top." He smiled to himself.

She cleared her throat. "Can I have the booklet please?"

"Not brought your copy?"

She pictured it sitting on the chair next to her in the sitting room, under her book.

"Sorry."

He sighed. "Very well." He pulled a drawer open next to her and pulled out a booklet, placing it in her hand. "Borrow it, for this session. But bring your own next time, please."

She flicked through the opening pages. *Let's get this over with*, she thought.

"I confess that I have been disloyal to the British state."

"Good. Tell me what you did, please." He was pacing again, moving from side to side in front of the window. The dim light filtering through was enough to silhouette his face so she couldn't see his expression.

"I hid my son who was suspected of membership of a proscribed organisation."

She paused, waiting for him to pick up on the *suspected*.

Instead he clapped his hands together. "Good! Now for Step Two, why not?"

She turned the page, scanning the words. She'd gone over this already. After the first group session she'd realised that she was expected to come up with something better than she'd planned on her first night. She hadn't wasted any time.

"OK. I accept the sovereignty of the British state. I understand that it has my best interests at heart."

He leaned over her, narrowing his eyes. "Do you?" He was so close she could see the grey roots in his hair. His tone was friendly though, inquisitive.

"I do. Of course I do. I've spent most of my life serving the state."

"Do you think that's true?"

She frowned. This wasn't in the handbook. "Yes. Of course."

"It hasn't occurred to you that some of the things you've done might have – let's say – damaged the British state?"

She stared back into his eyes. What was he getting at?

She thought of John, then of Michael and that vote of confidence.

"Is that what you want me to confess to? Should I go back to Step One?"

"That would be a little unorthodox, I think. No, let's stick with it. You know what your crimes are. You heard them in court, and you've just confessed to them. What I need you to do now is accept the love of the state."

"The love?"

"Yes." He put his fist on his chest. "You need to feel it. Accept it."

"The love?"

She thought of Leonard Trask, sneering at her in the corridors of Westminster. There was no love there. Then she remembered Catherine, his minister. Her friend.

"Alright."

He raised his eyebrows. "Good. This isn't so hard, is it?"

She said nothing. *Think of Catherine*, she told herself. *Focus on her friendship*. On what she risked. Think of John Hunter, her old boss, and everything he did for her. She had to ignore what had come after that.

Mark sat in his chair, and scratched his forehead. "Stand up, please."

She pushed her chair back and stood, her hands on the worn wood of the desk.

"Move to the middle of the room."

She gave him a puzzled look then did as she was told.

He leaned back, raising his hands and interlacing his fingers. "Go for it. Tell me again."

"Sorry?"

"Step Two."

"Oh. Right." She dug into herself, working through words she could use. Words that wouldn't sound insincere.

She knew that telling ninety per cent of the truth was the best way of letting the ten per cent lie slip through undetected.

She sniffed and looked up at the wall, over Mark's head. The photos were still there, and a diploma. She resolved to read that when she had the chance, to find out what his qualifications were.

"I accept the sovereignty and love of the British state." She thought of John. "I know that it cares about me and has my best interests at heart."

Mark was beaming. "Good. Now what does that mean, for you?"

She went over the booklet in her head. *Understand that it is in your interest to be loyal*, it said.

"I understand that it is in my interest to be loyal to the state."

"Oh, come on."

She could feel herself tensing. "What's wrong?"

"You can't just parrot the words in the booklet. It has to come from inside you. You have to mean it."

"I do mean it."

"Show me then."

She puffed out a few quick breaths. *Do it*, she told herself. *Give him what he wants*. It was just words.

"I accept the love and sovereignty of the state. I understand that the state has my best interests at heart and cares about my welfare. I know that if I do my best for the state, it will do its best for me."

He stood up. "Fabulous! Almost Kennedy-like." He paused. "You weren't copying Kennedy, were you? Ask not what your country can do, and all that?"

She shook her head. That speech hadn't even occurred to her. "No. Honest."

He put a hand on her shoulder. "Well done. Now I'll need you to do that in your next group session on Thursday. Think you can manage it?"

She went over what she'd said in her head, memorising the words. "Yes."

CHAPTER ELEVEN

"Come in."

Rita looked up from her seat in the basement corridor. Her new counsellor's door was open and he was looking out at her, his face blank.

She'd been wondering – hoping, maybe – that yesterday would turn out to be a mistake, that Miss Ashgar would reappear at some point. She'd hated Miss Ashgar, despised her for whatever it was she had to do to get through the programme and end up working here. But now, the younger woman was officially a figment of her imagination. That changed things.

She shuffled in to find the office unchanged from yesterday. Same desk against the wall; same two chairs placed diagonally; same photos and diplomas as decoration. The empty space in the centre of the room made it feel cold and unwelcoming.

"Don't get comfortable," he said.

She felt her shoulders droop. Was she being taken to another office? Was he going to lie to her, tell her she'd imagined ever being in here?

The previous night, lying in bed, she'd worked through her first day here. What was it – two, three days ago? Maybe four. She'd replayed it all, careful not to miss anything out. The two policemen; the one dominant, the other nervous, embarrassed when he'd got the wrong entrance. The broad sweep of the driveway. The crawl round the back, squeezing the car past the hedge until they stopped at the rear entrance. The orderly. He was real. Even Dr Clarke didn't deny his existence.

Then Miss Ashgar. Her hijab, the way she'd tucked her hair inside it when irritated. The potted plant – fake, in the artificial light. The story she'd told, of how she'd gone through the programme and been rewarded with a job here. What was it she'd done? Had she said? Rita couldn't remember.

She'd made sure she had everything she could remember in her head, and then she'd moved on to her first proper session with Miss Ashgar. The oath. The shifting feeling in her spine when she found herself close to reciting it. Her refusal. Had they fired her counsellor because she hadn't persuaded Rita to comply? Of course not. She can't have been the first.

If she had to rehearse those days in her head every night from now on, she would. It was important to remember, to reassure herself. Seeing the empty office yesterday had jolted her confidence, but emptying an office was easy. She wasn't imagining things. She was sure of it.

She watched the counsellor, waiting for his next instruction. Bossy bastard. The kind who would lord it over their wives and kids, to make up for their inadequacies at work. Now he had Rita to hold dominion over. Well, she wasn't going to let him.

"Why not?" she asked.

"Because I'm taking you to your first group session. Come with me."

He breezed past, not making eye contact. She turned to watch him sweep into the corridor. Would she follow?

There was a moment's silence as his footsteps stopped. She heard a theatrical sigh from outside the door. He peered round it.

"If you know what's good for you, Rita, you'll come with me."

She pursed her lips. It would be good to meet some other prisoners. She'd find out more about this place, and what was going to happen to her.

"Alright."

～

She followed him along the corridor and up a wide flight of stairs. Not the one she had come down; that was narrow and in a dark corner of the building. This stairway – one she'd been told not to use – ran up the centre of the house. It had a deep mahogany railing, in need of a polish, and ornate spindles coated in fading cream paint. The stairway smelt of bleach mixed with dust, underlaid by a faint tang of sweat. She could hear voices above her, on the upper floors – was someone singing?

At the top of the first flight he turned into a wider corridor, without looking back to see if she was following. The floors here were polished, with dark patches where there'd been rugs. The tall walls loomed down at her, feeding her sense of isolation. Did anyone know she was here? Even Mrs Toft would have no idea. And would Ash be looking for her? He lived in Worcester, twenty miles from her, and they weren't due to meet for a week. He might not even know she was gone.

Suddenly she felt very alone.

They were at the front of the building now, and as each of the tall windows flashed past she grabbed a look outside. It was raining, the green of the lawns little more than a blur behind the wet glass. How far was the nearest town?

Finally he stopped at a door. It was heavy and old. He smiled at her then pushed it open and stood to one side for her to enter.

She hesitated.

"Go on," he whispered, his hand hovering behind her back.

She pulled away then walked past him, her eyes sweeping the space.

The room was large, with a huge window at the other end flanked by pale blue curtains. There was no furniture except for a circle of familiar orange chairs in the centre. She blinked at them, counting. One – two – seven in all. Five were occupied. The chair nearest her, facing the window, was empty, and another one, two along from it. Between them sat a woman, craning her neck to see. She was short and plump, with pale grey skin and bulging eyes that made Rita's stomach turn.

Beyond her were four more women. A middle aged black woman, humming to herself with her eyes closed. A tall, slender white woman with mousy blonde hair and grey roots showing. A petite woman who was repeatedly wrapping her long black hair around her neck one way and then the other. And a slight, blonde woman, younger than the rest, glaring at her with undisguised disdain.

She felt herself hollow out. Was this what she would become? Or did she look like that already?

"Everybody," said Dr Clarke, heading for the chair closest to them and motioning for Rita to sit between the grey-faced woman and the angry blonde, "meet your newest group member. This is Rita."

Rita's cheeks grew hot and she looked down. She had sat on her hands, and felt stupid for it. She pulled them out from under her thighs and placed them in her lap, tugging at her thumb.

The women were stirring; she could hear feet shuffling and a couple of coughs. She wondered how long these women had known each other, how long they'd been here. How long she would be expected to stay with them.

"Look up please, Rita." His tone was clipped, but not as hard as it had been in his office. She dragged her head up and looked over the women's heads. At the wall opposite. It had a damp patch creeping down from the ceiling.

She glanced down to see the tall, mousy woman opposite her, giving her a nervous smile. She blinked and looked away.

"Rita?" Mark sounded impatient this time. She muttered under her breath and brought her gaze back up to the woman. Under Rita's stare, she squirmed, less certain of herself now. Her smile had dropped. She looked familiar.

Rita looked down at the woman's hands, which were resting on her knees. Her thumb was drilling into the skin of her palm, and there was a bright red weal beneath it. The woman wore jeans that were a size too large but a few inches too short. Her hands were red raw.

She risked an upwards glance to see that the woman was looking at the counsellor now. This gave Rita the opportunity to examine her face, to work out where she'd seen it before. Her skin was pale and blotchy, her hair just above shoulder length with grey roots. She had full, confident-looking lips and large blue eyes. If she wasn't so skinny, she'd be good looking. But Rita still couldn't place her.

"Can we welcome Rita, please?" said Dr Clarke. He raised his arms to beckon the women up. She shuffled in her seat, clamping herself to it.

Slowly the women rose. The tall woman opposite her first, followed by the angry looking blonde next to her. Tension radiated off her. Then the woman next along, brushing her black hair with her hands. Last was the grey-faced woman next to Mark. Rita flicked a glance at her to see that she had a scar over her right eye.

"Bel?"

Mark had turned to the woman next to him, who was shaking her head, muttering. Rita drew in a long breath and watched her. She looked unhinged; had she been like that before arriving here? Was that why she was here? Rita resolved to speak to her afterwards, to try and find out. Then she stopped herself; she had no intention of making friends. She was getting out of here. As soon as she could speak to a lawyer.

Bel said nothing, but stopped muttering. The tall woman, who was standing next to her, bent and whispered something in her ear. Bel looked up, startled. She whimpered and let the other woman pull her gently to her feet.

"Thank you," said the counsellor. "Let's welcome our newest group member then."

A shimmer of reaction passed through the group. The grey-faced woman next to the doctor frowned at Rita and the tall woman cocked her head, blushing.

"Go on, then."

"What sort of welcome, Dr Clarke?" It was the slight blonde woman, the angry looking one. She shifted and her fingers brushed Rita's arm. Rita tensed.

The counsellor sighed. "Just a welcome, ladies. Not too much to ask, is it?"

The woman turned to Rita. "Welcome." There was a note of menace in her voice. She looked back at the counsellor who motioned her down with his head. She sat.

Each of them in turn repeated the welcome; even Bel. They sat down again.

"Thank you," said the counsellor, injecting brightness into his voice. "Now let's work on the steps, eh?"

The angry woman next to her straightened in her seat; it reminded Rita of Saskia, hauling herself up in her seat to answer a question in class. Dr Clarke looked at her.

"Rita first, I think. But first, introductions are in order."

The woman nodded and simpered at him. Rita felt a shiver travel down her back.

The counsellor turned to the grey-faced woman next to him and raised his eyebrows.

"I'm Paula," she said in a dull monotone.

Rita was next. "Rita," she muttered, superfluously.

The blonde brightened. "I'm Sally," she trilled. Bel started to moan. Mark put a hand on her knee and she stopped.

A murmur came from the next woman along, who had wound her hair around her neck again.

"Louder, please," said the counsellor, irritated.

"Maryam," she said. Her voice was scratchy, making her sound older than she looked. Rita took the opportunity to peer at her around Sally; she was staring back at the counsellor, her eyes huge and the skin around them dark. Rita wondered if she slept.

There was sniff from the next woman along and the counsellor nodded at her. "I'm Jennifer," she said, giving Rita a blank smile. "I'm new too."

"Shh." The counsellor gave her a warning look. "I didn't ask for biographies."

Jennifer, thought Rita. *Jennifer*. Where did she know her from? Maybe she was one of Ash's friends. Maybe she'd been there in the pub one of the times the group had gathered.

How much did they know about Ash and his friends? Was that why she was here? Maybe it was nothing to do with the school at all.

Her chest grew heavy. Ash was too gentle for a place like this, too good. But the authorities wouldn't think that.

Jennifer turned to the woman next to her, who had bowed her head and was sitting in silence. She looked between her and the counsellor.

"This is Bel," she said to Rita.

"What did I say?" The counsellor was angry now. Jennifer gave him a shrug. "Sorry. I just wanted to help."

Rita narrowed her eyes, trying to get the measure of this woman. Who was she trying to help: the counsellor or Bel? Rita decided to steer clear of her. There was something about her that felt untrustworthy.

The counsellor clasped his hands together. "Thank you everyone. I think we'll do that every time we get someone new, yes?"

No-one spoke, but Sally nodded her head vigorously. He ignored her.

"In fact, it's emboldened me to break with convention again," he continued. Sally stopped nodding and Paula jerked her head towards him. Jennifer stiffened but didn't move.

He smiled. "I'm going to ask our new member to show us Step One. I know that we normally ask the more –

seasoned – members of the group to go first, but today I feel like changing things up a little.”

Rita stared at him. The other women said nothing, but all looked towards her. Except Bel, who seemed to have lost consciousness.

She shook her head, anger rising in her chest. Why was he singling her out like this?

“No,” she said, her voice low.

“I’m sorry?”

She swallowed. “No.”

He gave her an incredulous look. “I’m afraid that isn’t the answer I’m looking for.”

She looked around the group. Sally had her hand up to her face; was she laughing? Jennifer was giving her a concerned look. She wondered how old she was; not old enough to be her mother. She didn’t need to look so patronising.

“Miss Ashgar asked me already,” she said, “and I told her the same thing.”

She was finding her voice now, and had stopped caring what these women thought. Who were they to judge?

“I need to speak to a lawyer before I do anything you tell me to. You should tell me what I’ve been charged with. I have rights.”

Jennifer smiled, chewing her fingernail. Rita remembered: politician. Disgraced. Son who—

She stopped, wondering what they’d all done. What had brought them here. Jennifer Sinclair was in prison, she’d read it in the news. Was this a prison?

She stared at the counsellor. “I’ve told you. I’m doing nothing until you let me exercise my rights.”

She thought of the evenings in Ash’s flat, the long discussions between him and his friends. She hadn’t paid much attention; she wasn't doing anything wrong, after all. But she'd listened when they'd talked about their rights, about what they should do if they were ever arrested.

"You need to tell me what I'm charged with and let me speak to a lawyer. I should have gone before the magistrates by now. I'm eligible for bail."

The counsellor shook his head. "Oh Rita," he said. "You really haven't been paying attention, have you?"

CHAPTER TWELVE

Jennifer watched Mark push his chair back and stride towards Rita. Standing in front of her, he put his hands on her shoulders. Jennifer watched, torn between admiration and pity.

Rita was unblinking, glaring back at the counsellor. Her cheeks had reddened and her nostrils were flaring. She was as angry as he was.

"Come with me," he said. "Now."

Rita sniffed and said nothing. She didn't move. He pulled at her arm, hauling her upwards. But he wasn't strong enough to lift her.

"Go on," whispered Maryam. Rita turned to her. A flash of understanding passed between the two women and then Rita stood quickly, almost sending Mark off balance. Sally, between Rita and Maryam, was smirking.

"Alright," Rita said. But she was at a disadvantage now; standing so close to Mark, she was staring into his chest. Mark wasn't tall; Jennifer's height, in fact. But Rita was short. And young. Jennifer watched her, wondering if she was closer to Samir's age or her own.

Rita turned her head to look at Jennifer. She'd recognised her. Jennifer blushed and looked away. Rita wouldn't be back. Not after that outburst. And once she was gone, Jennifer could proceed with her own plan.

Mark grunted at Rita then looked around the group, finally alighting on Jennifer.

"Jennifer," he said. "I'll be a few minutes. I'm trusting you to make sure there's no trouble while I'm gone."

Sally snorted. He flicked his head round to her. "That includes you, Sally."

Her eyes widened and she nodded, chastened.

"Right. I'll be right back. You keep quiet while I'm gone. All of you."

He tightened his grip on Rita's shoulder and pulled her out of the room. She struggled to keep up with him, to walk instead of being dragged. But her jaw was tight with defiance.

The door slammed and the room fell quiet. Bel was breathing heavily, still unconscious, but otherwise the women were silent, looking between each other.

Sally broke the silence. "Silly bitch."

Jennifer glared at her. "Shush."

Sally laughed. "Oh, Jennifer," she intoned, mimicking Mark. "Look after the group while I'm gone." She straightened in her chair. "Who's the teacher's pet now then, eh?"

Jennifer felt her cheeks heat up. "It's not like that. Anyway, just be quiet. Please. We don't want to get into—"

"Oh for fuck's sake." Sally scratched her head, pulling out a few strands of her thin hair.

Jennifer dug her thumbnail into her palm but said nothing.

Sally continued. "You really think anyone cares if we

talk to each other? It's not as if we're going to plot our escape or something, is it?"

Maryam sniffed. Paula was watching Sally, her expression calm.

"As if I'd help you bunch of inadequates escape."

"Now, Sally," said Paula. "That's enough."

"Let her continue," said Maryam. "Dig herself a hole. She likes that."

"Shut up, you jihadi bitch."

Jennifer's eyes widened. "Sally, take that back!"

Sally smirked. "No. I know you, Jennifer Sinclair. You're just as bad as her. All of you deserve to be put in a boat together and shipped off somewhere. Maybe you'll die on the way. Maybe you'll see sense and jump overboard."

Paula stood up. "Sally. I really think you should—"

Sally stood and approached her. Jennifer stayed in her seat, glancing at the door. If Mark came back now, this would all be her fault.

"I don't get why you're sticking up for them," Sally said to Paula. "You're not like them."

"I'm not like you."

"You're an idiot. Just like that stupid bitch Rita. None of you know what's good for you!"

Jennifer leaned forward. "Does anyone know where he'll have taken her? Will she be OK?"

Maryam shook her head. "I don't know. I hope so."

Sally turned to face Jennifer. High dots of red pricked her cheeks and there was a sheen of sweat on her forehead. She was like a cornered animal.

"Why do you care?" Sally asked her. She paused then cocked her head. "Oh, of course. I forget. You think you're one of them, don't you?"

Paula's hand was on Sally's shoulder. "Sally, I think you should—"

Sally shrugged it off. "Eh? Speak, Jennifer Sinclair. High and mighty MP."

"I'm not an MP anymore."

She wondered if they were planning the by-election already. If John had filled her shadow cabinet job. Of course he had; she'd been gone for – how long?

She frowned, realising she wasn't sure. Apart from the monotony of the days, there was no indication of time passing here; clocks but no calendars. And no familiar phone or laptop to remind her of the date every morning. She'd sometimes longed for freedom from the calendar, for a simpler life. Now she knew that longing had been wrong.

"You heard him," Paula said to no-one in particular. "Fast-track."

"That's not good," said Maryam. "She'll never get through it."

"What's fast-track?" asked Jennifer.

"They skip all the steps," said Maryam. "Take you straight to the end of the programme."

Jennifer frowned.

"She'll have to do it all," sneered Sally. "In public. All six steps, with no practice." She chuckled. "She'll crash and burn."

Jennifer looked at the door again, torn between her instructions and her curiosity. She leaned in; the women were all again now. Bel had woken up and was scratching her chin, pulling her fingers away and staring at them every few seconds.

"Then what?" Jennifer whispered. "What happens to her?"

A shadow passed over Paula's face. "She'll fail."

"And?"

A shrug. "Depends on how lenient they're feeling. If she's lucky, she'll have to start all over again."

"She won't," said Maryam.

"Won't what?" asked Jennifer.

"Won't be lucky. Won't pass. You saw her. Poor girl."

They sat in silence for a moment, looking at the door. Even Sally was quiet.

"And if she passes?" asked Jennifer.

Maryam grunted. "If."

"Yes. If? If she passes?"

Sally turned to her. "Well, then she gets to leave us. Go home."

Jennifer felt her eyes widen. "Leave? Just like that?"

"It's not that simple," said Paula. "She won't pass. That's the whole point. Set an example."

"But," continued Jennifer, her mind racing. "But what if she did – what if someone did pass? If they were fast-tracked, and then passed? Would they get out?"

She thought of Samir. Of Yusuf and Hassan. Was this her answer? Her heart was pounding against her rib cage.

"Don't get any ideas," said Paula.

She stiffened. "Why not?"

Maryam put her hand on Jennifer's arm. "It's rare for anyone to be fast-tracked. I've only seen it once before."

"And?"

She shrugged. "We don't know. We never know what happens, afterwards."

Jennifer tried to push down her irritation. She wanted answers.

"Look," she said, her eyes travelling between the other women. "How do I get to be fast-tracked?"

Sally sneered. "You'll fail."

"Why? Why should I?"

She went over the programme in her mind, all six steps, rehearsed in her room. She had them all by heart now, and knew she could do it. All she needed was the opportunity.

A sound came from outside. They all sat straight, eyes darting towards the door. Even Bel.

They all stared as voices passed outside the door, then receded. Jennifer felt herself breathe again.

"Why should I fail?" she whispered.

"You know that," said Sally.

"I don't know what you're talking about."

Sally leaned towards her, hissing through gritted teeth. "Of course you effing do. You're responsible for this place. The programme. You were there when it all started."

She shook her head. "I'm not. I wasn't." A pause; they were staring at her. "I voted against it."

Paula's eyes softened. "But you were responsible. Weren't you?"

Her stomach felt hollow. Was it really all her fault?

"It wasn't just me," she said. "I had support. From the public. People like you, probably."

Paula shrugged. "Yes but we didn't know any better, did we?"

Jennifer struggled to find words that would reassure the other women, convince them that she'd acted with the best intentions. She was interrupted by the door opening.

Mark strode in. The women's eyes fell off each other, gazes thrown to the floor.

"Well," said Mark. "I'm glad to see we're all behaving ourselves."

Jennifer looked at him, determined to get answers from him at her next one-to-one.

"Jennifer has been keeping us in check," Sally said.

Jennifer glared at her. Sally looked back, her face full of false innocence. "You'll fail," she mouthed, and smiled.

CHAPTER THIRTEEN

Yonda Hughes was a tall, well built woman with a stare that almost pierced your skin. Today she was wearing a yellow blouse under an emerald green jacket, topped by a shimmering necklace and earrings that caught the light when she spoke. Her dark skin, almost black at this time of year, seemed to recede against the vibrant clothes.

Mark had known the occasional doctor like her, in his last job. Once they rose through the ranks and achieved the status of Consultant, they felt they could let their inhibitions go out of the window and wear what they wanted. The brighter the better, in fact, as it made them stand out among the dreary junior doctors they almost always had in tow.

Here, Yonda's outfits made him think about the changes this building had gone through, the paintings that would once have adorned the walls and the plush carpets that would have softened their footsteps. In the governor's office there was just one concession to the past; a single framed painting on the wall behind her desk. It looked like an

Impressionist, but Mark was no expert and had never got close enough to look at the signature.

Yonda was perched on her desk, files stacked next to her and another in her hand: Rita's.

Mark had worked with women like Rita before. He felt sorry for her. She mistakenly believed that she still had some rights, that the law didn't allow him to do what he wanted with her. He could only hope she would reconsider soon, and make things easier on herself.

Judging by Yonda's attitude in this patient review meeting, that wasn't looking likely.

"I'm bored with women like this," she said. "Why can't they just cooperate, make things easier for all of us? I've got targets to meet."

Mark shrugged. She knew the answer and he wasn't about to waste his time by going over it.

She slapped Rita's file on top of the pile and sighed.

"Let's show her how things work."

Mark raised an eyebrow.

Yonda turned to his colleague, sitting next to him opposite their boss's desk. "Meena, what was your take on her when she got here?"

Meena blushed. This was only her second month in the job and she was struggling to get used to Mark as a colleague rather than as her counsellor. He was proud of Meena; she'd been a success story. Even Yonda had given him a pat on the back when she'd graduated, the first to do so. Senior management had been cock-a-hoop.

"She didn't want to recite the oath," Meena said. "At first she said she would, then she refused. Then in her second meeting, she kept asking when she would see a lawyer."

Yonda slipped down from the desk, her flesh jiggling as

she did so. She walked between Mark and Meena and started pacing the floor behind them. Mark shifted in his chair, craning his neck.

"But I do think there's hope for her," Meena continued, stumbling over the words. "I'm sure you remember what I was like at first."

Yonda smiled. "Oh God Meena, that we do. Right pain, you were."

Meena allowed herself a nervous smile. "I think she'll see sense. Once she understands that she can't see a lawyer, that there won't be a trial. She's bright. I've looked at her file."

"Hmm." Yonda turned to Mark. "What was she like in group? Make any headway? If anyone can get them to play along, it's you."

He ignored the compliment. "Nope. Nothing."

Yonda shook her head. "Right, then." She walked back to her desk and hauled herself onto it again, pushing a file off with her bottom. "Let's fast-track her."

Meena gasped.

Mark nodded. "That's what I told her would happen if she refused to cooperate."

"Hmm. You should have waited to speak to me first. But yes, that's what we need to do."

Next to him, Meena was trembling. She'd seen the fast-tracking system before, but from the point of view of a patient. He tried to remember which ones she'd been there for. Then he remembered: Ashira Ghazi. No wonder she was trembling.

He reached out and brushed her arm with his fingers. She flinched and turned to him, tucking her hair into that hijab. Her eyes were hard.

"Sorry," he whispered. "It'll be fine. Rita won't pass, but it won't be like Ashira."

She gave a tight nod. Was there a tear at the corner of her eye? Meena Ashgar, not as tough as he'd thought. Well, that might help her in this job.

Yonda stood up. "Oh, Meena. It'll be fine. I promise you. She's not like you. You got it, quickly. After the first week, you were the perfect patient."

Meena's face had hardened and her blush had gone. She wasn't meeting Yonda's eye. She blinked a few times then nodded.

Yonda cocked her head. "Good. Get it sorted, you two. I'm due in a conference call in five minutes, so I need you out."

They stood up. Yonda cleared her throat.

"Mark, could you stay behind for a moment, please?" Her voice was casual. He glanced at Meena, who blushed and headed for the door. He took his seat again.

Yonda piled all the files in the centre of her desk then took the chair Meena had vacated. He could smell her perfume, rich and heady. Her dark brown eyes, flecked with yellow, bored into his face.

"I need you to help me with something. One of the patients."

"Mm-hmm."

She glanced at the files and then crossed one leg over the other. Her tights made a shuffling noise against each other and the chair creaked. Mark tried not to pull back.

"Jennifer Sinclair."

"Yes." This wasn't a surprise; the governor was bound to be interested in a disgraced former MP. He wondered if her file was the thick one, in the centre of the pile.

"What's she like?"

He scratched his chin. "Well, she seems to be doing OK. I've got her to step two in less than a week. I think maybe we could fast-track her. I think she'll pass."

Yonda looked alarmed. "Oh no."

"Sorry?"

"You mustn't do that."

"Why not? Surely the sooner we can get her cured and out of here, the better?"

Yonda brought a pink fingernail up to her lips and tapped them. "Not for this one, no."

This made no sense. The purpose of this centre was to help women through the programme and rehabilitate them. Passing them and sending them back out was good for everyone; the women, the staff, the general public. Not to mention the company that ran the place. Surely a reformed MP would be their biggest and best advert yet.

"But if we manage to cure a former MP—"

"Let me stop you there. You don't think we can ever tell anyone she was here, do you?"

He frowned. "Well, I hadn't really thought about—"

Yonda shook her head. "As far as the outside world is concerned, she's in prison. Bronzefield." She chuckled. "The irony."

She pulled her finger from her lips and reached out towards Mark, then thought better of touching him. "She can't be allowed to pass."

"Why not?"

"Come on Mark. I can't answer that question. But I've been given instructions, and I'm passing them to you. Slow her down. Make it difficult. Put any obstacle you can think of in her way."

He sighed. Suddenly he had a mental image of Jennifer's

face online, captured in the Houses of Parliament as she was being arrested. She was wide-eyed, her face pale in the light of the camera. She looked older now, in the flesh, more frail.

"What would happen, if she left here? Surely she'd just go back to prison?"

Yonda waved a hand. "That's what I thought. But it seems they don't want her out of here. Not in prison, and not back in the spotlight. And certainly not released."

"OK." He didn't feel comfortable about this. The clinical aspect of the job was what got him out of bed in the mornings; as a psychiatrist, he knew he could help these women, rehabilitate them. He didn't like being told how to do his job.

But there was no point in arguing.

"Has anyone been asking after her?"

Yonda narrowed her eyes. "Why d'you want to know that?"

He felt himself blushing. "Sorry. Just curious, that's all."

"Well if you know what's good for you, you'll stop asking. As far as the powers that be are concerned, Jennifer Sinclair has left the spotlight. And they want it to stay that way." She wrinkled her nose. "I didn't tell you any of this, right?"

"Right." A pause. "Any specifics? For keeping her back?"

"No. I'll leave that to your expertise."

"OK." He checked his watch; more than five minutes had passed and there was no phone call. "Do you need me to leave now?"

Yonda stood up and smoothed her skirt over her thighs. It had deep creases running across it with repeated sitting. She tossed the files into a cabinet and moved round her desk. Her chair was large and ornate, dating from the original house. It contrasted with the one he sat in, also old, but in a way that made him imagine it might collapse at any moment. She leaned back, smiling.

"Please. Thanks, Mark. I know I can rely on you."

He nodded and turned for the door. Behind him, Yonda had started humming something to herself.

"Hang on a minute."

He turned round. "Yes?"

"Just one thing. Keep her away from that Rita woman. I don't like the thought of the two of them influencing each other."

He shrugged. Jennifer and Rita had shown no sign of becoming friendly. "No problem."

CHAPTER FOURTEEN

Rita sat alone at breakfast. The other women from her group were at a table in the opposite corner, quietly talking between themselves. Except Paula; she was sitting at another table with another woman, short and dark with a high pitched laugh.

She'd slipped past them without making eye contact and found this small, solitary table near the exit. She watched them as she ate her soggy toast. Sally, the one who'd looked at her like she was a piece of gum stuck to her shoe, was gazing across at Paula and her friend as if she wished she were with them instead. She hardly spoke, only seeming to answer questions with monosyllabic grunts.

Bel, of course, wasn't taking part in the conversation. She stared at the other women, her eyes round, and shovelled spoonfuls of cereal into her mouth without looking down. More than once she spilled food down herself, but seemed not to notice. Instead, Maryam would lean over and sponge the food off with a paper tissue. It only made things worse, the paper mixing with milk to form a scratchy white stain on Bel's blue shirt.

Jennifer and Maryam were the only ones making anything resembling conversation. They muttered to each other, Jennifer's eyes flicking around the room as Maryam spoke then falling back on her companion's face. Maryam was still playing with her hair, tucking it into her collar between bites of toast. Jennifer was ignoring it in a way that looked deliberate.

Rita was torn between watching these women, trying to get the measure of them, and ignoring them, focused instead on her own release. She still hadn't been told what rights she had, and was beginning to wonder that maybe she had none. Ash hadn't prepared her for this.

She was watching Jennifer leaning in towards Maryam, asking her a question, when suddenly Jennifer's eyes rose to meet her own. Rita stiffened, feeling as if she'd been caught out. Then she mentally berated herself and arranged her face into a look of nonchalance. Jennifer responded with a smile.

Rita looked down at the table, uncomfortable. Could she leave without finishing her breakfast, or would she be punished? She decided to wolf the food down as quickly as she could. She was hungry.

She caught movement from the corner of her eye and looked up, expecting to see Jennifer standing over her. Politicians, she thought. Always such busybodies. The local MP had visited her school once, throwing the headteacher into a tizzy of panic, tidying classrooms herself and snapping at the staff to neaten themselves up for the day. She wondered if those people ever got to see the world as it really was.

But it wasn't Jennifer. Instead, two orderlies stood in front of her. She sighed. Was it time for her one-to-one, already? This new counsellor, the man, was hard faced and would surely lose patience with her non-cooperation soon. She had to hold out until she could find a way out of here.

One of the orderlies gestured at her tray. "Eat up. Then you have to go to your room."

She looked at the half eaten toast and cooling mug of tea; she wasn't all that interested in finishing them. "Why?"

The orderly looked at his colleague, then back at her. "To prepare."

She leaned back and folded her arms across her chest. Her heart was pounding. "Prepare for what?" Was she going to be released? Did she have a visitor, maybe?

"OK," she blurted, and stood up.

"Get rid of that," the orderly said, looking at the tray. She picked it up and took it to the waste counter, where she piled her plate on top of others and threw the remains of her breakfast away.

"Good. Come with us."

She glared at the orderlies. Why did they need two of them, just to take her up to her room? And what sort of preparations would she be expected to make, once she got there?

"I'm capable of walking up there by myself."

"We know that. But we've been told to take you."

She shrugged, feeling a shiver run down her back. She glanced across the dining room to see that Jennifer and the other women had gone. The room was emptying fast, women muttering among themselves. They were heading along the corridor towards the back of the house, where she'd been taken for that group session two days ago. Why weren't *they* being taken to their rooms?

She looked at the orderlies again then headed towards the stairway to her room on the second floor. It was tiny, no more than a box room, with a slim single bed that still took up so much room that she had to squeeze round the door to get in. When she sat up in bed, her head would hit the sloping ceiling. It smelt of damp, and the droppings of some unidentified rodent. But at least when she was in there she was free to roam her own mind, to convince herself that she wasn't going mad. She'd found a piece of charcoal under her bed and used it to mark off the days on the wall behind her headboard, where no-one would see. Five so far.

When they arrived at her room the orderlies waited outside while she squeezed herself in. She looked round the half-open door at them, wondering what would happen next.

"Wait there," said one of them. She realised his colleague had stayed silent the whole time. She looked at their name badges: Tim and Roy. Roy she'd met before; Tim was new.

She sat on the bed, looking around the room and wondering how long she would have to wait, and what she was expected to do. She didn't have any personal belongings to gather together, in anticipation of release; her clothes had been taken off her when she arrived and shoved into a clear plastic bag, filed away somewhere. Would she get them back, or would she have to leave here in the jeans and t-shirt she was wearing now? It was chilly, a spring mist like a thin veil outside the windows.

She looked out of the tiny roof window above her bed, the only source of light. All she could see was the blank sky above. A plane passed overhead, its trail thin and distant in the white sky. Five days. Already the normality of aeroplanes, trains, buses and cars seemed so distant. She wondered who was covering her class. It had been a Wednesday when they arrested her, but today was a – she had to stop and think – Monday, and the children would have been without her for three days. Would she slip back into her old job as if nothing had happened, or would she be denied that? Even Saskia would be a welcome relief, after this. Even Darius Williams. She allowed herself a smile at the thought of the boy's misdemeanours, so irrelevant now.

She pulled the headboard back to check the tally on the wall. Hopefully she wouldn't be adding a sixth mark. But the wall was bare. She frowned and pulled the bed back further, leaning over to get a better look. Was she imagining it? Had she marked the wall further down than she remembered? But even when she scraped the bed all the way back from the wall – quietly, so as not to be heard – there was nothing.

She shoved the bed back in and lay face down on it, her mind blank. She was sure she'd made those marks, could picture them in her mind. The charcoal she'd reached for under the bed, after searching every inch of this space on her first night. Her sudden resolution to mark the time here, to leave some sort of record. It was gone.

There was a noise in the corridor outside. She sat up and wiped her eyes, sniffing. She had to keep it together.

A quiet knock came at the door. She almost laughed at the incongruity.

"Come in."

The door was pushed open and a head appeared around it. Male, with pale skin and dark, wavy hair. Her counsellor. She felt her heart sink.

He smiled at her. "Hello, Rita."

"Hello."

"How are you feeling?"

She shrugged. "OK." Why was she behaving like one of her pupils? This place seemed to turn her into a petulant little girl. She sat up and squared her shoulders.

"I'm fine, thank you. I've been told to prepare for something. Where are you taking me?"

His eyes crinkled; there were deep crows' feet either side of them. "Back to the room we were in yesterday, for the group session."

"Oh." She hadn't been expecting this. "I thought maybe I had a—"

"Sorry. Can I come in?"

She shrugged again. Why was he being nice, all of a sudden?

He shifted into the room and sat down next to her on the bed, far enough that they weren't touching. He examined his fingernails, which were short and bitten.

"You understand that it's my job to help you get through the programme?"

"Yeah."

"Well, we haven't been making much progress so far, have we?"

He turned to her. She refused to meet his eye, shaking her head instead. "You know what I want. I want to see a lawyer. I'm entitled to a proper trial."

Her voice was lower now and she felt less sure of herself. Was there something she hadn't paid attention to, on the news? She cursed herself for not keeping abreast of current affairs. If some law had been passed that meant she had no rights...

"That's not going to happen, Rita." His voice was harder now. She pinched her lips together.

"We've decided that you need to be made to understand that. To realise the reality of your situation."

He scratched his head. She didn't move. On the roof above her head, there was the rattling sound of birds roosting.

"You know that the programme has six steps, right?"

"Yes."

"So, once you've worked through those, there's a ceremony. It's called Celebration. It's where you show your colleagues in your group, and your counsellor, that you're better. That you've been cured of your negative and unhelpful thoughts."

She looked up. "There's nothing negative about my thoughts."

He raised an eyebrow. "Look Rita, it'll help if you cooperate. It's been decided to fast-track you. Which means your Celebration is going to happen today. This morning."

"What?"

"You and I are going to talk through the entire six steps together. There'll be an audience. Your group."

She frowned.

"And other groups," he continued.

She remembered breakfast. How many women had been there; twenty? Thirty?

"There are more groups?"

"Of course. This is a big house. Did you think there was just the six of you?"

She stood up, almost hitting her head on the ceiling. "I'm not doing it."

"I thought you'd say this."

She faced the wall not six inches from her face. "You can't do this to me. This is ridiculous."

He stood up and put a hand on her shoulder, pushing her back on to the bed. She rubbed her shoulder. "Don't touch me."

He looked down at her; his cheeks were red. "I don't like having to do this."

"Do what?"

He squatted in front of her, his eyes just below hers. "Tell me, Rita, are you going to cooperate? It will be easier for you if you do."

She looked at him through her eyelashes. "No."

He stood up again. "Very well."

He opened the door and spoke to someone outside. She stiffened.

He glanced back at her then slipped outside. The orderlies from earlier on came in, their bulk filling the room.

"Stay sitting on the bed, please," Tim said. He was well-built, almost a foot taller than her. He was wearing a short-sleeved shirt today, and she could see a tattoo poking out from it.

"Why?"

"Because I say so."

She glared at him but stayed where she was. Leaving the room was impossible now, and they could easily overpower her. She wondered if the counsellor was still outside, or if he had conveniently disappeared.

The second orderly was pulling something from a bag he had slung over this shoulder. He placed the bag on her bed and she glanced it it; it looked medical. She didn't need any medicine.

"What are you doing?"

"Hold still, please."

Tim was gripping her shoulders now, pushing her down. She felt as if she was being ground into the bed, but managed to stay sitting. She looked at his colleague, Roy, and tried to stay calm.

"You can't do this."

Tim's face was impassive. "We can. Your doctor has told us to."

"I don't have a doctor."

"Your counsellor. He's your doctor. Dr Clarke."

"Not without my consent! You can't do this! Leave me alone!"

She considered pushing against his grip, making a dash for it. But as soon as she shifted her weight, his grip tightened.

"Don't move, please."

She stared into his eyes and then at the object his colleague held in his hand. It was a syringe.

"Stop it! I'll cooperate." She raised her voice. "Dr Clarke! Are you out there! I'll come with you!"

Tim smiled. "Too late for that. He's gone. He'll be waiting for you, downstairs."

Her body tensed as she realised the hopelessness of her situation. She had no idea what was in that syringe.

"What are you injecting me with?"

"Just a sedative. Don't worry. The serum will come later."

"What serum?"

But his response was a blur. She felt a sharp pain in her shoulder and the world started to fade in front of her eyes. Helpless, she fell onto the bed.

CHAPTER FIFTEEN

The breakfast room was bleaker than the room they'd been in for group session. At the back of the house the ground floor had lower ceilings and a dingy, uncared-for feel. There were no patches from missing pictures on the wall and the paint was peeling in places, dusty marks betraying damp.

Jennifer sat with the other women in her group, glad of the company. In Parliament she'd tended to keep to herself, lacking confidence in her ability to network, to trade on easy relationships the way John did. But here she felt an affinity with these women. She'd only known them for a few days yet she felt relaxed in their company, for once comfortable to be herself.

The group wasn't complete. Rita, the newcomer, sat alone in a far corner, staring at them from time to time like a frightened animal. And Paula was with her buddy Mandy. The two of them sat at the next table, laughing at each other's jokes and touching each other's arms and hands in a way that made Jennifer miss Yusuf. She wondered if relationships were allowed between the women, or if her roommates had to hide the way they felt about each other. It was fairly obvious from where Jennifer was sitting.

Breakfast was better than it had been in prison, or at least it was fresher. She'd helped herself to a couple of slices of toast and a smear of marmalade from a catering size jar, along with two cups of strong coffee. She hadn't slept well last night, disturbed by Paula and Mandy's coordinated snoring and haunted by her worries for her family. She knew that she wasn't going to get any visitors here, but was hopeful that they might allow Edward in, and that he could give her news.

The room wasn't large but they'd managed to squeeze in a number of small tables, women huddled around them and leaning over their trays. There were possibly thirty women in here, all talking amongst themselves. Most were in groups of five or six – counselling groups, she guessed. They were a mix of ages and races, with a high proportion of Asian women. Some wore headscarves, others didn't, which made Jennifer wonder about Maryam.

She watched Maryam eat with one hand, the other in her hair. Maryam was a Muslim name, and she looked like a woman who was missing her hijab. Why wasn't she allowed to wear it? Was it something to do with her crimes outside, with what had brought her here, or was it punishment for some misdemeanour inside? Jennifer knew how vulnerable Maryam would feel without it, even when the male orderlies weren't present. They may be surrounded by women, but they were strangers.

She resisted the temptation to ask Maryam about it and instead focused on continuing the conversation they'd had two days ago, about Rita and the programme. But Maryam was wary today and reluctant to answer Jennifer's questions. Something about Rita's behaviour had loosened the other women's tongues. But now they were still.

As she was finishing her toast, the other women started to move. As one they were standing and taking their trays to the waste station, forming a quiet, orderly queue. Jennifer frowned; at previous meals this had been a slow, haphazard process, accompanied by as much noise as the meal itself.

"Get up," Maryam whispered. "We all need to go."

"Go where?"

Maryam allowed herself a small smile. "You'll find out."

Sally and Bel stood up, Sally reluctantly catching Bel's arm as she nearly slipped and fell. The four of them headed for the waste station. Paula slipped in behind, with Mandy disappearing into another group. Jennifer looked across the room for Rita. Surely she would join them. But Rita was still alone at that table, or not quite alone. Two orderlies stood in front of her, talking down at her. Her face was contorted, her cheeks flushed. Jennifer felt her heart skip a beat.

The women filed out of the room and into the corridor along the back of the house. Orderlies flanked them, watching in silence, with the occasional frown for bad behaviour. Jennifer's group were near the back. She could see over the heads of the women in front of her and knew that they were turning into the room where she'd had her group sessions. She looked at Maryam next to her, raising an eyebrow in question, but Maryam put a finger to her lips and glanced at the orderly closet to them.

As they approached the room, the silence broke. Coming from inside was the sound of dozens of excited voices. Chairs scraped against the floor and there was a rumble of pounding feet. She felt herself grow cold.

Inside, the noise was deafening. In front of her,

arranged in semi circular rows, were dozens of chairs. Most were taken, women jiggling in place and craning their necks to see the front. Feet slammed against the floor and hands were clapping, the rhythm like a chant. Moving around the crowd were more orderlies, pumping their arms in encouragement. They looked sweaty, even more excited than the women.

As they passed through the gap in the centre of the chairs, she looked at the women's faces. Some of these women had been in the dining room with them, but other faces were new. Where had they all appeared from? She counted the rows – ten of them, with maybe ten women on each. More towards the back, where the semicircle grew bigger.

The women's faces glowed with sweat and emotion; some were afraid and others excited. All of them looked at the orderlies, and at the row of people standing at the front. Five people, all wearing suits. Two men and three women, one of whom wore a green hijab over her grey suit. She was the only one of them who wasn't white. Her expression was different from the others': she was scanning the rows of women more intently, as if looking for someone. The others next to her looked across the tops of the women's heads, smiling nervously. She imagined they were counsellors, but where was Mark?

An orderly ushered her group to the front row and waved his arms at them, encouraging them to make noise. Paula and Sally started thumping their feet, their faces tight. Bel shuffled her feet on the floor, her eyes wide and her head stiff. Maryam allowed herself to relax and started clapping. Jennifer followed suit.

She leaned in towards Maryam, sitting next to her. "What's going on?"

"Celebration." Maryam had to shout into her ear to be heard. She watched the nearest orderly as she spoke.

"What's Celebration?"

"Final stage. Once you've gone through the six steps."

Jennifer frowned. There was nothing about this in the booklet.

"There's nothing in the book—"

"They don't want to scare you."

"Why would you be scared?"

Maryam paled. "Don't worry."

"What do you mean, this is the last stage? What happens after this?"

"Pass this, and you get out."

She felt her eyes grow wide. "All of us?"

Maryam turned to look at her, then quickly looked to the front again. "No, silly. Her." She pointed towards the empty space at the front.

"Who do you mean?"

"They'll bring her in in a minute. Hopefully she'll be walking. But there's no bed."

Paula leaned across Maryam. "That means they've had to sedate her."

Jennifer was feeling increasingly confused. "What do you mean? Why would you be sedated, for your release?"

Paula smirked. "Not everyone gets out."

"Sorry?"

"You don't necessarily pass. Sometimes they like to put someone through it who's not ready. Make an example of her."

Jennifer shuddered. "Do you— Have any of you done this?"

Maryam was quiet. Paula looked at her, her expression wary.

"Maryam?" Jennifer asked.

Maryam nodded. "How d'you think I got this?" She pulled her hair towards Jennifer.

So that was the situation. This was the last stage of the programme. If you passed, you got out. If you failed, they punished you.

"What did you do wrong?"

She knew she was being nosy. But the noise here gave her a boldness she hadn't felt in the quiet of the dining room.

Maryam shook her head. She rubbed an eye. "I wasn't ready."

Jennifer nodded and looked back to the front. The counsellors had shifted into a huddle and were talking among themselves. Then they pulled back and formed a row again. One of them – a man, thin and blond, with translucent skin and an unhealthy look about him – put up a hand. The room fell silent.

The door opened behind them. The counsellors looked round but stayed in their line. The orderlies hustled to arrange themselves around the room, evenly spaced. Jennifer craned her neck. Behind her the women were quiet, a silence broken by the occasional *shush* of admonishment.

A large black woman walked through the door. She wore a red and yellow floral blouse and a red skirt that was tight on her large thighs. Her height – she was almost as tall as Jennifer – was exaggerated by a pair of red platform heels. Her face glowed and her curly dark hair was piled on top of her head.

The woman smiled and the room grew quieter.

"Thank you, ladies," she said. "It's a pleasure to see you all here today. Celebration is my favourite time."

She looked around the room like a proud teacher surveying a class of well behaved six year olds. Then she took a couple of steps forward, passing the row of counsellors. They watched her, looking uncomfortable.

The woman approached them and scanned the front row. Her gaze settled briefly on Jennifer then moved on. Jennifer shuffled in her seat, unnerved by the flash of recognition that had passed over the woman's face.

Finally she stepped backwards. The counsellors parted to let her stand in the middle of the row.

"Some of you are new here." Again her gaze flicked to Jennifer, then quickly away. "You may not know who I am." She paused as if waiting for a response, then smiled and clasped her hands together. "My name is Ms Hughes. I'm the centre's governor. It is me you have to thank for these wonderful counsellors who are helping you all to get better."

She swept her hand along the row of counsellors, who shuffled in place. The women were silent. Somewhere behind her, Jennifer heard someone mutter 'bollocks'.

Ms Hughes turned back to the women, pacing in front of the counsellors.

"So," she said. "A treat for us all. A Celebration." She licked her lips. "Something I know you all look forward to."

She cocked her head as if waiting for an answer. "Don't you?"

Someone shouted 'Yes!' Ms Hughes smiled over the heads of the women. "Now that wasn't good enough, was it. Tell me, are you looking forward to this?"

More voices. "Yes!" Jennifer looked at the women either side of her, wishing they hadn't been put in the front row. Ms Hughes' eyes kept returning to her. She breathed in and cried, "Yes!" but it came too late, and rang out after the other women's cries had stopped. Ms Hughes looked at her again, for longer this time, and gave her a patronising smile. She blushed.

"Good," cried the governor, her hands clasped above her head. "Now show me just how much you're looking forward to this!"

Jennifer was thrown into a sea of noise. Feet thumped, hands clapped, there were whistles and shrieks. Maryam joined in, standing up and clapping. Jennifer followed suit, daring a whistle. She felt ridiculous. Did these women really feel this, or were they pretending? She risked turning to look at the faces behind her. Some were bright with emotion but others were hard, not matching their owners' gestures.

"Good, that's fantastic," Ms Hughes exclaimed, then swept her arms to an abrupt halt. The women fell silent. "Now for the star of the show."

Jennifer felt herself squirm. Was this how they were referred to, as a star? She wondered how it would feel, to be the one up there at the front. Would it feel like making a speech in the Commons chamber? She doubted it.

There was another hush. A woman panted behind her. Maryam sat down next to Jennifer, who had already slumped into her seat.

She leaned towards her. "Where's Mark?"

Maryam nodded towards the door. "He'll be with her."

"Who?"

Maryam looked at her, her brow creased. "Rita, of course."

CHAPTER SIXTEEN

Rita opened her eyes to see a high ceiling some five feet above her. This wasn't her poky room.

She blinked a few times, her mind working over her body. Her wrists and ankles hurt, and her neck was sore. Her head felt dull and heavy, as if she'd been asleep for hours. She realised she was moving, and fought back a wave of nausea. Next to her, looking ahead, was her counsellor. Behind her, at one end of the gurney, one of the orderlies. Beyond her feet, the other. They were wheeling her along a corridor in silence.

She stretched the muscles in her neck and looked around as best she could. She was on the ground floor, she was sure; the blank patches on the walls, the high ceiling with ornate plasterwork at its edges.

"Where are you taking me?" Her voice was blurred and thick.

The movement stopped and she felt herself lurch. Dr Clarke turned to her.

"Don't talk. Not yet."

She pulled against the restraints, feeling the pain in her wrists sharpen. "Tell me why you've got me tied up!"

He shook his head and nodded at the orderly beyond her feet. The movement started again.

She fell back, her head slumping on the thin pillow. The footsteps of the orderlies echoed in the empty space. The wheels squeaked beneath her. But then she heard it, an unfamiliar sound. Coming from up ahead, and growing louder.

She frowned and closed her eyes to listen. Voices. A cacophony of voices. Shouting, cheering, stamping of feet.

"What's going on?"

Dr Clarke raised a finger. "One moment."

They paused at a door which he elbowed open, standing back to let the orderlies push her through. She waited for the noise to increase, for its source to appear. But as the door closed behind her, it dimmed.

She pulled up and looked around. They were in a small, featureless room, with no furniture except two plastic chairs and her gurney. Dr Clarke gestured at the orderlies and they left, their feet shuffling on the wooden floor. Rita could smell air freshener mixed with something more medical; antiseptic? She wasn't sure.

She allowed her head to fall back and blinked up at the ceiling. "Please will you untie me," she said.

She couldn't see his face now, but could hear his breathing rasping in the small space. He was a smoker.

"Please," she said. Hating herself.

"If I do, will you be sensible?"

"Yes."

He leaned over her. His aftershave was musty, making her gag. As his hand passed over her she saw damp patches under his arms and smelt sweat. She closed her eyes, screwing up her face.

He paused and drew back, looking into her face. "The orderlies are right outside," he said. "No funny business, right?"

"Right."

He looked towards the door and then loosened the restraints on her wrists. She pulled at them, relieved to feel their grip loosen.

"My feet?"

He grunted and did as she said. She wriggled her toes. One of her feet had pins and needles; the urge to scratch was excruciating.

"I'd like to sit up."

"No."

"I won't do anything, I promise." Her limbs felt heavy; she wasn't sure if she would be able to sit up anyway. But lying here like this was too much to bear.

"No. Sorry."

She let out a breath. "Why have you brought me down here? I thought I was supposed to be preparing for something."

He was standing over her now, looking down. His tie moved in front of her eyes, its thin blue stripes blurring.

"You are." He pulled one of the chairs over and sat in it, bringing his eyes level with hers. "You're about to undergo something called Celebration."

She frowned. "What?"

"It's the final stage of the programme."

"But I haven't even done the first stage yet." Her energy was returning. "Look, will you just let me off this bed? You have to tell me what's going on. You can't do this."

But she could hear it in her voice; the loss of hope. If

they were prepared to sedate her, to drag her down here on a trolley, there would be no solicitor, no case before the magistrates. She cursed Ash, and then herself. Why hadn't she paid attention, all those nights in the pub when he'd been complaining about the government with his friends? Their friends. She agreed with them of course, but the detail of it bored her. Unless it related to school.

"I can, I'm afraid. And there's a lot more I can do. Legally. You need to listen to me, Rita, You need to see sense."

See sense. Patronising bastard. She pulled at her restraints again; they slackened.

"Stop it," he said.

"OK," she breathed. "So what's this Celebration, then?"

He leaned in and smiled. "That's better. I'm going to take you into a room. The room where you were with me for group, you remember?"

"Yes." How stupid did he think she was?

"I'm going to ask you some questions in there. There will be witnesses."

She nodded. The group, again.

"More witnesses," he said. "Not just your group. All the women here will be present. There's quite a crowd. I'll need you to keep calm."

She nodded again; holding his eyes with hers while she pulled gently at her wrist restraints. He'd loosened them too much.

"What do I need to do?" she asked.

"Just answer the questions."

"Truthfully?"

He chuckled. "Yes. Of course."

She felt her right hand come free. Beyond the door, there was a sound; the orderlies?

She had to act fast. She looked around the room quickly, trying to spot anything she could use. Anything.

There was only the other chair. She couldn't get to it, not with her legs tied up.

"Alright," she said, bringing her eyes back to his. "I'll be a good girl."

He started to smile and then his face fell. He wasn't buying it. Quickly she yanked her left hand upwards, freeing it, and brought her right hand up to meet it. She clenched the two of them in a fist and slammed it into his face. As it made contact she saw his eyes widen.

He crashed backwards, falling off his chair. She pulled herself up and bent to reach her ankles. The straps were secured with buckles, like a watch. She could undo them easily.

A hand fell on her shoulder and pulled her backwards. She tugged against it, screaming.

"Stop it, you stupid bitch." The larger of the two orderlies, the one with the tattoo – Tim – was behind her, pinning her down. His colleague had her other hand and was strapping it down again, tighter this time. He tugged at the strap, testing it. It hurt.

The counsellor rose from the floor, glaring at her. "You're going to regret this."

He looked at the orderly. "Let's get her in there. Quickly."

The orderly pushed the gurney through the door, slamming her head into it. She cried out. Back outside, she could hear the rumble that had disappeared when they'd gone into that room. It grew louder as they sped down the corridor. She took in gulps of air, desperate not to be sick. Lying here like this, she could choke in her own vomit.

But why hadn't they sedated her again? She thought

about what he'd said. *Answer some questions.* They needed her conscious.

She'd answer his damn questions. But she wouldn't give him the answers he wanted.

At last the gurney came to a stop. Next to her, Dr Clarke was panting, sweat dripping from his chin. His nose was swelling but not bleeding.

The noise had stopped, and she could hear a single voice through the doors in front of them. It was a familiar door, one her counsellor had led her through before. But there was more than just her group beyond it.

She strained to hear. The voice was a woman's, deep and sonorous. *Show me,* she heard. Then the voice was drowned out by sound. Raised voices, whistles, hoots, hands clapping, feet stamping on wooden floors. Was this for her? She felt her stomach lurch.

Then, just as abruptly, it went quiet.

"Now," breathed Dr Clarke. The orderlies propped the door open and pushed her in.

It was the same room, alright. But this time, even though she couldn't see anything except the high, cobwebbed ceiling, she could sense that it was full. Whispers skidded over her head, accompanied by shuffling of feet and the occasional cough. She tensed. Who was here?

Mark bent over and whispered into her ear. "I'm going to unfasten your wrists. If you move, Tim there will lean on your ribs. Clear?"

She swallowed. "Clear."

He unfastened the restraints, his eyes staying on her face. She lifted herself up and blinked against the brightness of the sunshine that poured in from the window at the far end of the room.

A shiver travelled through her gut. In front of her, wide-eyed and staring, were over a hundred women arrayed in concentric rows. Next to them and in front was a neat group of people in suits. Two men were closest to her. One of them sneered at her from a face so pale he looked like a ghost. The other was short and obese, sweating profusely. Next to them were three women. Two were nondescript, wearing almost identical black trouser suits beneath dark brown bobbed hair. The third – Rita gasped – wore a green hijab.

She pointed at her. "You're real!" she cried.

The woman paled. The people around her looked at her and a wave or murmurs worked its way through the woman.

"Miss Ashgar. My counsellor. You're real!" she repeated.

Dr Clarke passed in front of her. He pushed her back down to the gurney. "Hush now."

She glared at him. "You lied to me. You told me I was making it up. There she is! She's real!"

He shook his head. "I don't know what you're talking about. Of course Miss Ashgar is real. She's a counsellor. My colleague."

He turned briefly to look at Miss Ashgar, whose eyes widened.

"Now then, what's going on? I think we need to move things along a bit."

Rita turned to see another woman approaching her. She looked nothing like the other counsellors; tall and flamboyantly dressed, she reminded Rita of someone she'd once taught with.

"Who are you?"

The woman chuckled. "I'm Yonda Hughes. Centre Governor. I"m here to help you with your Celebration."

Rita gulped. "I thought he was going to do that."

The woman glanced at Dr Clarke. "Oh, of course. We're all here to help you, my dear."

Rita narrowed her eyes. The governor looked at Dr Clarke and nodded.

The orderlies grabbed Rita's arms and pulled her up. "Stay there," said Tim.

She sat staring at her audience, who stared back. It reminded her of those awful workshops she had to do with parents, but a hundred times worse. She felt an itch start up in her leg, and reached down to scratch it.

"Don't move," snapped Tim, balling his fist. She blanched and pulled back.

Dr Clarke had moved to the other side of the room, and was bending over a table, his back to her. His arms moved; he was doing something, preparing something. What?

Finally he turned, holding a glass of water.

Rita felt her vision blurring. *Don't pass out*, she told herself. She panted in a few sharp breaths, willing herself to focus on his face, not on the audience.

He approached and then turned to the group. "This is Rita Gurumurthy. Today is her Celebration."

She thought of the programme that he and Miss Ashgar had told her about, the six steps. They'd only asked her to answer the first one, and she'd refused. She'd seen one of the other women – which one? – answer the second. She had no idea what the rest of them were.

Dr Clarke smiled and held out the glass.

"Here. Drink this, and then we'll get started."

CHAPTER SEVENTEEN

Jennifer struggled with her emotions as she watched Rita being wheeled in. Part of her was being swept up by the excitement and anticipation of the crowd, but a greater part felt fear for Rita. She'd only spent a matter of minutes in the other woman's company, but already she felt an almost maternal protectiveness towards her. Rita reminded her of herself at her most naive. Hopelessly ignorant of the law and how it applied to her, she was persisting in the belief that by resisting she could get herself out of this place.

Jennifer knew that was foolish.

Rita pulled herself up from the gurney as they brought her in. Her face was pale and her eyes rimmed with dark shadows. Her normally light brown cheeks were blotchy and stained with tear tracks. But her eyes blazed and she looked as defiant as ever.

Mark bent to whisper in Rita's ear then released her wrists. She sat up and stared at them all. Her eyes flew over Jennifer and the rest of the group and came to rest on the counsellors.

The tall, pale man was shuffling nervously. He looked as if he might lash out at any moment. The young woman in the hijab had paled.

Rita shouted at her, crying out her name. Maryam gasped. Behind her, a woman called out, echoing what Rita had said.

Around her, the women stared at the counsellor, then back at Rita, who was continuing to shout at Mark.

Jennifer's eyes stayed on the counsellor. She was facing Rita now, standing side on to Jennifer, and it was difficult to make out her features. Her features were familiar: sharp nose, the wide eyes ringed with thick eyelashes.

She stooped to whisper in Maryam's ear. "Do you know her?"

"No. Shush."

She stared again at the young woman, who was pushing a stray hair under her hijab.

A rumble ran through the crowd, muttering voices this time, and not clattering feet. Mark was approaching Rita. He passed her a glass of water and she drank from it. She wiped her lips and sat back. The gurney had been rearranged so Rita was upright now, facing the audience.

Mark took a tissue from another counsellor and wiped Rita's cheeks. He looked into her face with a surprising tenderness.

"Rita. Can you hear me?" he asked.

"Yes. I can hear you."

The hush deepened as they strained to hear Rita's voice, which had grown small and childlike.

Mark turned and walked towards the window. He picked up a chair and carried it over to Rita's gurney. Everyone held their breath.

Rita turned her head to him and the audience beyond.

Her face was clear, her eyes half closed and her muscles relaxed.

"Good," said Mark. He glanced up at the governor who gave him a tight nod. Then he shuffled his chair in towards Rita. He didn't lower his voice; he knew that the whole room was listening.

"Now, I'm going to ask you some questions. I need you to answer them for me, in your clearest voice. OK?"

"Yes." Rita's voice rang across the room. Mark placed his hand on Rita's.

"That's perfect," he said. "Let's start with Step One. Can you tell me what you did, Rita? Your crime?"

Her brow furrowed. "Which one?"

Whispering came from the crowd. The governor looked up and the room fell silent.

"Don't worry, Rita," said Mark. "I mean the crime that brought you here. Why were you arrested?"

"I didn't say the oath. With my class."

He nodded. "Which oath is that?"

"The British Values oath."

"Can you say it for me now?"

"I could."

"Yes?"

"But I don't want to."

"I'd like you to, please."

Rita shook her head. "No thanks."

"Alright," said Mark. "Let's go back to Step One. Have you been disloyal to the British State?"

"Depends who you mean."

"Sorry?"

"This is nice."

Whispering rippled through the room. Maryam had

started trembling. Jennifer reached for her hand, and felt hers being gripped tightly.

"I know it's nice," said Mark. "But that's not what I need you to tell us. Have you been disloyal to the British state?"

"I don't think so."

Mark's shoulders dropped. "But you broke the law."

"Yes."

"You don't think that's disloyal?"

"No. Not when it's a stupid law." Rita's voice was still soft.

"Alright," Mark said. "Let's try the next step. Do you accept the sovereignty of the British state?"

"Of course I do. I love this country. My parents came from India, you know, and they struggled to—"

Mark put his hand on her chest. "Yes, I'm sure that's all great. But that's not what I need. I'm glad you accept the sovereignty of the state."

"Not of this crappy government though."

The governor stepped forwards, clapping her hands. "Alright, I think we've heard enough."

Mark looked up at her. The back of his shirt was dark with sweat.

"I need to go through all six steps," he said. "Otherwise it's not valid."

The governor raised a well-groomed eyebrow. "Really? We're going by the book, are we?"

"Yes," he replied, his voice taut.

"Very well. But let's get it over with, for everybody's sake." She looked up at the assembled women. "Be quiet now. All of you."

A woman coughed behind Jennifer, who clamped her own lips together.

Mark dipped his head back down to Rita's.

"Step Three now, please."

Rita frowned. "I don't know what step three is."

The counsellors shuffled nervously. Even the governor looked perturbed. "Get a move on," she snapped.

"I'll help you," Mark said to Rita. "I need you to accept my support. And the support of your group."

Rita's eyes widened. "What group?"

"The group you sat in the other day. Paula, Jennifer, Sally, Maryam and Bel."

Jennifer felt eyes upon her from behind. Maryam's grip on her hand tightened. She was using the other hand to all but strangle herself with her hair.

"Oh. Them. OK then."

"You accept their support."

Rita shrugged. "Guess so?"

"And mine?"

"No."

"Sorry?"

"Not you. I want *her* back." Her arm wafted in the general direction of the counsellors. "Miss Ashgar. I liked her."

"You accept her support?"

"Yes." Rita closed her eyes.

"Stay with me, Rita. I'll be quick."

She opened her eyes again.

"Step Four. Who have you harmed? How will you make amends?"

Rita frowned. 'I haven't harmed anyone."

"I need you to answer the question."

"Unless you mean that girl I stole Ash from. She hated me. I guess we broke her heart."

Mark cleared his throat. "No, that's not what I mean.

How did you harm the children in your class, by not saying the oath?"

Rita's eyes widened. "I didn't harm them. Opposite."

"Sorry?"

"Opposite to harm. Of harm. They're better off. Me. 'Cause of me."

Mark glanced at the governor, who was tapping a foot. Her platformed shoe looked out of place in this dreary room.

"OK Rita, we need to wrap things up," he said. "Steps Five and Six together, OK?"

Rita waved a hand. "Whatever. 'S nice, this."

Maryam sniffed and wiped her cheek. Beyond her, Bel was shaking.

"I need you to tell me how you'll change. What you'll do differently. And I need you to promise to spread the message outside here. To tell people how we've helped you."

The governor frowned. "That's not quite—"

Mark put up a hand. "Rita?"

"Dunno. Not going to change. Maybe change. Will it stop me coming here?"

"Maybe."

"Alright then. I'll change. Won't steal Ash again."

"Again, Rita, that's not what I mean."

"Oh." Rita closed her eyes and slumped onto the gurney, unconscious.

The governor stepped forwards, eyeing the orderlies. "Let's get everybody out of here. Take the patient away."

Mark stepped back and the two orderlies who had brought Rita in wheeled her out again. The women followed, quietly this time.

CHAPTER EIGHTEEN

"Morning."

Rita sat up abruptly, banging her head on the ceiling. She put a hand to it, wincing. Her brain felt thick and her vision was blurred.

"Aah," she groaned.

She forced her eyes open. She was back in her room, in her bed. She lifted the sheet and fumbled her hands down her body. She was wearing pyjamas, the regulation blue. Had she undressed herself?

"Do you want to know how you did?"

"Huh?" She let the room come into focus. Someone was sitting at the end of her bed, facing her. A man, tall and dark haired, with pale skin. He swam into focus. It was Dr Clarke, her counsellor.

She pulled the sheet up higher.

"Don't worry," he said. "I've not been here long. One of the orderlies put you to bed. A woman."

"How many people?"

"Sorry?"

"Were there two of them?" She knew enough about

safeguarding from her training at school to know that if you were undressing a pupil there should be two people present. "Undressing me?"

He shrugged. "I guess so."

She grunted. That would have to do. "How long have I been asleep?" She tried to remember the previous day, but it was foggy. She remembered breakfast, and being brought back up to her room. Then her memory jumped to a room, and her counsellor threatening her. She'd tried to attack him, hadn't she?

After that, the day descended into a grey mist. Had they sedated her, after she attacked him?

"A day and a half," he replied.

She stared at him. "You mean a day. You put me out yesterday morning."

He shook his head. "No. The day before. We decided it was best to keep you calm yesterday. You were screaming blue murder at me."

She narrowed her eyes at him. She had a mental image of his face close to hers, of him asking her questions. She couldn't remember what they were.

"What did you do to me?"

He stood up, brushing imaginary dust from his trousers. His suit looked freshly cleaned. "Don't worry, Rita. We just asked you some questions. You had Celebration. You won't remember it."

So he'd been poking around in her head. "I hate you," she told him.

He laughed. "Not lost any of your spunk then."

"You're not going to do that to me again."

He shrugged. "Maybe, maybe not. For now, I suggest you keep your head down. Think about what you've done. Or haven't done. Maybe try a different tactic."

"Tactic?"

"Your policy of noncooperation. It's not working."

She felt herself deflate. The memories were becoming sharper now; a sea of faces behind his. A large woman in a brightly coloured jacket. But she couldn't remember any questions.

"Who was watching?"

"You're remembering, then."

"Who was watching?"

"Everyone. It's how Celebration works. I'm sure you'll get the chance to spectate yourself."

She had no idea what he was talking about. Whose were those faces? Who was the woman she remembered talking to him, clapping her hands together? The more she tried to picture it, the more her head hurt.

He stood up. "Anyway, you won't be surprised to know that you failed. No release for you, I'm afraid."

She shook her head. "What about my rights?"

"Oh, Rita." He ran a hand through his hair. A tuft stayed up, poking up at the back. "Give up on that, now. The British Values Act applies to your crime. The sentence is to be brought here, and to undergo a rehabilitation programme. The six step programme. Once you get through the programme, you're free to go."

"Alright. So how do I get through this programme, then?"

He smiled. "That's better."

He tossed a small booklet onto the bed. She squinted at it: *British Values Programme.*

"Read that," he told her. "We'll be working through it together. In your one-to-one sessions, and your group."

She looked up. "My group?"

"Yes. The women you met four days ago. They're going

to help you. You're going to help them. Get through the programme, and you get another Celebration. Another crack at the whip."

"Alright." There had to be a way around this, a way to manoeuvre herself into another Celebration. She'd pass next time. She wouldn't attack him.

"Only one more go, mind."

"Sorry?"

"You get two chances. After that, it's a mandatory sentence."

"How long?"

He smiled. "Ah, you don't need to worry about that, do you? You'll help me out, and you'll pass. Next time."

She picked up the booklet and pretended to read it, ignoring him. He stood up.

"Now, time for breakfast. Get dressed, and go downstairs."

He clattered out of the room, squeezing through the half open door. She tossed the booklet onto the bed, trying not to cry.

She pushed herself up from the bed, pausing to gain control of her quivering legs, and grabbed her clothes from where they'd been piled into the bedside cabinet, the only other piece of furniture that would fit in this room. She dressed carefully, easing her sore muscles into the tight fitting clothes. When she was ready, she pushed the door open to find an orderly outside. Roy.

She stared at him. "I can do this myself."

He shrugged. "Sure you can. But he told me to keep an eye on you."

She pushed past him and made her way to the stairs as fast as she could. Occasionally she had to put a hand out to the wall to steady herself.

The dining room was full. She joined the queue at the serving hatch, eyes on the ground. The women in front turned to look at her, sharing whispers. She ignored them. When she emerged with her tray she scanned the tables, trying to find a secluded spot. There were none.

She scanned the room again. Her group were huddled round a corner table, all of them except Sally. She steeled herself. It would be easier without her.

She weaved her way between the tables, catching the pauses in conversation as she passed. Her eyes were on her tray and the floor immediately beyond it. As she approached the table, Jennifer stood up.

Their eyes met; Jennifer's were full of pity. Rita was torn between anger and tears. What had they all witnessed? What had she done, in front of all these women? What had she said?

Jennifer pulled out a chair. "Hi Rita," she said. "Good to see you. Sit down."

Rita sat. Paula was on one side of her, with an unfamiliar woman sharing her chair. On the other side was Maryam, who looked as if she might cry herself. She shuffled her chair in and focused on her bowl of cornflakes. They tasted like dry cardboard.

"How are you?" asked Maryam.

Rita shrugged. "OK."

She could sense the women at the neighbouring tables watching them, talking about them. Paula stood up, making the woman sharing her chair almost topple to the floor.

"Nothing to see here, girls," she said. "Get on with your breakfast."

Rita smiled, wondering if Paula had worked in the police.

"Thanks," she muttered.

"It's fine." Paula sat down again, and the woman sharing her chair grabbed her hand. "This is Mandy, by the way."

Rita looked up and nodded at Mandy. Mandy nodded back. She had a thin, ruddy face topped by a shock of short ginger hair. She was skinny, her elbows sharp on the table. Paula, on the other hand, was short and plump, with rolls of fat protruding from her collar. It was a tight squeeze on that chair.

Rita looked down at her food, hoping the women would go back to their conversation, that they'd ignore her.

No such luck.

"How much can you remember?" asked Jennifer.

She looked up. None of your business, she thought. She shrugged.

Jennifer nodded. "Would you like us to fill you in?"

Did she want to know what she'd said, in front of all those people? Or was she happier with it being a blur?

"No. Please, just let me eat my breakfast."

"Oh, of course. I'm sorry. You won't have eaten since—"

She looked up. Had they been watching for her, waiting for her to return? She wondered if she'd been fed, up in her room. Had she been conscious at all yesterday?

"Tell me," she said. "Tell me what happened."

Jennifer looked at Maryam and then Paula. She cleared her throat.

"OK. I don't know much, as it's the first time I've seen a Celebration. But they brought you in on a trolley. I think they sedated you. Then Mark asked you some questions."

"Mark?"

Jennifer blushed. "Our counsellor."

Paula leaned in. "He took you through the six steps. You gave him hell."

"What do you mean?"

Paula chuckled. "You were just as difficult as you were in group."

"What do you mean?"

Paula licked her lips. 'OK. Let me see. You told him you'd accept our support – thanks, by the way – but not his. He didn't like that."

Maryam was opposite her. "You said you'd only talk to one of the other counsellors. You seemed quite shocked to see her."

Rita frowned at her. "She was my counsellor when I got here. He told me I'd imagined her."

Silence.

"So I didn't imagine her?"

"No. She was there, yesterday." A deep flush covered Jennifer's cheeks and neck, and she was holding herself very still. "Who is she?"

"Just a counsellor. What else did I say?"

Jennifer opened her mouth to speak but Paula interrupted. "You kept talking about someone called Ash."

Rita felt herself melt. "My boyfriend."

"Was he arrested too?"

Shock jolted through her. Could Ash be in one of these places? "No. No, it was nothing to do with him. They arrested me 'cos of my school. I wouldn't say the oath."

Paula nodded. "That's what you said, in Celebration."

"What else?"

Jennifer leaned across the table. "Did they tell you if you passed?"

"I failed."

Jennifer nodded. "Can I ask you something?"

Rita nodded.

"I mean, I know this is difficult, with it being so soon, but... why didn't you go along with it?"

Rita lifted her head. "What do you mean?"

"Well, if you'd lied. Told them what they wanted to hear. Then you'd be out of here by now."

The other women shifted in their seats.

"It's not as easy as that," whispered Maryam, scraping her fingers through her hair. Jennifer's blush returned.

"Who are you to tell me what to do?" asked Rita. Her energy had returned, and she was angry. This was none of Jennifer's business.

Jennifer put her hands up. "Sorry. I'm really sorry. I didn't mean to—"

"She doesn't know," said Paula. "It was her first."

"It was my first too," said Rita. She looked at Jennifer. "Tell me what I said. Why you think I was such an idiot."

"I didn't say you were an idiot."

"You implied it."

Jennifer slumped back, saying nothing.

"Go easy on her, Rita," said Maryam. "It's hard on all of us."

Rita glared at Jennifer. "Is that what you think I should do? Roll over like a good dog? Do what they want us to? Is that what you'll do?"

Jennifer frowned. "Sorry. I didn't mean to offend you. I just thought it would make more sense to say what they wanted you to. You could have passed. You could be out of here."

Rita shrugged. "From where I'm sitting, I'm the only one who's lost the last two days to whatever drugs they gave me, and who had an audience watching her saying stuff I can't remember." She was trembling.

Maryam smiled. "I've done it too."

"Then why are you still here?"

"I failed, like you. They took my veil away."

Rita looked at her hair, wound around her neck. "Oh. I'm sorry."

"You need to let us help you."

Rita nodded.

Jennifer sat up again. "Next time, maybe just lie to them."

"Lie to them."

"Yes."

"Has it occurred to you that I couldn't?"

"What do you mean, couldn't? Did they threaten you?"

"They sedated me, before they wheeled me in. I felt like they'd given me a bottle of wine. A whole bottle. How good are you at lying, when you've had a whole bottle of wine?"

Jennifer shook her head. Rita remembered where she'd seen her before and laughed.

"Oh, of course," she said. 'That was your job, wasn't it? Drinking fine wine at the taxpayer's expense then trooping into the House of Commons and lying to us all."

Maryam stiffened. "That's not fair."

But Jennifer was silent, returning Rita's stare across the table. Rita hated herself, but she hated Jennifer more. Bloody politicians; the reason everyone was in this mess.

"Forget it," she said, and stood up, leaving her breakfast things for the others to clear away.

CHAPTER NINETEEN

After everything that had happened over the last few days, a one-to-one with Mark felt like a waste of time.

He was garrulous today, pacing his office and talking to her at length about the programme, the steps she needed to take to get out of here. His dark hair caught the sunlight each time he passed the window, and she caught fragments of sound from up there, outside in the yard. Doors slamming, voices calling. It made her feel claustrophobic.

Jennifer watched him, pulling her energy together and preparing her request. Rita's accusations had knocked some of the wind out her sails and she was suffering a failure of confidence. Maryam had told her to ignore it but it wasn't so easy. The idea that this place was of her making kept nagging at her, like a persistent itch. If she'd thought twice before resigning, before opposing John and Michael, where would they all be now?

Finally Mark stopped talking and sat in the chair opposite her, rubbing his knees.

"Anyway," he said. "What's morale like? Among the rest of the group."

"Haven't you already seen Paula and Bel this morning?"

"Yes, but they aren't as talkative as you."

She frowned. Did she talk too much?

He looked at her. "Oh I didn't mean it like that. Just that, well, with your background and everything, it's easier to talk to you. You're a model patient. Cooperative. I wish they were all like you."

She felt her skin crawl. She didn't want to be this man's model patient. She wanted to do what was necessary to get out of here and find her family. The thought of him developing any sort of fellow feeling with her made her feel sick.

He rubbed his nose. "Anyway. Tell me, how is the group doing? It's not every day we get a fast-tracked Celebration. It sometimes has knock-on effects."

She shrugged. "You forget I haven't been here long. I haven't seen any other sort of Celebration."

"Of course. How forgetful of me." He gave her a meaningful look. "It isn't normally like that. Most people pass."

"Why didn't she? Rita?"

"She wasn't ready."

Jennifer looked at him with disgust. Of course she wasn't ready. "So why did you put her through that?"

"Not my idea. The governor thought it would show her how things worked. Set an example."

Jennifer remembered the governor; difficult to forget her. A woman in a man's world, dressed like a canary to avoid becoming wallpaper. It was familiar from Parliament, all those female MPs in their bright jackets and baronesses in their uniform of patterned scarves.

She smiled. "So you did as you were told."

He blushed. "Of course. That's what we're all here for."

"Are we?"

He stood up. "Yes. And here's something I'm telling you to do." He moved away from the desk and stood facing the window, his head silhouetted in the angled sunshine.

"Yes?"

"Keep away from Rita, if you know what's good for you."

"Why?"

He turned, not meeting her eye. "She's a bad influence. You don't want people like her holding you back."

"Alright," she said. "I'll keep away from her." Rita didn't want anything to do with her anyway. "Anything else you need me to do?"

He laughed. "Other than the usual, no."

"Talking of that."

"Hmm?" He was looking at his fingers. There was a pale band of skin on his ring finger. She looked up at those photos again, of the boy. One of them was torn at one edge; an ex-wife?

"I want you to fast-track me," she said.

He looked at her, startled. "I'm sorry?"

"You said I'm a model patient. I can get through the Celebration thing. Let me try. Fast-track me, like Rita."

He shook his head. "Oh, I could never—"

"Why not? I can be a success story for you. Fastest ever progression through the programme. That would be a feather in your cap, wouldn't it?"

He chewed his lip, considering. Then he straightened his back and adopted a stern tone.

"No. It's out of the question."

"Why?"

He glared at her. "Just accept it, alright? If you want to get through this, you have to do as I say."

She wouldn't have this chance again; she had to convince him. She stood up and approached him, softening her voice. "Can I tell you something?" she said.

He gave her a puzzled look. "Of course. That's what I'm here for."

"I'm desperate."

His neck blushed a deep pink. She smiled to herself. "Desperate?" he asked.

She nodded. "To find my family. To be reunited with my husband."

His blush faded. "Oh."

She nodded. "My son was arrested just a few hours before me. My husband – Yusuf – said he'd find him but I'm not so sure. And my younger son, he was with social services last time I heard. I want to know if they're OK. I want to get out of here as quickly as I can, so I can find them."

She drew in a breath, aware that she'd garbled her words. Had she said too much?

He nodded. "I understand." His face was no more than a foot from hers, and his pupils were dilated. She forced herself to stay where she was, not to shrink back.

"Can you help me?" she asked.

He frowned at her, regaining his composure. "Sit down, please."

She did. He took his own seat to face her.

"You have to understand that it isn't as simple as that," he said. "Everyone here has someone they want to be reunited with. Everyone wants to go home. Some more than others. Even I—"

She widened her eyes in encouragement but he changed the subject. "I can't fast-track you," he said. "I'm sorry, but I can't. You're not ready."

She slumped back. "But nor was Rita. I'm way more ready than she was."

"I know. You don't imagine I don't know that, do you? But Rita was fast-tracked precisely because she wasn't ready."

He blushed again; he shouldn't have told her that. But she could work it out. Maybe if she tried the same for herself...

"OK," she said. "I'm new too. Almost as new as Rita. If I'm not ready, you can make an example of me too. Think of it; humiliating the fancy politician in front of all those women. They'd love it."

"Don't be absurd. You don't want to be humiliated like that."

"I don't care. If it gets me closer to finding my family, I'll do anything."

He leaned back, watching her. "Look." He paused, pursing his lips. "What if I help you another way?"

She recoiled. "What do you mean?"

"You're desperate to find out where your family are."

She nodded.

"Well, what if I talk to the governor, see if I can find anything out for you. That way you can at least satisfy your curiosity."

"It isn't enough. I need to be with them. You can help me get out of here. I know that's your job. Surely you have performance management here? Won't it look good for you, if you help me pass through the programme quickly?"

He stood up. "Don't you understand, it's not as simple as that!"

She flinched. Why so angry?

He sat down. "Sorry. The situation with Rita has frayed my nerves. Look, I can help find out about your family. I'll see what information I can get for you. That's all I can do though."

She said nothing.

"Did you hear me?" he asked.

Again she said nothing, but stared at him instead. He lowered his eyes.

"And then I can apply for Celebration?" she asked.

He sighed. "No, Jennifer. I'll get you some information. But that's all I can do. You'll have to put up with it."

CHAPTER TWENTY

It wasn't one of Mark's scheduled slots to meet with the governor. She didn't like interruptions, but today was different.

He knocked on her door, waiting for her to call him in. She didn't look as surprised to see him as he had expected.

"Mark, come on in. What can I do for you?"

She was behind that monstrous mahogany desk, the one they'd dragged into her ground floor office from a former study on the first floor. Behind her was a huge bay window, draped with red curtains. He wondered if they'd been there before or if she'd had them brought in; they matched her clothes. The low sun shone behind her head, dazzling him and shrouding her in light.

She was the only staff member with an office up here; the rest of them were relegated to the basement. He craved daylight and fresh air; the high window in his office had been painted shut years ago. Still, at least he had a window. Perks of seniority.

"Morning, Yonda. I need to—"

"How's our new girl? Rita. She made quite a spectacle of herself in Celebration."

He shook his head. "She's coming round. Starting to get the message." Yonda cocked her head, not speaking. "Slowly," he finished.

"Why did she react to Meena like that?"

"Oh. Yes. Well, I told her that she'd imagined Meena. That I'd been her counsellor all along."

"That's a little unorthodox, isn't it? I know we want to get inside their heads but she'd only been here a couple of days."

He blushed. "I thought it would help to subdue her. She was aggressive towards Meena, refusing to cooperate."

Yonda waved a hand. "I know all about that. Took me two days to fill out the paperwork. How did you expect to carry on with the lie, given that she was bound to come across Meena eventually?"

"Cross that bridge when I came to it, I guess."

"Hmm. It didn't help, at her Celebration. Shocked the other women too. And I've had to deal with another complaint from Meena."

"Sorry."

"Wish I'd never taken her on, between you and me. Did you see her scanning the crowd at Celebration?"

He shook his head.

"Hmm. Looking for her old group mates, I imagine." She pulled off her reading glasses and placed them on the table. "We need to watch her."

"Meena?"

"Yes."

"Fair enough."

A sigh. "Oh, Mark. I mean you need to watch her. I'm

too busy here. Do you have any idea the pressure I'm under from management? They arrested six women involved in that vehicle attack last week and they'll be here any day now."

He looked at her desk. There was nothing on it except a pristine laptop and a small porcelain figure of a dog; a Yorkshire terrier.

"Surely you aren't surprised?" she asked.

"No." He was as much drawn to the news as anyone, despite his better instincts. There was nothing good happening; more attacks, more unrest, more distrust. Forval, the company that employed Yonda and the orderlies, was making a fortune from it.

"So. You sort out your troublemakers. I want Meena to take them on once you've calmed them down, but first I need to know if we can trust her." She paused. "Or do you want to add a whole extra group to your roster?"

"No. I'll watch her," he said, pulling at his collar.

"Anyway," she said, closing the laptop. "What did you come here for?"

He pulled in his chest. "Jennifer Sinclair."

"Ah." She smiled and stood up, rounding the desk and perching on it. Today she was wearing a flowing green dress, with red collars. Her shoes matched it, gleaming against the threadbare rug.

"She wants to get out."

Yonda laughed. "Of course she does. They all do."

"I mean it. She's desperate to be reunited with her family."

"Well, that's not about to happen. I already told you—"

"I don't think she'll take no for an answer."

Yonda frowned. "Did I not make it clear the other day,

Mark? She's got to stay here. I've got instructions. So have you."

He scratched his nose. "I know. Yes, I did understand." He told himself to keep calm; Yonda responded to professionalism. She only treated him with respect when he subtly reminded her that he'd come here via a medical career and her via a none-too-successful management one.

"I offered her a compromise."

She raised an eyebrow. "A compromise? Since when were we negotiating with prisoners?"

"Patients."

"Whatever. I think you're forgetting what this place is."

He felt his body slacken. Was he getting soft? Had they got to him? "I'm not. I just want to keep things running smoothly. We don't want her causing us trouble."

"You didn't offer her," – she wrinkled her nose – "sexual favours, did you?"

He blushed. "No. Of course not."

"You know what happens if I get wind of anything like that again."

His blush deepened. "That's irrelevant."

"Hmm. Anyway, I don't think this is a good precedent. We don't start making bargains with them."

He swallowed. She stood up again, stretching her heavy legs, and slid back into her chair. She opened the laptop and started scrolling through her screen. Was he being dismissed?

"Shall I tell you what I offered her?" he said.

She sighed. "Oh, go on then. If it makes you happy."

"I suggested that if I give her information about her family, then that would be enough."

"Enough?"

"I made it very clear that she can't be fast-tracked. That's what she wanted."

Yonda snorted. "That's not happening."

"I know. Which is why I suggested—"

"And exactly what *information* about her family do you think we should give her? The truth?"

"Well, that depends."

"On what."

"On what the truth is."

"Let me see. I've had an email about her, this morning."

He leaned forward. She gave him a warning look and pulled the laptop closer to her, clicking between windows.

"Does it give us anything I can use?" he asked.

She put up a hand. "Wait. Let me read it." She picked up her reading glasses and slid them onto her nose, frowning as she shuffled them into place. They made her look older, more intelligent. He wondered if that was deliberate.

She sat back, running a hand across her forehead. The fingertips were light on her skin, scratching it with her long nails. Did that hurt, he wondered.

"What is it?" he asked.

She looked up as if surprised to see him there. "Tell me what you propose," she said.

"OK. I'm not saying we tell her the truth about her family. But if we give her something that makes her believe it's not in her interests to get out of here quickly, she could stop pushing for fast-tracking."

"What do you think would do that?"

"I don't know." He looked around. "Mind if I sit?"

She waved a hand and he pulled one of the easy chairs towards the desk. As he dropped into it he immediately regretted it, as he was now a good four inches lower than her. He lifted himself up and perched on the front of the seat.

"Well, there's her husband. Yusuf Hussain. I think she's worried he may have been arrested too, after her. For helping to hide their son. But the son, Samir, he's what she's most worried about. I think. And then there's the younger one. She thinks he's in care."

"Do you know where he is?"

"No. I thought you might."

"With the grandmother. Jennifer's mother. Family services thought it best that he didn't go back to the father."

He nodded. It wasn't uncommon for the women here to have children moved between homes, poor things. He thought of Olivier, somewhere in Canada with his mother, and felt his heart harden.

"If we told her all that, maybe she'd be satisfied."

"I'm not so sure. Anyway, we have bigger fish to fry."

"What?"

"This email. She's going to get a visitor. An important one."

He frowned. "Why?"

She shrugged. "Don't ask me. I didn't think they dirtied their hands with coming here. But we need to prepare."

"Who is it?"

She raised an eyebrow. "Ah-ah. Sorry." She looked back at her laptop, her eyes scanning the screen. "Shit." She turned back to him. "Look, Mark. Do what you need to do to keep her quiet. Sit on any ideas about fast-tracking. And make sure she reflects well on us."

He stood up. "Of course."

"I mean it, Mark. I'm relying on you. We need to be squeaky clean for this. No sign of that Rita woman. Jennifer is going to be our ambassador, and she'd better do a bloody good job."

He nodded, heading for the door. "I'll warn her."

"No!" Yonda had stood up. "Don't tell her. Don't tell anyone. Just get the staff ready, and keep Jennifer Sinclair happy."

He looked at her. High pricks of red dotted her cheeks and her brow was damp. This was big. "OK," he said.

CHAPTER TWENTY-ONE

"I thought you'd tell her I need to be fast-tracked."

Mark pulled a hand through his hair. "No, Jennifer. That isn't what I told you. We agreed that I'd get you information on your family. If I could."

She'd been anticipating this for the last four days. He'd been cagey after the last group session, refusing to answer her questions when she'd attempted to pull him to one side at the end. Glancing nervously at the other women, he had whispered to her that she needed to wait. She didn't like waiting, when her family could be in danger.

"It's not good enough," she said. "Whatever you tell me, how can I be sure it's the truth? The only way for me to know what's happened to them is to get myself released. And the only way to do that, as you well know, is Celebration."

He gave her an uneasy look and shuffled some files on his desk. Had he even spoken to the governor?

"Have you spoken to her?"

He looked up. "To who?"

"To Yonda Hughes. The governor."

"You have to realise that you're not the only patient here. You're not her only concern, or even mine. I've got Rita to—"

"I know." Rita wasn't doing well. In group she'd been taciturn, refusing to engage with anyone. The resistance was gone, the angry rebellion. But it had been replaced with a bleakness that worried Jennifer. She still didn't understood why the other woman couldn't lie her way out of here. Why none of them could.

"You did promise me," she said.

He nodded. "Look. I have spoken to her."

She felt her heart lift. "And?"

"And she wasn't happy. She's refusing to even consider fast-tracking you. Just like I said. It's not as easy as all that, you know."

"It was for Rita."

He cocked his head. "You know that Rita was never going to pass."

"So maybe I should do the same thing. Act difficult, shout at you in group. Then you'll make an example of me. Yes?"

"Nice try. But no."

"I thought not." She closed her eyes. She couldn't stop thinking about Samir, wondering if he was going through this somewhere. Was there another place like this, for men? Or was he in prison? Had he been deported? Had they all?

"But I did get some information on your family," he said.

Her head flicked up. "Yes?"

He licked his lips then brought a finger to them, biting the nail. "It wasn't easy. I'm not supposed to do this sort of thing, you know."

She could guess what he was getting at. "So you're saying I owe you something, in return."

He shook his head, blushing. "No. Well, yes. If I give you this information, you have to promise to stop badgering me for fast-tracking. Your best bet is to stay calm, work through the programme with me. Who knows, if you do that you might be able to get your own Celebration anyway."

"Might? Why wouldn't that be definite?"

His blush deepened. "I didn't mean it like that. Just that we can't say for sure if you'll succeed. Unless you try." He leaned back and looked at her. "Will you try?"

She eyed him. "If you tell me where my family are, yes."

"Good."

She caught him glancing at the files on his desk. "Is that my file? Is there information on them in there?"

"What? Oh no, That's something different. Not your concern."

She raised an eyebrow. There was plenty around here that wasn't her concern. She wished she'd taken the time to make it her concern, back when she could.

"Go on then," she said, impatient.

He sniffed. "Right. Well, your husband, Yusuf Hussain." He looked down at his knees.

"Yes?"

"He's awaiting trial." He looked up. "There's nothing you could do to influence that, even if you do get out of here. They don't want you as a witness. If you got out of here, he wouldn't be waiting for you."

She frowned. She'd worried he might be arrested too, but logic told her that it would have been at the same time as her. "What's he on trial for?"

Mark looked startled. "Similar crime to you, I imagine."

"But he didn't hide him. Not knowingly. Not once they'd issued a warrant. That was all me."

"Oh." Mark scratched his chin. "Well, I can't say. All I can tell you is what I've got."

"Do you know when it'll be? The trial?"

He brought his head up to look at her, his eyes steady on her face. "No."

She nodded. "What about Samir?"

He relaxed. "He's in a detention centre, near Manchester. I think he was there when you were brought here."

She shrugged; she hadn't been told much in prison.

"Hang on a minute," she said. "Why is Yusuf getting a trial, and I'm not?"

He froze. "I don't know."

"It makes no sense."

He shrugged. "Sorry. You just said it was you that hid him. You pleaded guilty, didn't you?"

"Yes."

"So did he."

"Did he? Why?"

"How can I know that?" he asked, his tone harried.

Samir had run away from their house in her Birmingham constituency before the police turned up. He had come to her flat in London and she'd let him hide there. By the time Yusuf arrived, he was gone. And as far as the outside world was concerned, Yusuf had never known that his son was under suspicion, not until he was arrested. Only three people knew the truth about that: Yusuf, and her. And Catherine Moore, her friend in the Home Office.

"Samir. Are they going to deport him? When? His MP

can help with that. He has rights." A pause. "Who is his MP now, anyway? Have they had the by-election?"

Mark shook his head. "You know more than me about that, I'm sure. All I know is that he's in a detention centre. Sorry."

She plunged her fingernail into the skin of her thumb, willing herself to breathe.

"What about Hassan?"

He frowned at her, saying nothing. She could sense him working through something, as if coming to a decision.

"Do you know where he is?" she urged.

He looked down. "He's fine," he said. "He's with your mum."

She felt her chest lighten. Thank God. "Not with social services?"

He shook his head. She gave him a tight smile. "Thank you. I appreciate it."

She tried to imagine Hassan dealing with the disappearance of his parents and older brother. He wasn't close to her mum; she lived fifty miles away, and was an infrequent visitor. She'd been a distant mother to Jennifer, too busy scratching out a living after her father left. What would she be like with her grandson?

"Why couldn't Yusuf's parents have him?"

Mark pursed his lips. "They're Muslim."

"What? That's ridiculous."

"Sorry. Just the way things are. Look, Jennifer, this is bigger than you. I know you want to know about your family, but you need to trust me, trust the system. I've got other things to worry about, besides your desperation to get out of here."

"Like what?"

"Like— Like everything."

"I'm sorry," she said.

"That's OK."

"No," she replied. "I really am. Not for you – you're doing alright out of this, with your cushy job – but to everyone. All the women here. Yusuf. Samir. Hassan, even. It's all my fault."

"It's really not."

She stood up. Her head wasn't far from the low ceiling and she towered over him. He shifted in his seat.

"Sit down, please," he said.

She shook her head and walked to the window, looking up through the smeared glass. Outside she could see car tyres, and a shock of daffodils drooping under the weight of recent rain. She wished she could be allowed outside.

"I don't think you realise how much you should be blaming the others," he said.

"What others?" she asked, not turning from the window. She was feeling relaxed now, different from when she'd first arrived. She could work on this man, develop his trust until finally he let her prove she was ready to be released.

"Well, Michael Stuart for one."

She laughed. "Yeah. Him I can blame."

"If he hadn't introduced that bill you'd never have rebelled against him. They forced you to do it."

"You think so?"

"Maybe."

She thought about the look on his face in the Commons Chamber when she'd beaten him, more than two years ago now. The sneering triumph on Leonard Trask's face as she passed through the same voting lobby as him. If she hadn't stood up to Michael, he would still be Prime Minister.

Trask wouldn't be. And there'd be no British Values Act. Probably.

"I know what you're thinking," said Mark.

She turned round. "Really?"

"You're blaming Trask. That's stupid."

"Why?"

"Well, you always knew what he was. He could be relied upon to do what he did. You should be blaming the people closer to you. People who should have stopped you."

"Like who?" Did he mean Yusuf? She thought of all those arguments they'd had, all the tense silences. All the doors Samir had slammed. Yusuf had been even angrier than her; he'd only encouraged her.

"Like John Hunter."

She snorted. "If only you knew." John, her old boss and now the Shadow Home Secretary, had secretly agreed with her. Not that he'd had the guts to tell Michael. Yes, John could share some of the blame.

"And Catherine Moore."

She approached him. "Shouldn't you be careful, talking about her?"

He shrugged. "Free country."

"Is it? Really?"

"Yes. And just because she's the Home Secretary now doesn't mean I can't say what I think of her."

"Home Secretary?" This was news. Last time Jennifer had seen Catherine, she'd been a junior minister in the Home Office.

"Yes. Reshuffle."

"Right." She thought about what Catherine would know, in her new role. What would she make of this place? "She's your boss. Indirectly. How many rungs above Yonda is she?"

He blushed. "It doesn't work like that. She probably doesn't even know about this place."

"Oh, she does."

"Do you know that?"

"No. But I know Catherine. Eye for detail."

"Yeah well, maybe with all that detail she could have warned you. Told you to back off."

She frowned at him. Did he know what Catherine had done? That she'd broken the Official Secrets Act to tell her that Samir was under suspicion?

No. If he did, she wouldn't be Home Secretary. She shook her head. "It's not as simple as that. It wasn't her fault."

He shrugged.

There was a knock at the door and they both looked at it, startled. Jennifer shrank back towards the window. There was a clock on Mark's wall; it wasn't an hour yet, not time for the next woman to arrive.

Mark cleared his throat. "Come in."

The door opened and Yonda Hughes appeared. She was smiling, simpering even.

"Ah, hello," she said. "Thought I'd find you here."

Catherine stared at her. The governor only ever ventured out of her office for Celebration, as far as Jennifer could tell. And what was this about finding them here?

Mark stood up, brushing imaginary crumbs off his jacket. "Hello, Governor."

Yonda nodded at him then looked at Jennifer through narrowed eyes. "I need you to come with me."

Jennifer gave Mark a startled look. She looked up at the camera; in her agitation, she'd forgotten it was there. Had Yonda been listening in? Mark had turned pale.

Jennifer pulled on a smile. At least she had the governor's attention. "With pleasure."

She followed the other woman along the dim corridor towards the stairs. Yonda's bulk and flamboyancy filled the space, throwing its grimness into stark relief. Jennifer wondered how often she came here; she seemed to be picking her way along the scuffed concrete floor as if repulsed by it.

Finally they arrived at the narrow staircase and Yonda stood back to let Jennifer go in front. She was smiling, but there was worry in her eyes. What was going on?

She made her way up, hearing Yonda's heels clipping behind her. By the time she reached the top she was six steps ahead; this staircase wasn't designed for those shoes. She waited patiently, listening to her own heightened breathing.

Yonda gave her another smile as she passed. "Walk with me, Jennifer."

Jennifer fell into step next to the governor, waiting for her to speak first. They passed a group of women heading to their group meeting. The women stared after them, open-mouthed. Jennifer tried to ignore them, and Yonda was oblivious.

"So, Jennifer. How are you getting on here?" Yonda asked finally.

She licked her lips. Small talk, really? "Very well, thank you."

"Good."

"I'm making fast progress through the programme. In fact, I believe I should be fast-tracked. Like Rita."

The governor smiled. "Of course you do."

They arrived at her office at the back of the building, in its centre. Yonda opened the door and beckoned Jennifer inside, not saying anything. Jennifer looked at her, frustrated, and passed through.

The office was large, almost as large as the room they'd used for her group season and the Celebration ceremony. At one end was a bay window that made her think of the Oval Office. It had bright red drapes, made out of a smooth material that absorbed the light. There was a rug on the floor, modern and abstract. It looked wrong on the rich wooden floor, surrounded by heavy antique furniture. The walls were empty except for a solitary painting, an Impressionist. Tasteful. Plundered from elsewhere in the house, no doubt.

Yonda sat behind her desk, gesturing towards a low wooden chair in front of it. "Please, take a seat."

Jennifer sat. She could barely see the other woman over the desk now, so hauled herself upright. "What's this about?"

"The direct approach. I like it. I'm sure you know that you aren't our normal run of the mill patient."

Patient. Prisoner, more like. "Yes." She ran over her conversation with Mark in her head; had she said anything indiscreet?

"We feel honoured to have you here."

Jennifer could have laughed. "Why have you brought me here? Are you going to release me? Am I special enough for you to do that?"

"Sorry to disappoint you."

Yonda raised a finger and fumbled in the pocket of her jacket, which was short and tight. She brought out a buzzing mobile phone and held it to her ear, closing her eyes.

"Yes. Yes. Fine."

There was a pause while the person at the other end

spoke at length.

"Are you sure?" said Yonda. "I really don't think—"

Another pause. Yonda was trembling. What was going on?

"Alright." She slid the phone back into her pocket and looked at Jennifer, brightening her expression. "You stay here, please. I'll be back shortly."

Jennifer watched the door for a few moments. There were no sounds from outside; the wood was too thick. She wondered if the governor was in the hallway, talking to someone. Should she go and check?

Finally she stood up and walked round the desk to the window. The sun had disappeared behind a cloud, throwing the lawns into relief. They were edged by herbaceous borders, their low, brown shapes not yet woken by spring.

A solitary figure walked along a path towards the house. She watched, envious. It was an orderly, the short white clinical jacket unmistakable. For the first time she wondered where the staff came from, whether they lived here. They seemed to be in the middle of nowhere. She wondered how they had found themselves here, and what they thought of it. Did those orderlies come from the Department of Health, or the Home Office? She shuddered.

Behind her, there was a creak as the door opened. She turned, waiting for Yonda to scold her for getting out of her seat.

It wasn't Yonda.

She stared, mesmerised.

"Catherine?"

CHAPTER TWENTY-TWO

Rita had grown to hate her room. The ceiling pressed down on her. She had to stand on her bed to see anything other than the sky, which made her feel more confined than if there'd been no window in here at all.

Worst of all, the door was never locked. Day and night, anyone could come in here. Even as she slept, her body was on alert, like a cat twitching its ears in slumber when someone passed.

She hadn't bothered to record the passing of the days again; they could rub her marks off at any time. Besides, the charcoal had disappeared.

She heard a faint bell hum along the corridor and raised her wrist, despite knowing there was no watch on it. Only the bells for mealtime ruled her internal clock here. That, and the orderlies reminding her to go to a group session, or a one-to-one with her counsellor.

She pushed herself up from the bed, rubbing her eyes, and made for the door. Outside, the corridor was filling up, women making their way down for lunch. She held her head down, not wanting to attract attention. None of the women from her group were on this floor and she didn't want to make new friends.

As she reached the staircase, pulling back to let a pair of women pass who were engrossed in sharing a joke, an orderly stepped in front of her. She looked up to see it was Tim. Her heart sank.

"Hello again," she said, then regretted it. His face was hard.

"Not you," he said. A woman pushed past her and stared at the two of them, wondering what was going on. Rita pulled into herself, humiliated again.

"Why not?" she asked him. But he said nothing, instead watching the women file past in silence. At last they were gone and she was alone with him. She could hear branches knocking on the roof above their heads and the distant sound of the wind. But even on a windy day, it could get close up here when the sun shone. The orderly was sweating, an ugly kind of sweat that filled his white coat with grey dampness and poured off his forehead. He wiped his chin and sniffed at her.

"Can I go now?" she asked, pushing against his hand with her chest.

"No. You have to stay here."

"But I need to eat." She willed herself to stay calm. A few days ago, she would have railed at the injustice, insisted that he was violating her rights. Now, she knew there was no point.

"Later," he said. He looked from the empty stairwell back to her. "You'll get your chance."

This felt ominous. Was it something to do with her failed Celebration? She thought she'd been punished for that already. Mark believed she was going to try harder next time, didn't he?

He grabbed her arm. She tugged it away and he whistled.

"You're a feisty one, aren't you?"

She shrugged. "I'm not going back there."

"Fair enough. You can go back to your room or you can sit out here on the floor. With me."

Which was worse, the confines of her room, or the company of this man?

"Alright." She turned back towards her room and shuffled along the corridor, her arms brushing the walls. These would have been servants' bedrooms once. She wondered if they had been treated better than her.

"Good. Sensible girl." She wrinkled up her nose, but didn't turn to let him see.

Back in her room, she stood on her bed and pushed at the roof window with all her strength. It had a catch which she had been able to pry open, but try as she might she couldn't push the window up. She needed air. She reached up both hands and stooped to put her back into the effort, pushing as hard as she can.

There was a sound behind her as the door banged into her bed.

"What are you doing?"

She turned. "Nothing. I want some air, that's all."

"Are you trying to escape?"

"No." She was three floors up here; the roof of this house would be uneven and might lead down to the lower levels, but going up that way was too risky. Especially feeling as weak as she did.

He rounded the door and took a step in, reaching out to grab her wrist. He yanked her down and onto the bed. Her arm twisted beneath her.

"Ow!" she cried. "You're hurting me."

She thought of the day of her failed Celebration, the lengths he would go to. She shrugged him off, rubbing her arm.

"Sorry," she said. She sighed. What had happened to her? "I'll stop."

"Good."

"At least get me a glass of water."

"Jesus Christ, what do you think this is? A hotel?"

"No. But I'm thirsty, and you've stopped me from going down to the dining room. The least you can do is get me something to drink."

He smirked. "Too big for your boots, you are."

He turned and closed the door. She yanked it open again. He was walking away from her, his boots echoing along the corridor.

"What about that drink?"

He didn't break stride but instead lifted his right hand, giving her the finger. She scowled and drew back into her room.

She looked at the window, considering whether she would be able to open it. She was feeling shrunken somehow, and having difficulty breathing. It felt as if there was a hand around her throat.

"Help me!" she croaked. "I need help." Her heart was thumping now, and her limbs aching. She felt like she was about to be sick.

She slumped onto the bed, not hearing the door open again. A hand was on her back. She bucked violently, shaking it off.

"Rita? What's wrong?"

She turned on the bed to see Miss Ashgar standing over her. She blinked and rubbed her eyes. Was she imagining things again?

"Miss Ashgar?"

The counsellor nodded. "Call me Meena. Are you OK?"

She shook her head violently and brought her hand to her neck. "Can't breathe."

"One moment." Miss Ashgar left the room. There was the sound of raised voices and then she reappeared with a glass of water.

"Sit up. Drink this."

She sat next to Rita on the bed and supported her with her arm, raising the glass to her lips. Rita drank, only some of it dribbling down her chin.

"Thank you," she gasped. "They've imprisoned me up here."

Meena shook her head. "I wouldn't say that."

"Have you come to take me downstairs?"

"Not yet. Sorry."

Rita looked at the counsellor. She looked even younger than she had before. "Are you real?"

Meena put a hand on Rita's cheek. It was cool. "Does this feel real?"

Rita nodded. "Why are you here? What made you come up here?"

A shrug. "I was asked to check up on you."

"Oh." Rita reached out for the glass and Meena handed it to her. She drank eagerly, then wiped her lips. "Who by?"

Meena's expression didn't change. "Dr Clarke. Your counsellor."

"He's still my counsellor? Not you?" Her throat felt dry, despite the water. "Can you get him to open the window? I need air."

Meena frowned but slipped out and brought Tim back

with her. She looked uncomfortable. But she was clearly his superior.

Meena pointed at the window. "Open it, please. She needs fresh air."

"But—"

Meena raised an eyebrow and the orderly shrugged. "It gets closed when you leave."

"Of course."

He drew a bunch of keys from his pocket and leaned over the bed. He brought one of them up to the window and pushed it open with ease. Rita cursed herself.

She stood to push her face into the gap, breathing in the damp air. The angle of the window kept her dry but the occasional raindrop rebounded against the roof below and onto her chin. It felt wonderful.

"Come down, please," said Meena. "It isn't safe."

Rita let herself drop to the bed. Meena was sitting at the end of it now, wiping her damp hands on a tissue.

"Why are you here, again?" asked Rita.

"I told you. Dr Clarke."

"I don't get it. He wanted me to think I'd imagined you. Why does he send you up here now, when I'm being kept away from everyone?"

Meena shrugged. Sounds came from above Rita's head, through the window. The crunch of car tyres on gravel, followed by voices. She sprang up, ignoring Meena's restraining hand on her leg.

Pushing herself up to see over the lip of the roof, she could make out the driveway below. Her room was at the front of the house and so she had a view of the lawns that swept up from the road, and the gravelled area where she'd waited while the police had tried to bring her in by the wrong entrance.

Four cars were parked below, gleaming black in the wet. They were large and official-looking. She frowned.

"What's going on down there?" she asked, not taking her face away from the window.

"What do you mean?"

"Those cars."

Meena put her hand on Rita's calf. "Get down, please. It's not safe. There's nothing going on."

Rita turned towards her, banging her head on the window. "Ouch." Meena winced.

She sat down to face her old counsellor. "Have they banished you up here too?"

"Don't be silly."

"They have, haven't they?"

Meena's expression hardened. "No, Rita. You're being paranoid."

"I'm not. You're just as bad as me, in their eyes. That's why you're up here with me."

"Don't be silly."

"I'm not. All the other counsellors are white. Does anyone outside this place know that they gave you a job, after you passed?"

Meena frowned. "Of course they do. Now stop it. I need you to behave yourself."

"You're being naive."

"No, Rita. You're being naive." She stood up, and called Tim back. "Shut that window please."

Tim did so, grinning at Rita. Meena thanked him and turned back to Rita. "They don't hate you for the colour of your skin, Rita. They don't hate me because I wear a veil. It's what you did that's the problem. What I did. Whoever you are, if you can show them that you're willing to make amends, that you can be loyal, they'll forgive you. They'll let you go."

Rita snorted. "If only it were that simple." She thought of Ash, the angry music he would listen to condemning white supremacy. She hadn't paid much attention at the time, but he was right. And Meena had been brainwashed.

"You'll see," she said, as Meena retired. "I'll prove you wrong."

Meena gave her a withering look and closed the door. Rita rose to pull the door open and tumbled into the corridor. Meena was retreating, heading towards Tim at the top of the stairs.

"They hate you!" Rita cried. "They hate us all!"

CHAPTER TWENTY-THREE

Catherine looked even more demure and professional than she had last time Jennifer had seen her. This wasn't the nervous, clumsily dressed woman who had emptied her bag onto the table in their train carriage when they had first met.

She gave Jennifer a smile that dripped with aloofness.

"Jennifer. How are you?"

"I'm coping."

Catherine's smile deepened but there was a vacant look in her eyes, as if her mind was elsewhere. She pushed the door closed behind her and approached Jennifer. She put her hands on Jennifer's shoulders and held her out to look at her. Catherine's heels were high, which meant they were at the same height. Jennifer glanced down at her feet; neat blue designer heels, with sensible tan tights and a straight blue skirt in the exact same colour. Over it she wore a long grey coat that looked like cashmere. A white scarf was knotted at her neck, and in her pale ears were small pearls. Her makeup was still subtle, but very slightly heavier than in the past, with a pink blush brightening her cheeks and brown eyeshadow making her eyes look darker.

Jennifer looked at her, wondering. Was this the Catherine who'd risked everything to warn her about Samir? Or the Catherine who'd betrayed her in the Commons Chamber?

"Your hair's grown," Catherine said.

Jennifer allowed herself a laugh. She had to believe that Catherine was here as a friend. "That's just the half of it. What about *you*?"

Catherine shrugged and looked down at herself. "Goes with the territory." She looked back, into Jennifer's face. Her eyes were dancing now, and had lost that abstracted look. "I'm Home Secretary. Did they tell you?"

Jennifer nodded. "Yes. Since when?"

"Last week." Catherine gave a shy smile. Jennifer imagined what it would have been like with the two of them on opposing sides, trading barbs across the chamber. Then she remembered that debate, the day of her arrest. She pulled away.

"Why are you here?"

"To see you, of course. Oh, and a sort of social visit. At least, that's what I told Ms Hughes." She leaned in. "What does she think she looks like, a parrot?"

Jennifer stared at her. Sure, she didn't have a lot of time for Yonda, but when she was a minister she never would have talked about her staff like that.

Catherine pulled back. "You look well, Jennifer. Better than I expected. I assume this place is treating you better than prison?"

Jennifer winced. "Yes."

"Come. Let's sit down." Catherine moved towards the two easy chairs beyond Yonda's desk, shrugging off her coat and letting it slide onto Yonda's chair. Beneath it she wore a blue jacket in the same colour as the skirt, with a black blouse. The scarf was pulled off too and it joined the coat on the desk.

Jennifer sat down, pulling her knees back so they wouldn't touch Catherine's. "Thanks for coming."

"Least I could do." Catherine pulled a mirror out of her handbag – smaller than the monstrosity she'd been carrying when they first met but still roomy – and dabbed at her eyelid with a forefinger. "I thought you might need a bit of support."

"Well, more than that. I imagine."

Catherine put the mirror back in her bag. "Sorry?"

"How's Yusuf? I take it you know where he is? And Samir?"

Catherine frowned. "I can't tell you that."

"Why ever not? I'll be seeing them soon."

Catherine looked into her eyes for a moment then blinked, pulling on a smile. "Yusuf is fine. He's at your house."

"What?"

A shrug. "Why wouldn't he be?"

"But wasn't he arrested too?"

"Briefly. But he didn't hide your son. Samir. Your lawyer managed to produce evidence that Samir ran away before the police told Yusuf they were looking for him. So as far as the court was concerned, he had no knowledge, and so he didn't hide him."

Jennifer stared at her, waiting for the nervousness to show, the recognition of the truth. Yusuf had known, of course, and because Catherine had told Jennifer. Wasn't she going to acknowledge it?

Catherine's eyes roamed the room, covering every inch; ceilings, walls, floor. Looking for a camera.

"Good," said Jennifer. "That's wonderful news. What about Samir?"

Catherine's head dipped. "I told you I can't tell you."

"Has he had an appeal?"

Catherine stilled. "Jennifer, you understand the seriousness of what he did, right?"

"He did nothing. He had some friends, that was all. No-one has been able to prove anything different."

"No. He was associated with a prohibited group. That's different from having friends. You saw that photo of his girlfriend."

Jennifer felt her neck grow hot. She thought of Miss Ashgar, of Rita shouting her name at Celebration. If it was really her, then surely Catherine would know. Unless she'd been deliberately sent here, to watch Jennifer...

Change the subject, she thought. *Don't make things worse for Samir.*

"So. When will I be going home?"

"Going home?"

She nodded. "I owe you, Catherine, I really do. Now I can get them back. My family."

Catherine stood up. A sound came from Yonda's desk; a mobile phone vibrating inside the green jacket draped over the back of the chair. Jennifer hoped Yonda wouldn't come back to answer it. Where was she, anyway?

"What makes you think you're going home, Jennifer?"

Her mind raced. "Not today. I understand. How it has to look. But it'll be soon, right?"

Catherine shook her head. "It isn't like that."

Jennifer stood up. Catherine had moved to the window

and had her back to her. Outside, she could hear a car starting up.

"Do I have to go through the motions? Have one of those Celebration things? I understand."

Catherine was shaking her head. Jennifer stayed where she was, with the desk between them.

"What do you need me to do, Catherine? Just tell me."

Catherine said nothing. Jennifer clenched her fists.

"Say something. Tell me what's going to happen."

Catherine turned. "I haven't come here to get you released."

Jennifer glanced at the camera over the door. "Of course not. Just get me fast-tracked. I'll pass Celebration and I'll be out. Fair and square."

Catherine gave her a pitying look. "I know what you're trying to do."

The back of Jennifer's legs hit the easy chair she'd been sitting in. She let herself drop into it. How was Catherine going to tell her what to expect, with the camera watching?

She scanned the desk; nothing on it except that laptop and the ugly dog statue. What could she write with? She had an idea.

She stood up and beckoned Catherine, heading back to the window. She stood close to it and breathed out, her breath fogging the glass. She moved from side to side, making circles with her face and fogging up as large an area as possible.

"When go home?" she wrote. She turned to Catherine, smiling and pointing at the window.

Catherine frowned. She held her finger out to the window; it was pale, and neatly manicured.

"You won't," she wrote.

Jennifer frowned. "No, rlly," she wrote. The window

was clearing now; she took a moment to fog it up again. "Understand," she wrote. "Secret."

Catherine swallowed. "No secret. Stay here," she wrote, and then lifted the sleeve of her jacket to wipe the window clean. She leaned in to inspect it, checking that all traces of their conversation were gone.

Jennifer turned to her. "What do you mean?" she whispered.

"You have to stay here." Catherine's voice was low. She wouldn't meet Jennifer's eyes. "You can't leave."

Jennifer put a hand on her shoulder. Catherine stiffened but didn't pull away. "I don't understand," she said. "I thought you'd help me."

Catherine met her gaze. "Don't you understand?" she whispered. "I can't help you." She pulled back and walked towards the desk. "I'll ask them to go easy on you. I know how hard it can be for politicians in these places. There hasn't been any trouble, has there?"

Jennifer felt sick. She stared at Catherine, her hand on her stomach. "Not here. Prison," she managed to say.

Catherine's eyes creased. "I'm sorry. What did they do to you?"

Jennifer shook her head, dumb. There was a moment's silence. Yonda's jacket vibrated again. They ignored it.

Catherine picked up her coat from the desk and draped it over her arm. "Anyway, I have to go."

Jennifer glared at her. "You helped me before, Catherine. Why won't you help me now?"

Catherine gave her a warning look. "Sorry. I don't know what you're talking about." She wound the scarf around her neck.

"I'll get out," said Jennifer. Her voice had come back; it was hard and even.

Catherine shook her head. "No. You stay here. I'll make sure you're treated well, but you won't be leaving. Sorry."

"Will you bloody stop saying you're sorry?" She ran at Catherine, lifting up her fists. Fear crossed Catherine's face before Jennifer stopped in her tracks.

"I will find my own way. This programme isn't as tough as you think it is. I'll get through it, I'll do the Celebration, and I'll get out. You'll see."

"It won't work."

"Of course it will. It already is. My counsellor, Mark, he's pleased with my progress. Thinks I'm doing well." Her voice trailed off as she remembered Mark's refusal to fast-track her. She squared her shoulders. "Once I get through the six steps, they won't be able to refuse me."

Catherine shook her head. "We're too alike, you and me."

"No. We really aren't."

A smile. "I know what you're doing. What you're trying to do. I get reports. No-one's surprised that I'm taking a special interest in the former MP. Your progress in here reflects on all of us, after all."

"I don't care what you think."

Catherine sighed. "What do I have to say to convince you?"

"Nothing. You've said enough."

"Alright then. I'll show you."

Jennifer waited for Catherine to put her coat down, to make some sort of gesture. What was she going to show her?

"I don't get you," she said.

"Your plan," replied Catherine. "It won't work. You'll see. Just wait."

CHAPTER TWENTY-FOUR

Mark raised a hand to the wood.

"Come in."

He sniffed and pushed the door open. He was expecting this; Yonda would want to debrief after the Home Secretary's visit. A post-mortem. He wondered if the other counsellors had already been summoned or if he'd be first in, given that the MP was in his group.

Sitting at Yonda's desk, in her chair, was a neat-looking woman with dark hair tucked behind her ears. She smiled and stood up.

"Hello. You must be Mark Clarke. Catherine Moore, Home Secretary."

She reached across the desk and he shook her hand. She hadn't needed to introduce herself; this woman's sudden ascension to one of the top four political jobs in the country had been all over the news for the last week. She was only thirty-two and a first term MP. He wondered who she'd had to kill to get there.

"Pleased to meet you," he said, slipping into his doctor persona. There'd been plenty of ministerial visits to the hospital, especially when elections were looming. They'd often skipped the psychiatric ward but on a couple of occasions he'd been graced with the ministerial presence. No cameras though; his patients weren't suitable.

"Take a seat, please." She gestured towards the two low chairs. He turned to see Yonda sitting in one of them. She gave him a look that warned him not to pass comment.

Catherine leaned back in Yonda's chair. A coat that he presumed was hers was draped over the desk and the dog statuette had been pushed to one side. He could only imagine how Yonda felt about this.

"Thanks for letting me visit," she said.

Yonda leaned forwards. "Not a problem, Minister. We like to demonstrate just how smoothly this centre is run."

Catherine nodded. "Of course." She turned to Mark. "You're a counsellor here?"

Yonda interrupted. "Mark is one of my more experienced members of staff. We give him some of the most difficult patients."

Patients. Not a word Yonda was always accustomed to using.

Catherine nodded impatiently. "Tell me about your – patients, Dr Clarke."

Yonda took a deep breath and sat back in her chair. She was gripping its arms. The seat was all wrong for her; she had to lift her knees up to accommodate those heels and it made her look intensely uncomfortable. Mark wondered how the minister had managed to steal that precious desk.

"Well," he said. "It's not much different from working in a clinical setting really. I have three groups of women. Each of them has six members. I work with them, individually and as a group, to help them overcome negative thoughts.

Negative emotions. The aim is to enable them to leave here as fully functioning members of society."

"Of course," the minister said, bringing her fingers together. They looked like they'd been scrubbed; you could perform surgery with those hands. "And what techniques do you use?"

He glanced at Yonda. Was some sort of accusation being made? She nodded at him and turned to the minister.

"The programme, of course," she said. "We work through it with them in one-to-one sessions with their counsellor. The aim is to form a bond that enables us to get through any barriers. Then they help each other to progress, in group sessions."

"And the Celebration ceremony? How does that work?"

Mark frowned; surely the Home Secretary would know this? He racked his brains, remembering the manual. Was there anything they were doing differently?

"It's a wonderful event," Yonda continued.

Catherine held up a hand. "Thank you, Ms Hughes, but I was asking your doctor here. You're here because of your background in psychiatry, right?"

"Yes. But other colleagues – quite a few of them – are counsellors. Not medical practitioners. I'm the only one, in fact."

"Which is why the governor here relies on you so much."

"I wouldn't say—" interrupted Yonda.

"Carry on," said the minister. "Tell me about Celebration. Can I call you Mark?"

He nodded. *I bet I can't call you Catherine*, he thought. "We bring all of the women together, all of our patients. Those ready for Celebration are given the opportunity to show everyone their progress. Their commitment. It's very motivational."

"And the drugs. You use the recommended dose?"

"Of course."

"They work? They achieve the desired effect?"

He thought about Rita, the way she had told him exactly what she thought of him, lying on that gurney. "They do."

"Good." She swept her hand across the table as if wiping off dust, then peered at her fingers.

"Can I ask a question?" he asked.

She looked up. "Of course."

Yonda frowned at him. He swallowed. "One of our patients is a former parliamentary colleague of yours."

The minister's eyes sharpened. Yonda's grip on the chair arm closest to him tightened.

"Indeed," said the minister. "In fact, Ms Hughes here let me speak to her. Alone. I thought it would encourage her."

"Oh," he said. "Does that mean that our instructions have changed?"

The minister's gaze was hard. "How do you mean, changed?"

"Well," he said. "My understanding was that she was to stay here for some time. Fully understand the nature of her crimes. I've been ensuring she doesn't progress as quickly through the programme as she'd like to."

There was silence while they stared at each other. Mark wished his chair was higher.

"Was that the right thing to do?" he asked.

She stood up, brushing her fingers across the desk again. Her coat fell to the floor and she looked at it as if about to pick it up. Then she moved away from it, leaving it next to the desk.

She rounded the desk and perched on it, pushing the dog further towards its edge. Yonda coughed.

The minister stood up, brushing her skirt as if she'd got it dirty. "Oh I'm so sorry," she said. "You probably don't want me sitting on your desk."

Yonda stood up. "No, that's fine, of course. Make yourself at home." Mark could see her eyes flitting to her chair; she longed to sit in it, to regain control of the room.

"Right," said the minister. "Where were we?"

"Jennifer Sinclair," said Mark.

"Of course. Going back to Celebration. A patient gets two cracks at it, right?"

He nodded. *You don't need me to tell you this*, he thought. Then it occurred to him; she'd been Home Secretary for a matter of days, at a time when terror threats were an almost constant fact of life and the prison population was rising exponentially. She might not have read the relevant files yet.

In which case the reason she was here wasn't for a formal visit, but to see her old friend.

"Will we be releasing her?" he blurted.

"Who?"

"Mark, please," muttered Yonda.

Mark stood up, not happy with being the only one sitting down. Now they were all at the same level, in the centre of the room. Yonda scratched the back of her head.

The minister turned to him. "Here's what I want you to do. I believe that Jennifer Sinclair has seen the error of her ways. I've spoken to her, and she's ready."

"Ready?" he asked.

The minister cocked her head. "For her Celebration."

CHAPTER TWENTY-FIVE

The noise was unbearable. All around them, people were stamping their feet, clapping their hands, whistling through their fingers. Rita put her hands to her ears, deafened.

Maryam leaned towards her. "Horrible, isn't it?" she shouted.

Rita nodded. "Was it like this when I had mine?"

"Yes. Just the same. It always is."

"Why?"

Maryam shrugged. "Gives us a chance to let off some steam, I suppose. Break in the tension. They like to control it, stop us from releasing it when we shouldn't. At who we shouldn't."

"But the poor woman. The victim."

Maryam arched an eyebrow. "Is that how you see it?"

"It was for me. I didn't want to be there." She sniffed, looking at the empty space in front of them. There was a bed in the centre of it, empty and waiting. She didn't remember being transferred to a bed.

"Will they move her onto that?" she asked, nodding towards it.

"No. She'll walk in."

"That's not what happened to me."

"You were resisting."

"And Jennifer isn't?"

"What do you think? She's been gunning for this since day one."

Rita nodded. Jennifer had been kind to her, after her own Celebration, and she'd reacted with angry hostility.

The door opened and the noise abated. It started again when the women realised that it was only two counsellors, hurrying to take their places at the front. One of them was Meena. She scanned the crowd and then nodded when her gaze hit Rita. Rita glared at her.

"Who's that?" asked Maryam.

"She was my counsellor. When I got here. She's an idiot."

"Are you sure?"

Rita turned to face Maryam, puzzled. Maryam pulled her closer and whispered into her ear. "Only she was an inmate, when I got here."

Rita stiffened. So she hadn't been imagining things. They really had given a job to a woman who'd gone through the programme and come out the other side. Well, she wouldn't be accepting any job, however cushy.

"Were you at her Celebration?"

Maryam nodded.

"What was it like?"

"Textbook. They loved her."

"Who was her counsellor?"

"Dr Clarke, of course."

Rita watched Meena talking to the other counsellors.

The two men looked awkward in her company, tripping over themselves to be polite but with a wariness in their eyes.

The door opened again and a large black woman in an emerald green suit walked in. Piled on her head was a floral headscarf.

"Who's that?"

Maryam screwed up her nose. "Yonda Hughes. Governor. She's in charge of all the counsellors."

The governor raised her arms, beaming. The noise abated, orderlies picking their way into the crowd to hush those who were slow on the uptake. It reminded Rita of school assemblies, Mrs Toft glaring at children who didn't sit quietly, legs folded and arms crossed. She almost expected the governor to put a finger to her lips.

After a moment's quiet she moved towards the women, pacing in front of them. Rita and Maryam were in the front row with the rest of their group and Rita could hear the swishing of the governor's tights as she passed.

"Good morning, everybody," she exclaimed. Rita closed her eyes, half expecting a singsong *Good Morning, Mrs Hughes.*

The governor gestured towards the window behind them. "Isn't it a beautiful day? Perfect for a Celebration."

She beckoned one of the orderlies over and muttered in his ear. He crossed to the window and pulled the curtains shut while one of his colleagues flicked a light switch.

As the governor passed in front of them again Rita remembered something from her own Celebration – a canary, she'd imagined it to be. Was it this woman, in her bright plumage?

She leaned in towards Maryam, her eyes on the governor, who was looking over their heads.

"The sedative they gave me, for Celebration."

Maryam nodded. "Shh."

"You got one too, right?"

"Shh."

Yonda's gaze moved to them. Rita pulled back and adopted her most innocent smile, wondering if the governor remembered her from last time.

She raised her arms again. "Come on ladies, let's show our lucky celebrant our appreciation!"

Rita took the opportunity to turn to Maryam, her mouth close to the other woman's ear.

"Maryam, did you need a sedative?"

Maryam shook her head.

"So did you get drugs?"

Maryam shrugged. "I'm not sure. I wasn't aware of any, but I didn't feel... right. You know?"

Rita looked across at the bed, the small table next to it. There was a jug, a glass and an unmarked box.

"Did they make you drink first?"

Maryam frowned. "I'm not sure."

"They made me drink a glass of water. It tasted odd, I assumed that was because of the sedative."

The doors opened and the room descended into hush. Behind them, a woman coughed. Another giggled and an orderly muttered something.

There were dim figures beyond the door; two people, walking. Unlike her. She looked back at the table, the box. What was it for?

"Maryam," she hissed. "How did you feel? Was it like you were drunk?"

Maryam stiffened.

"Sorry. Was it, I don't know, was it like—"

"It reminded me of the time I took sleeping tablets. After my mum died."

Rita blushed.

Yonda was talking now, facing the door where the two figures lurked.

Maryam continued. "I felt woozy, light-headed. Delirious, almost."

Rita nodded. She remembered it, now.

"And you know what else?" Maryam said, as if only remembering it herself for the first time. "I felt an overwhelming desire to tell the truth."

CHAPTER TWENTY-SIX

The noise enveloped her before they even opened the doors. She thought of Rita. Wheeled in here, the things she'd said to Mark. Poor Rita.

This would be different.

She squared her shoulders, looking between the two orderlies standing either side of the double doors. The corridor was in darkness, the only light coming through the window in the centre of each door. They were stained glass, and in need of a clean. All she could make out beyond were dim shadows.

There was a hush and then she heard Yonda Hughes' voice, sharp and echoing in the high space. Jennifer swallowed. She closed her eyes for a moment and imagined she was standing outside the Commons chamber, waiting to enter those double doors. Preparing for a big speech. A frisson of excitement ran through her. This time tomorrow, she would be out of here. Home, with Yusuf. She clenched her fists and pushed back a smile.

The light through the windows dimmed and the doors were opened. She glanced at Mark, standing next to her. He nodded her through. She hesitated. Yonda was still talking, her voice clear. She wondered if Rita had heard any of this, or if she'd been sedated, lying out there on that gurney. She couldn't remember.

"Many of you will have seen today's celebrant in the news," Yonda said. Jennifer hardened her jaw; was she going to use her notoriety against her?

"Forget about that," the governor continued. Jennifer relaxed. "Today she is one of you, one of us. Today she needs your support. Now show us how excited you are!"

The frenzy rose again. This time, Jennifer could see the faces in the dim room, and pick out her own group in the front row. Rita and Maryam were whispering to each other, their eyes on the governor, who was pacing back and forth in front of the assembled prisoners, revelling in it all.

When I get out of here, thought Jennifer, *I'll get this place closed down.*

Mark gave her a light push in the small of the back and she ventured through the doors.

She kept her head high, waiting for the roar to subside. It didn't. She looked at Rita and Maryam in the front row, wearing worried expressions. She broadened her smile, encouraging them to join her. This was a celebration, wasn't it? She was going to get out of here, and then she was going to help them. They should be pleased.

Maryam shook her head. Rita mouthed something at Jennifer, her lips distorted. Jennifer shrugged and Rita pulled a hand up to her face, wiping her eyes. What was wrong?

"This way," Mark muttered, and she turned to follow his gaze. In the centre of the floor, facing the crowd, was a bed. An empty bed, with a small nightstand next to it. Waiting for her.

She shuddered and looked at Mark. "But I walked in. I came willingly. I don't need a bed. I don't need to be strapped down."

Her heart rate was rising with the noise, and she could feel sweat on her brow. Why would they need to restrain her, if she was happy to do this? Why would she need to lie down? Surely she could do this sitting in a chair, or standing even? Yes, standing would be good.

She stepped towards the crowd and opened her mouth. The noise stopped and the women froze, many with their hands mid-air. The orderlies tapped shoulders and dipped into the crowd, jostling the women.

Yonda Hughes turned from her spot at the front, and looked at Jennifer. She frowned.

"Get back there!" she hissed.

Jennifer stepped towards her. "I can do it here. I'm happy to stand. I'd prefer it."

"Don't be stupid, girl. Now get back there and do as your counsellor tells you."

Mark was standing behind the bed, watching her. He looked concerned. She curled her lip.

"Go," urged Yonda. Jennifer heard the sweep of her clothes as she turned to orchestrate the crowd. The noise started up again.

Jennifer closed her eyes then opened them again, stepping towards Mark. He looked like he was miles away. Finally she was next to him. She tried not to look at the bed.

"Why?" she asked him.

"Procedure, Jennifer. It's how we always do it. Please, just go along with it. For your own sake. And mine."

He glanced at the orderly who was standing at the opposite end of the bed. She recognised him: Tim. He'd been rough with Rita, last time. He was thickset, with a heavy blonde moustache. He gave her a smile that didn't extend to his eyes.

She steeled herself to look at the bed. Its top half was angled into a reclining position. There were straps at the bottom edge and the sides, for arms and legs.

"I won't need those."

"We'll see," muttered Mark.

She swung round, her eyes wide. "I won't. Don't tie me up. Please."

He put a hand on her shoulder. "You'll be fine. Now please, sit on the bed."

She took in a deep breath and let it out again slowly, thinking again of the preparation she'd done for big speeches. The day she'd saved her career, despite the death at Bronzefield. The day she'd brought her own government down. The day she'd been arrested. She gritted her teeth and clenched her fists. Her nails had grown and they dug into her skin. The pain was good; it anchored her.

She put her hands on the bed and heaved herself up to it, thinking of hospital beds, of the three births she'd gone through. This had to be easier.

Perched on the bed, she looked at Mark. He looked back into her eyes. "Well done. You'll be fine. I'll help you. I promise."

She nodded at him, resentful of being patronised like this.

"Now," he said, "I need to tell you what's going to happen."

Beyond him, Yonda waved her arms and the women started clapping; a rhythmic, regular clap that made her feel as if they were booing her. It wrapped her and Mark in a cocoon. He bent down to get closer.

"I'm going to ask you some questions," he said. "I suggest you drink this first."

He lifted a glass of water off the nightstand.

"No thanks. I'm not thirsty."

He shook his head. "You need to drink. It will help you."

"What if I refuse?"

He glanced at Tim. "I wouldn't advise it."

She stiffened. "What's in it?"

She eyed the glass; there was a viscous substance dissolving in it. She recoiled.

"It'll help you relax," said Mark. "It'll clear your mind. After about five minutes you'll fall asleep. That's all. But in those five minutes, we need to work through the six steps. Can you do that?"

She felt her eyes pricking. "Yes."

He lifted the glass to her lips.

"I can do it."

He nodded. She took the glass and drank. It tasted bitter.

"And the rest."

She glanced at Tim again then finished the glass off.

"Good. Now sit back."

"No."

He sighed. "Please. If you don't, you could fall."

She frowned. "Alright." Anything to get her out of this place. Anything to get her back to Yusuf.

She let him ease her back and shuffled her feet. She was aware of them sticking out of the clinical gown she'd been told to wear, facing the women, and hoped she was decent. She closed her eyes and swallowed. The room was quiet now. She heard a cough echo around the space, followed by shushing.

Mark turned to the front of the room.

"This is Jennifer Sinclair. She has worked through the programme with me and agreed today to undergo the Celebration ceremony. I hope you'll all support her."

There was a murmur of assent. Jennifer stared up at the ceiling, wondering what Maryam and Rita were doing. What Rita had been mouthing at her.

Mark turned to her.

Her head had begun to feel heavy, as if she'd been drinking.

"Now, Jennifer. How do you feel?"

She examined her body mentally, wriggling her toes and fingers. There was a lightness to her limbs. It felt nice. "Good. Thanks."

"Good. Now, we're going to work through the six steps, just like we did in your group sessions, and your one-to-ones with me. OK?"

"Okey dokey," she said, then put her hand to her mouth.

"It's OK," he whispered. She remembered Rita. Was she going to make a fool of herself, too? She realised she didn't care.

"Step One," Mark said, his voice louder. "Do you accept that you've been disloyal to the state?"

"I certainly have. First there was John, then Michael, and I brought my—"

He put a hand on her arm. "Shush. That'll do."

She nodded, smiling.

"What did you do wrong? Why were you arrested?"

"Oh. I was arrested because I hid my son, Samir. They accused him of being a terrorist. He had this girlfriend, see—"

She heard a commotion beyond her feet somewhere. Mark put his hand on her lips. She kissed it, then laughed.

"Sorry."

"It's OK. Let's just keep things brief, shall we?"

She nodded, looking up at him. His eyes were a bright blue. Lovely.

"Now, do you accept my support? The support of your group?"

"I sure do." She reached a hand up to touch his face. He brushed it away.

"Who have you harmed?"

She frowned. "Well, that's a toughie."

"OK, let me rephrase it. By hiding your son, who did you harm?"

"Oh, that's easy. No-one. I had to hide my son. I'm his mother after all."

She thought of the words she'd prepared, the lies. They'd left her. Oh well. It didn't seem to matter now.

"Right," said Mark, his voice stern. "What will you do differently, in future?"

"Well I won't betray my own party, for one thing. And I'll get this place closed down."

There was laughter from beyond her feet. Jennifer smiled, then put a hand to her cheek. Was that what she was supposed to say?

"Finally, Jennifer, will you spread the message you've learned here? Will you encourage others to love the British state and be loyal to it?"

"That depends."

"On what?"

"If there's a change of government."

There was laughter followed by a series of slaps. She heard a woman cry out.

"Thank you Jennifer."

"Is that it? Have I finished?"

"You have."

"Oh. Thank you."

She reached a hand up again towards his face but it was heavy. She watched it descend back down towards her face, becoming less distinct. By the time it fell, she was unconscious.

CHAPTER TWENTY-SEVEN

Rita was sitting alone at the breakfast table when Jennifer arrived. She was looking the other way, checking for the rest of the group. *She's avoiding my eye,* Jennifer thought. Not that she could blame her.

She put her tray down.

"Mind if I join you?"

Rita feigned surprise. "Oh. Jennifer. No, not at all."

Jennifer ate in silence, aware that Rita kept turning towards the door. When she'd finished her toast, she cleared her throat.

"I'm sorry."

Rita spoke at the same time. Her voice was small and high-pitched. "How are you?"

"What?"

"Sorry? Oh. After your Celebration. How are you?"

Jennifer shrugged. "Disappointed." She picked up her mug of tea and drank from it, as much to shield her face as anything.

Rita shrank back. She started picking at the skin on the back of her hand. "What was it like?"

"I can't really remember. But look, I wanted to talk to you. Before the others arrive."

Jennifer wasn't used to this. She didn't have many friendships; it was Yusuf to whom she normally owed apologies. She'd learned how to frame it, when to pick the right moment. This was so much harder.

"Oh."

"Well, I know I was out of order. About your Celebration. I didn't—"

"Welcome back."

They looked up to see Maryam standing over them. Jennifer smiled.

"Thanks."

"Am I interrupting something?"

Jennifer felt her face grow hot. She glanced at Rita, who was looking down at her hands again.

"No," Jennifer said. "Sit down. Please."

Maryam placed her tray next to Jennifer's. "Has Rita told you?"

Jennifer looked between the two women. "No. Told me what?"

Maryam gave Rita a look. Rita nodded.

"We realised it when we were waiting for you to come in," said Maryam. "The drug. It's a truth drug."

Jennifer scoffed. "There's no such thing."

Maryam shook her head. "Not true. I know it sounds like the sort of thing you'd see in the movies, but it's real. I talked to one of the other women, she's a doctor. It's called Sodium Pentothal. If you take it, you can't lie."

"Can't lie! That's ridiculous."

Rita looked up. "Shush."

The room was empty, the kitchen team having cleared up and left. Jennifer wondered how inmates got on that team. She could be here for a while; she might as well keep busy.

Rita slumped in her chair, pulling at her skin. She kept whistling something to herself. She reminded Jennifer of Bel.

"Rita? Are you OK?"

Rita looked up at her, shrugged and bent her head again. Jennifer squeezed her eyes shut and dug her fingers into her hair. "Look, we have to come up with something."

"What do you mean?" asked Maryam.

"A plan. To get out of here. They can't keep us here forever." She looked up. "Can they?"

Maryam shrugged. "Dunno. I've only seen two women leave. They might have been released. They might not."

Jennifer shivered. She hadn't considered that getting out of here would mean anything other than going home to Yusuf. Surely once she convinced them to believe her that she'd repented, they'd be done with her?

Then she thought of prison, and Cindy. Maybe staying here was for the best.

She shook herself out of it. "I can't just sit here and wait for something to happen," she said. "I need to come up with something. That's what I do."

Rita sniffed.

"What's happened to you?" Jennifer asked her. "Where's the fire gone? When you got here I was in awe of your guts. Standing up to Mark like that. Refusing to cooperate."

Rita looked up. "Really?"

Jennifer blushed. "Well, if I didn't, I was wrong. I thought I could get out of here by lying, and look where it got me."

She looked across at Maryam, noticing that her friend

had dropped her habit of winding her hair round and around her neck. "I like your hair," Jennifer said. "It suits you. If you don't mind me saying that."

Maryam's hand shot to her hair. She looked around the room. "Thanks," she muttered.

Jennifer sat back, her mind blank. She didn't like not having a course of action to get started with. "How did you work it out?" she asked. "About the truth drug." She still wasn't convinced but it didn't do any harm to find out more.

Maryam shrugged. "It was Rita, really. While we were waiting for you to come in for your Celebration. I think it brought it back to her. She asked me about mine, and we realised what we had in common. She asked me if it felt like I'd been drinking!"

Maryam laughed and Rita blushed. "Sorry."

"That's OK." She turned back to Jennifer. "I told her it felt like when I took a sleeping pill." She cocked her head. "What was it like for you? Can you remember?"

Jennifer fished in her memory. It was only two days ago but it felt hazy, like something that had happened last year.

"I felt relaxed. Happy." She squinted. "Did I touch him? The counsellor?" She felt her cheeks grow hot.

Maryam chuckled. "Don't worry. It gets us all like that, a bit."

Jennifer considered. "It did feel like I was drunk," she said. "And I had an overwhelming urge to say everything that was on my mind." She paused. "What *did* I say?"

"Something about John, and Michael?"

"Oh hell. Ah well, I guess that was true." She had an idea. "Maybe there is a way around this."

Maryam shook her head. Rita slumped so far down that Jennifer thought she would fall off her seat.

"No, there could be," she said. "What if we find a form

of words that isn't lies, but is what they want to hear. There must be a way of framing it." She smirked. "If anyone can come up with the right words, it's a politician."

Maryam shook her head. "You can try, maybe. I don't think I can."

"Why not? Maybe I can help you." Jennifer leaned in. She heard a sound behind the closed serving hatch; somebody dropping something metallic. It clattered on the floor. Had they been overheard?

"Tell me what you're here for," she whispered. "Let me help you with the words. I can probably do yours easier than my own."

Maryam shook her head. "I'd rather not."

There was another noise, from the doorway this time. Jennifer looked up to see Mark standing in it. She paled.

Maryam turned round. Her eyes widened when she saw him. Rita did nothing.

He nodded at them and shuffled into the room, glancing at the kitchen hatch.

"Morning."

"Morning," they muttered.

"I've been looking for you, Jennifer."

She pointed at herself. *Who, me?* "Oh?"

He smiled. "Still yourself, I see." He glanced at Rita, his brow creasing. "Come to my office, please. It's time for your one-to-one."

She looked at Maryam, who was staring at her, shaking her head.

"No it isn't," she told him. "That's tomorrow."

"Well, you just failed Celebration, didn't you? You need an extra session. Come on."

Jennifer looked at Rita, who was leaning against her. She pushed her gently towards Maryam, who nodded.

She stood up. "Right."

"Good. Come with me."

They passed at least four other women on the way to his office, all of whom stared at her. She looked back at them, wondering what they were thinking, what they'd seen her say. She didn't like being the centre of attention. She was relieved to reach his office and duck inside.

"Please, sit down." He took a seat and gestured at the empty chair. She sat, leaning back.

"So, do I have to start all over again?" she asked.

He pursed his lips. "That depends."

"On what?"

"On whether you'll tell the truth this time."

"What did you expect? I wanted to get out of here. As far as I could see, saying what you wanted to hear was the best way."

"I understand. Believe me, I do. But it was never going to work."

"Did you know I was lying? Did you see through it, all along?"

He nodded. "Sorry."

"So why did you put me forward for Celebration?"

He blushed. "That wasn't my idea."

"You knew I wouldn't be able to lie. You knew you'd be giving me a dose of Sodium Pentothal."

He flinched.

"I worked it out. Or rather, Maryam and Rita did." She paused. "Are we the only ones here who've been through it?"

"Yes."

"Isn't that a bit of a coincidence? All of us in the same group?"

"I get the difficult ones." He reached a hand towards her. "I'm sorry, I didn't mean—"

"So, we're the difficult ones, are we." She smiled. She'd never intended to make life easy for him. Just for herself. "Don't worry. Someone's got to be. Didn't it occur to you that we'd work it out?"

He shrugged. "Of course it did."

"Why would anyone apply for Celebration, if they know?"

"Because most patients don't intend to lie. Most pass first time."

She raised an eyebrow. "How many? This place has been here, what, ten, twelve months? How many women have passed in that time?"

"Two, maybe three."

"Is that all? Two, or three."

He blushed. "Two."

She grunted. "So, what do I do now? How do I get past this goddamn system?"

He stood up. "Look, I never asked to come here, you know."

"Don't give me that. Only obeying orders. This country hasn't gone that far."

"It's true. I worked in a psychiatric ward before this. They closed it down. NHS cuts. I had no choice but to take whatever was on offer. Which was this."

"What did you do, in this psychiatric ward?"

"I was a psychiatric doctor, of course."

"And it doesn't bother you what you're doing here? Administering truth drugs to women and holding them prisoner until you can brainwash them?"

"I didn't design the system. It keeps prison crowding down. Surely you'd rather be here than in prison?"

She narrowed her eyes: so he'd read her file.

"I want to help you, Jennifer."

"You've already said that. Help me get through the programme. Which step is that? Oh yes, step three. Accept the help and support of my group and my counsellor. I need more than that, if I'm ever going to get my family back."

"I know. That's why I want to help you. And not that way."

She curled her lip. "What way, then?"

"I can't tell you." He looked past her shoulder towards the camera. "But I'm sure we can work something out."

"How the hell am I supposed to trust you, if you won't tell me? How do I know you won't go running back to that Yonda woman and tell her what we've talked about?"

"Why would I do that? I'd lose my job."

"No you wouldn't. I know you're picking your words. You know she watches you."

He turned to the wall next to his desk, and pulled one of the photos down. The one that was ripped on one side. He waved it in front of her face.

"Look at this, Jennifer. This is my son. His name's Olivier. He's five years old, but in this photo he's three. My wife left me six months after that photo was taken, said she couldn't bear living in this country anymore. I said I'd go with her but she told me that as far as she was concerned, I was the same thing. I represented everything shitty about Britain. So she took him to Canada."

"I'm sorry."

"Don't be. I'm a big boy. But I wanted you to understand that you're not the only one with problems. You're not the only one who's human. There's me, and all those women out there. We're real, Jennifer. We're not monsters."

She looked from the photo to his face. His eyes were

red. She thought of her children, of how it physically hurt to be away from them. "When did he leave you?"

"Eighteen months ago. I told you. I haven't seen him since."

She felt her muscles slacken. She nodded, her eyes lowered.

He attached the photo to the wall again, carefully. He touched the boy's face with his thumb as he did so.

She leaned over the desk, lowering her voice. "Alright. For the sake of everyone in here. Help me get out, and then I'll get them out."

CHAPTER TWENTY-EIGHT

The group was quiet today. Rita sat with her head hung low in front of her chest, ignoring them all. Across from her, Jennifer was shifting uneasily in her seat, while Maryam was still, smoothing her hair over her shoulders. Sally played with her fingernails, pulling at them as if it would make them grow. Paula, next to Rita, was staring into space, thinking about Mandy maybe.

Rita swung her legs below her chair, enjoying the swishing sound of her feet on the floor. She wasn't interested in talking.

The door opened and Rita sensed the others looking up. She continued staring at the floor, examining the scratches in the wood. Mark strode in, his footsteps slowing as he approached the circle of chairs. He sat down hastily and dropped his pile of files on the floor in front of his feet. They appeared in the corner of her vision, brown and dog-eared.

"Morning everybody," he said.

No-one replied. This wasn't Celebration, and he wasn't Yonda. No-one could force them to speak.

"Where's Bel?" asked Jennifer. Rita looked up for the first time, noticing the empty seat.

Mark gave Jennifer a grave look. "She's not very well. In the infirmary." His eyes brightened. "I'm sure she'll be back with us soon."

Rita grunted and looked back down. She pulled her feet out from under the chair and started to examine the tops of her shoes, which were grubby and worn. She wondered how many other women had worn them.

She considered Bel, in the infirmary. If that was where she really was. Bel had been quiet and moody, humming to herself; classic signs of mental illness. Rita paused. Was *she* heading that way?

She sighed. Maybe it would make things easier.

She felt the air stir as Mark stood up. The other women were fidgeting in their seats, watching him. He pushed his chair backwards and lowered himself to the floor, kneeling on it. She shuddered; was he trying to catch her eye?

Then he said something that startled her. "Everyone, let's sit on the floor. Change things up a bit."

There were murmurs around the circle.

"What?" asked Sally. "Don't be daft."

"Please," said Mark, his voice soft. Rita wondered if he cared about their predicament, if he too had been affected by the two failed Celebrations one after the other. Of course not; he could walk out of here at the end of the day and go home to his family.

Sally pushed her chair back, but remained standing. The others lowered themselves to the floor. Rita noticed Maryam putting a hand to her back as she went down.

"Rita?" Mark was on the floor across from her, looking up into her face. She shrugged.

"Join us, please."

She looked up at Sally, still standing with her hands on her hips and her lips curled. Better not to be like her. She pushed her chair back and slid off it to the floor, arranging herself in a crosslegged position.

"Lovely," said Mark. She frowned at him.

Sally was tapping a foot now, right next to Rita's knee. Rita tried to ignore it.

"You can't do this. It's beneath our dignity."

Jennifer looked up. "Come on, Sally. It can't do any harm."

Sally glared at her. Paula nodded towards Sally who finally shrugged and dropped to the floor, crashing onto her hands and knees.

"Happy now?"

"Thank you," said Mark.

This was too much for Rita. She knew they were all looking at her, thinking about her performance at Celebration. She hated that she couldn't remember it but everyone else could; it made her feel like a caged animal being watched from outside.

She sighed and lay down on the floor, relaxing as her head came into contact with the rough wood. It felt good. She pulled her legs out straight and arranged her arms at her sides. She closed her eyes and wiggled her fingers, resting them palms-up on the floor. She let her breathing deepen, like a tide washing over her.

There was few moment's silence broken by the sound of someone clearing their throat. Rita ignored it.

"Rita?"

It was Mark. His voice was over her, close to her. She felt herself tense and then pushed through her muscles, willing them to relax again.

"Sit up please, Rita. We can't have our group session with you lying on the floor."

She pursed her lips and whooshed out a long breath, feeling her stomach contract. She shook her head.

She heard Mark move back. What was he going to do? Would he continue the session with her lying there? She imagined them all staring at her, cursing her in their minds. Well, let them hate her. She hated them.

There was someone else next to her now, not Mark. One of the women. Her breathing was high pitched and she smelled of soap.

"Rita?" she whispered. It was Jennifer.

She screwed up her nose and tightened her eyes.

"I think you should get up," Jennifer said. She dipped down, her lips close to Rita's ear. It tickled. "Mark doesn't look happy."

"Fuck him," Rita whispered in response. Jennifer withdrew.

There were murmurs above her and then the room fell quiet again. A hand landed on her shoulder. It was large and rough; Mark.

"Get up now please," He said, his voice stern.

She shook her head. "No."

"We need you to participate in the group session. Everyone has to play their part."

She opened her eyes. His face was over her; his breath smelt of eggs. She gagged.

"What about Bel?" she asked, then closed her eyes again.

"Bel's unwell. I told you."

"She's not here, so I'm not going to be here either. Do it without me."

He was still holding her shoulder. Now he started to

jiggle it as if attempting to wake her. "I'm serious. I need you to get up. Join in with the others. If you don't help your group, they can't work through the programme."

"No point," she said, not opening her eyes.

"That's not true." His voice was shaky; he knew she was right.

"No fucking point," she repeated. "They'll all fail." She opened her eyes again to glare at him. "We're the difficult ones."

She caught his blush before closing her eyes again. He started trying to pull her up.

She opened her eyes to glare at him. "Leave me alone!" she hissed. "Don't touch me."

"I need to help you get up, Rita." His face looked tense and his skin had paled.

She batted his hand away. "No. Get off me!"

His expression was stern now. "Rita, you need to think about your actions. You don't want to get into tro—"

"Why not? What's the point? I'll be here forever and you know it. Do what you want to me, see if I care!"

He pulled back. She was sitting up now, propping herself up with one arm behind her. The other women had backed off and were looking scared.

"Please, Rita," said Jennifer. "I don't think this is a good—"

Rita spun her head to look at her. "Oh, shut up! Whatever plan it is you've got to get out of here, it won't work! You're stuck here, just like me."

Mark had backed away but now he was approaching her again, his hands in front of him. She widened her eyes. "Don't touch me."

He shook his head and came closer, grabbing her wrists. She struggled to pull them free but he had them gripped firmly and the movement ended up being more like a bizarre dance.

"Calm down," he said through gritted teeth. "It'll be OK. I'll help you." He looked wildly at the others, his hair falling over his face. "We'll all help you, right?"

"Right," said Jennifer, Maryam and Paula in unison. Sally said nothing. She was standing with her arms folded, grinning. Rita felt rage surge through her. She stopped trying to pull out of Mark's grip and lurched towards him, pulling her arms in and them outwards, He yelped and let go. She brought a knee up and landed it between his legs.

"Shit!" he cried, doubling over.

"Rita, stop it!" cried Jennifer. "This is madness."

"No," she hissed, turning to the group. "This place is madness." She pointed at Mark. "*He's* madness."

He was bright red now, backing away from her with an arm held up. He stumbled towards the door and pushed it open, leaning out. She realised what he was doing and lurched towards him, flailing for his leg.

"Help!" he cried. "Security! Code B!"

There was thundering in the corridor outside, the sound of running feet. Rita turned to the other women, staring madly. She was overcome with triumph mixed with dread. What now?

Three orderlies appeared; two men and one woman. One of the men had a yellow moustache. Tim. He grabbed Mark and pulled him out of the room, taking his weight. The other two approached Rita. The woman reached into her pocket and pulled something out. She made a snapping motion with her arm and the object suddenly lengthened; a truncheon.

Rita ran backwards, slamming into the wall. "Sorry!" she cried. "I didn't mean to."

Jennifer, Maryam and Paula rushed at the two orderlies, trying to pull them off. But they were like fleas on a rhino's back. The orderlies shrugged them off and continued towards Rita. When they saw that she'd given up they snapped the truncheons shut again. She slid down the wall, her hands pushing against the plaster, moaning. They picked her up and lifted her between them. She tried to struggle but it was no good; they were stronger than her. And besides, all the fight had left her. She felt like a deflated balloon, the air sighing out of her as they carried her out of the room.

CHAPTER TWENTY-NINE

Jennifer didn't wait for the previous woman to come out of Mark's office and beckon her in this time; she was a few minutes late and figured he'd be alone.

He was.

"Where is she?" she demanded, standing over him at the desk.

He pushed aside the papers he'd been working on and looked up at her. His face was red.

"Sit down, Jennifer."

She shook her head. "What have you done with her? She hasn't been at meals for two days now, she hasn't been in group. And I've just checked her room."

She paused, hearing her breathing in the air between them. Venturing upstairs to the second floor eaves rooms was forbidden; her room was on the first floor.

She didn't care.

"She's not in her room. I can't see any sign of her. What have you done with her?"

He stood and backed towards the window, not taking his eyes off her face.

"Please calm down. This is not going to do you any goo—"

She advanced on him, feeling her heart slow a little. He held his ground, regaining his composure.

"Tell me where she is. Last time I saw her she was being dragged out of group. What's happened to her?"

He shook his head. "We don't discuss the details of centre management with patients."

She licked her lips and sat down. Maybe a show of calm would achieve more.

"This is me you're talking to. I know how it works. I know what rights I have, and Rita has. I was an MP when they passed the legislation, for Christ's sake!"

He sat in his own chair. "You told me you weren't there."

"What?"

"You weren't there. You didn't know."

"You know what I mean. I was an MP. I know my rights."

"That doesn't mean you have the right to ask about Rita."

"I'll find out, you know. I'll find an orderly who's prepared to tell me—"

"You really think Mary and Tim will tell you?"

She felt her muscles tense. "There are two members of our group missing now, and we don't know where either of them are. How are we supposed to *accept the support of the group* if its members keep disappearing?"

"I told you. Bel is unwell. She's in the infirmary."

"Yes. This infirmary that I can't find any evidence of. None of the women I've spoken to has been there."

"Well..." She could sense him chewing over his options, deciding how much to tell her. "That's because we don't often have need for it." He looked up at her. "It's not some great big hospital ward, you know. It's just a room. Tiny. More of a sick bay than an infirmary, really."

"So is that where Rita is, too?"

His eyes widened momentarily. "Yes. You saw how unwell she was."

She shook her head. "No, she's not unwell. She's angry, and she's desperate. She wants to get out of here, and now she believes she never will." She slowed down, aware that she was garbling her words. "She needs her friends around her."

He arched an eyebrow. "Friends?"

"Yes. The group is the closest thing any of us has got to friends in this place. Unless you think we should consider *you* a friend?"

He allowed himself a chuckle. "I think you're getting a little past yourself, Jennifer. I'm your counsellor. You not long ago failed Celebration. You should be trying to keep in my good books, no? Not barging in here accusing me of all sorts of things."

"I didn't acc—"

"Strictly, no. But I'm not stupid. You think I've done something with Rita, something illegal. Don't you?"

"I just want to know where she is. And Bel."

"I have good news on that front." He stood up again and started pacing the room, avoiding her eye. He paused at the window and turned to her. "Look. Come with me. Let's take a walk."

"A walk?"

"Yes. It'll do you good. Fresh air."

She hesitated. She hated doing as he asked, but the thought of getting outside was almost too much to bear...

"OK."

"Good." He beckoned her up with his eyes and she followed him out of the room. They walked to the stairs at the end of the corridor and he headed up without looking back to check she was there. She followed, hating herself. Hoping none of the other women would see.

As they crossed through the lobby of the house, a space she had only had cause to venture into a couple of times, Mark froze. A door about ten feet in front of them was opening. He grabbed her arm and pulled her out of the front doors, shoving her outside. As he dragged her through she caught a glimpse of yellow emerging; Yonda Hughes?

She smiled to herself. If he was breaking the rules, then she had one up on him.

She shook her arm free and he glared at her. "Don't do anything stupid. This place is secure."

She sighed. "I'm not stupid, either."

"Let's hope so."

She followed him along a path that led away from the house to its side, passing through a gap between two hedges. Beyond them towards the back of the house, she could see a few women walking. Some were accompanied by orderlies, others weren't. What did you have to do, to be allowed out here?

Finally they arrived at a curve in the path and he stopped. He looked over her shoulder, checking they were alone. She followed his gaze. The house was hidden by trees and shrubs from here.

He turned to her. "Right."

"Why all the cloak and dagger?" she asked. "Surely you can say whatever it is you need to tell me inside."

"Don't you like being out here?"

She said nothing; that wasn't the point.

"Right," he said. "I think it's time we had a proper chat."

"A proper chat? Isn't that what we're supposed to be doing at all my one-to-ones?"

"Not that sort of chat. I want to tell you how I can help you. Get through Celebration. Get out of here."

She narrowed her eyes. A rustling sound came from behind her and he pushed her to one side, his eyes full of panic.

"Come on," he barked, and grabbed her hand. She tried to snatch it away but his grip was too tight.

"Let go," she grumbled, as he pulled her further way from the house. They crossed a small patch of lawn from where the corner of the house became visible again. He kept his head down, picking up pace. The sun hit the lawn, dappled as it was filtered through nearby trees. Soon they were among those trees, their foliage deadening any sound. How close were they to the road?

He stopped and she nearly stumbled into him. At last she pulled her hand away.

"Don't do that," she told him. "I'm not a piece of meat."

"Sorry," he shrugged, but she could tell he didn't mean it. She wondered what the staff here thought of the women, whether they saw them as individuals or just anonymous bodies to be processed.

"I don't want your help," she said.

"What? That's not what you said."

"It's different, now."

"How?"

"Christ Mark, can't you see? How am I supposed to trust you when you won't tell me what you've done with Rita and Bel?"

"I told you, Bel's doing well."

"You told me nothing. You dragged me out here with no word of explanation." She folded her arms across her chest. "What's going on? What are you up to?"

"I've got no idea what you're talking about. Look, I'm sorry. I was about to tell you about Bel. Good news. She's coming back to the group. She's a lot better."

"Really? And how did you make her *a lot better*?"

"Why don't you trust me?"

She barked out a laugh. "If you need to ask me that then you're twice as stupid as I thought you were."

He glanced around the clearing they were standing in. Bluebells lay in a carpet at their feet, and she could smell wild garlic. He shook his head and leaned in towards her.

"You don't seem to understand the situation you're in."

"How's that?"

"I'm your counsellor. It's up to me to recommend you for Celebration. No Celebration, no release. You need to show me a bit of respect."

She swallowed. "Seriously? After what you did to Rita?"

"I did nothing to Rita." He pulled a hand through his hair. "She'll be back, soon. We're helping her to get better, that's all. Stop worrying."

"I don't believe you."

He put his hands on his hips. "Jennifer, do you want to get out of here? Do you want to see your family again?"

She felt her chest clench. "Of course."

"Well, stop banging on about Rita. Stop bandying accusations around. And accept my help. Don't forget what it is you really want. Your family. I can help you with that."

"And my friends?"

"They'll be fine. Don't worry about them." A pause. His

blue eyes were drilling into her; there was a sheen of sweat on his upper lip. "Worry about Yusuf, and Samir. Hassan."

She shuddered. "Don't talk about them. They're not yours to talk about."

He sighed. "Don't you see? That's your prize. Accept my help and you'll get them back."

She hated him for using her family's names like that; but it had worked. She felt as if the high wind that had been billowing through her sails, powering her anger, had dropped like a stone.

She shook her head. "I don't believe you. You lied to me about Yusuf."

"What?"

"You think I wouldn't have asked Catherine, when she came here?"

"Catherine?"

"Catherine Moore. Home Secretary. She was here. I saw her."

"I didn't know—"

"She told me that Yusuf's fine. He's at home. He wasn't arrested, at least he wasn't charged. That's not what you told me."

"I didn't in as many words—"

She put up a hand. "Stop. You're lying, even now."

"Fine. Don't trust me then. You'll never get out of here though."

"I will."

"How? You already know that you can't lie your way out."

"I'll find a way."

"Well, good luck with that."

"Thanks."

He shook his head. "I'm being genuine, Jennifer. I hate what they're doing to you. I want to help you."

She frowned. "They?"

He blushed. "I mean the system. This place. You deserve better."

"I do? But Rita and Bel don't?"

"Oh hell. Just think about it. Your priorities. If you get out of here, you can help them much better than you can stuck in here."

She shook her head. "That's not true, and you know it."

"Sorry?"

"Look. If you're so desperate to help me, then the first step is to answer my question. Tell me what you've done to Rita. Bring Bel back to group. Show me that you're not lying. Then maybe I'll start to trust you. But if you can't give me that, then why should I believe you'll help me?"

He rested his hands on his thighs and leaned over, putting his weight on his knuckles. "Alright."

"Alright?"

He straightened up. He seemed smaller; despite their almost equal height she felt as if she was suddenly towering over him.

"Alright. I'll bring them back. Both of them. So will you accept my help?"

She looked up towards the treetops. She could hear birds calling to each other between them. Freedom was so tempting. She had nothing to lose, surely?

"Yes."

He relaxed. "OK. Here's what I can do for you."

He stopped talking at a sound behind her. She turned. Someone, or something, was approaching through the trees. She could hear footsteps, crunching on the low woodland plants surrounding them. She thought back to that flash of yellow in the lobby. She turned back to him, her eyes wide.

"Later. I'll tell you later," he hissed, and started running away from her. She paused for a moment, listening to the footsteps approaching, then ran after him, resisting the urge to call his name. But when she emerged from the trees, he was gone.

CHAPTER THIRTY

When Mark walked into Yonda's office for their
regular meeting, Meena was already there. The two women
were sharing a tense silence that made him wonder what
had passed between them in his absence.

"Morning," he said, trying to sound as breezy as possible. He'd just come from Rita's new room in the building's
basement, on a different and even bleaker corridor than that
of his own office. There were three small rooms down there,
set as far away from the rest of the house as possible. The
rooms were bare but clean, or at least they were when the
patients kept them that way. Rita, luckily, had used the
toilet at the end of her bed and not chosen to smear excre-
ment on the walls, unlike some of the previous occupants.
He was sure the smell still lingered, despite the application
of pints and pints of bleach.

Rita had refused her breakfast this morning; an orderly
had fetched him from his office, entreating him to help. But
when he'd taken the tray back in she'd thrown it to the floor
and spat on him. He'd had to retreat hurriedly and let Roy
work through the hazardous substances procedure with

him; swabbing his face, cleaning him with disposable wipes. Masks were recommended for visits to solitary confinement, but they just exacerbated the anger of women like Rita. He'd be fine.

"We were just discussing your latest troublemaker," said Yonda. She glanced at Meena, who shoved her hands under her legs and blushed.

"And?" he asked, intrigued.

"I was hoping you could enlighten us," Yonda replied. "Seeing as you're her counsellor and the esteemed psychiatrist."

"She's making progress," he said, ignoring the veiled insult. Would she be receptive to the idea of Rita going back to the group, after the way she'd spoken at her Celebration?

Failing Celebration was like poison for these women. They were the only patients unlucky enough to pass under Yonda's radar, and tended to stay there after failing. Which meant the pressure on them to conform was high.

"Really?" Yonda asked. He nodded.

"I thought she would," said Meena. "I know I only had a few days with her, but I could see potential in her."

Mark sighed inwardly. Still, having Meena as an ally on this one would be useful.

Yonda turned her stare on Meena. "Is that so?"

Meena nodded. "She reminded me of myself, when I arrived here."

Mark was glad Meena was facing away from him, and couldn't see his eyes roll.

Yonda didn't look convinced. "They're not all like you, you know."

Meena blushed. "I know that. I do. But Rita was angry and resistant. Like me. She's starting to calm down. Like me. I think we should give her some time, then she'll come round."

Yonda stood up, pushing her chair back. "Tell me Meena, how many times did you undergo Celebration?"

"Er, once."

"And you passed first time. With flying colours. No?"

"Yes."

"And how many Celebrations has Rita had?"

Meena's voice lowered. "One."

"Did she pass?"

Mark stepped forward. He'd been thinking about his conversation with Jennifer, his promise to bring Bel and Rita back to the group. He had to nip this exchange in the bud.

"I think Meena has a point," he said.

Yonda leaned on her desk, shaking her head. She put a hand out to stroke the porcelain dog next to her. Meena's eyes were on it, and her face was flushed.

"How's that?" Yonda said, looking at Mark. He sensed Meena relaxing; the spotlight had moved on.

"She's been in solitary for three days now. And her behaviour is improving." He paused. "She's eating, and she hasn't attacked anyone since her first day."

"*Hasn't attacked anyone*," repeated Yonda. "Is that how low we're setting the bar these days?"

"Give her a chance," he said. "Failing Celebration isn't a pleasant experience. It can hit some women hard."

Yonda tapped at her lower lip with a fingertip. Her nails were a glossy pink that matched her lipstick.

"I'm not denying that," she said. "But attacking her counsellor like that isn't acceptable. I want to get her out of here."

Mark stiffened. "No."

Meena's head shot up. He'd been too hasty.

"I mean, I don't think that's a good idea," he said. "I can work with her, rehabilitate her. Now that she understands the reality of what she's faced with – what she's done – I think she'll turn."

Meena was still looking at him, her eyes dark. She smiled at him. He flinched.

"OK, so you say that failing Celebration can hit them hard," Yonda said. "What about your other one? Jennifer Sinclair. Has she attacked you? Has she lost her marbles?"

"I don't think that's an appropriate way to—"

She raised a hand. "They're prisoners, Mark. They are not the patients in your old hospital. Answer my question, please."

He swallowed. "Jennifer is doing well. She understands her situation." He pictured her standing among those trees. Did she?

Yonda raised an eyebrow. "And how exactly do you know that?"

"One-to-ones, of course."

"Nothing more?"

He stiffened. Had it been her, behind them in the garden? "No."

She sniffed. "You've got form, Mark. Don't push it."

He glared at her. "That's hardly relevant here."

She raised an eyebrow. From the corner of his eye he could see Meena leaning forward in her chair, fascinated. "I know you're lonely, Mark, but these women are your patients. I stuck my neck out for you, made sure you kept your job. Don't blow it."

He nodded. "Of course not. You've got nothing to worry about." But he'd all but stopped breathing.

"So," she said, rounding the desk to sit behind it again.

She stroked its surface, muttering under her breath. "I believe Rita needs to stay where she is for a while. Then we'll assess her."

"If I can— I don't agree," said Meena. Mark's eyes shot to her.

Yonda gave Meena a warning frown. "You haven't been dealing with her for a few weeks now. You don't know."

Meena slumped back in her chair. Mark stepped towards the desk, putting his hands on it. "Rita is fine," he said. "She can be allowed back to her group."

"She's not," said Yonda, " and you know it."

He said nothing, but met her stare. She shook her head and turned her laptop around to face him.

"Watch this," she said. She tapped a key and a video of Rita in her new room burst into life. She was hurling herself at an orderly whose back was to the camera, screaming at him. The orderly grabbed her wrist and pushed her to the bed, where she started kicking his shins, lashing out like a cornered panther. Her hands were gripped in his, her head a wild mass of hair and black, screaming mouth. Then the orderly's hand went to her arm and she fell back, sedated.

Yonda pressed another key and the video stopped. Meena sheeshed in a long breath.

"When was this?" Mark asked.

"Last night."

He closed his eyes. He hadn't spoken to the night staff this morning, and hadn't looked at their log for the night. He'd been too busy getting cleaned up after Rita had spat at him.

"It's an anomaly. She's fine with me."

"Really? You want me to play another video?"

He shook his head. He hated that she could spy on him from her eyrie here on the ground floor. But he hated even more the fact that she felt it necessary, that she didn't trust him.

"Right," said Yonda. "I'm going to ignore the fact that you're lying to me. I'm sure you have your reasons. But don't do it again. Bel can go back to the group, but not Rita. Rita stays where she is. If she hasn't improved in three more days – *really* hasn't improved – then we assess her."

He shrugged. Meena's fingertips brushed his hand; sympathy, or pity? He shuddered.

CHAPTER THIRTY-ONE

Jennifer could hear the other women taking their places in the circle of chairs behind her. She'd arrived early this morning, eager to see Rita and Bel again. She'd told Maryam about Mark's promise to bring them back to the group, but not the others.

She stood at the long windows, watching the garden outside. If only she could go out there again, relieve the itch to be under the vast sky. She'd always thought of herself as an indoors person, shuffling from one office to another, sitting in cars and on trains. But this enforced imprisonment made her feel like a caged animal.

She turned to the group, suddenly decisive.

"Let's move the chairs over here," she said.

They ignored her. Sally was staring at her fingernails, legs twisted in front of her chair. Maryam held her arms at her sides; they twitched every few seconds with the urge to dart up to her hair. And Paula was relaxed in her chair, leaning back with her legs splayed in front of her. Her eyes were closed.

Jennifer sighed and crossed to her own chair. She

looked at the other women and then picked it up, carrying it over to the window.

Sally looked up. "What are you doing?"

"I thought it would be nice to sit near the window. I want to look outside."

"Why?"

"Beats looking into the middle of the room, I suppose. Come on, join me."

Maryam frowned at Sally then Jennifer, then stood up and dragged her chair next to Jennifer's. She gave her a conspiratorial smile then sat down, leaning forwards to look out at the gardens.

"I wish we could go out there," she said.

"Hmm," replied Jennifer. "Have you been out at all? Even once?"

Maryam shook her head. "Of course not. We're not allowed."

"So who are they? And why are they allowed?" Jennifer pointed to two women walking along the path towards the woods where Mark had taken her.

"No idea," replied Maryam. "Best not to think about it too much."

This frustrated Jennifer. "Why not? Surely if we find out how they got out there, we might be able to get out too?"

"I heard that it's just for inmates who are ill," said Paula. She placed her chair beyond Maryam.

"So why haven't we seen Bel out there?"

Paula shrugged. "Dunno. Anyway, shall we move the rest of the chairs?"

Jennifer grinned at her and stood up to fetch the empty chairs. First Rita's and Bel's. Then Mark's. They placed each in the same position it had been in the centre of the room, with the circle identical.

Sally stayed where she was, holding her chair back and watching through lowered eyelashes.

"He'll only get you to move them back," she said.

"Maybe, maybe not," said Jennifer. "Come on over. It's nicer here. Better light."

Sally muttered something but then moved her chair. She didn't place it in the space that had been left for her. Instead, she slid it between Paula and Mark's empty chair. Maryam frowned at her then shrugged.

"Morning all." Mark pushed through the door and then paused as he noticed the chairs. Bel was with him, a few steps behind. A gasp ran around the waiting women. Maryam stood up and crossed to Bel, whispering to her. Bel muttered something in response and smiled.

"What's going on?" asked Mark. "The chairs."

Jennifer gave him a confident smile. "We thought it would be nice to sit near the window. It's a beautiful sunny day."

She was right. The lawns gleamed as brightly as any of Yonda's outfits and the sky was a brilliant blue. In the silence while Mark gathered his thoughts, Jennifer saw movement in a hedge and spotted a tiny sparrow flying out.

He looked from Jennifer to Bel and then at the rest of the group. They looked back at him, their faces steady.

"Whose idea was this?"

No-one spoke for a moment. Then Jennifer stood up. "Mine."

He pursed his lips, glaring at her. She held his gaze, beginning to regret this.

He shrugged. "Why not."

Jennifer let out a relieved breath.

Mark didn't move. Instead he put a hand on the small of

Bel's back. Bel stiffened but didn't make a sound. Her eyes looked distant and glazed.

"Everyone congratulate Bel on her recovery," he said.

They flocked to her, muttering words of welcome and congratulations. Jennifer had never heard Bel speak and had no idea why the older woman had found herself here. She guessed that was about to change.

Jennifer sidled around the group to Mark.

"Where's Rita?" she whispered.

He kept his eyes on Bel. "Not ready yet."

"You promised me."

"She's still unwell. Give it time."

Her heart was pounding. Maryam was watching, knowing what they were talking about. Jennifer considered the wisdom of asking after Rita publicly. Then dismissed it.

"You need to bring her back," she hissed. "We need to see her better."

He nodded. "I will. Trust me."

But she couldn't. As she watched him encourage the other women to sit down, she couldn't help but notice how strangely he was acting. His face was pale and his hair unkempt, and he had dark shadows under his eyes. He kept giving her sidelong glances as he spoke to the other women, ushered them back into their chairs.

The group had finished congratulating Bel and was drifting back to the chairs. She watched Mark as she took her own; he looked pleased with himself.

Mark sat in the chair next to Sally, giving her an irritated look. He beckoned for Bel to take her habitual place on his other side. She shuffled into place, her eyes lowered.

"So," he said, pressing his hands together. "This is going to be a good session. It's so good to see Bel recovered and back with us."

The group smiled and nodded. Bel looked up and smiled back. She wasn't rocking, or moaning, or pulling at her skin. But her eyes looked dull, and her skin was blotchy.

"So," Mark continued. "Bel is ready to do Step One with us today. Aren't you?"

He turned to Bel, who took a deep breath. Mark raised his hand.

"Not just yet. We'll let some of the others go first. Ease you in."

He worked around the group, asking each woman in turn to recite her Step One mantra. When Jennifer's turn came there was an awkward silence as they waited for her to speak. Maryam nudged her arm as if thinking she'd forgotten, or not noticed that it was her turn. Sally leaned back and smirked at her. Paula nodded at her.

She licked her lips.

"Sorry," she said.

Mark nodded. "It's OK. Go on."

She glowered at him. She'd explored the building the previous night, creeping along corridors in search of any sort of infirmary. But all she'd found was a small room on the first floor with two spartan beds and a bored-looking nurse keeping watch. One of the beds was occupied, but not by Rita.

Where was she?

She shook her head. "No. Let Bel have her turn, please."

Bel had stiffened and was looking less confident. She glanced at Mark.

Jennifer looked at Bel, hating herself. "Alright," she said. "I'm sorry."

She closed her eyes as she took her turn, thinking of Yusuf. Wondering what he would think if he saw her doing this.

At last it was Bel's turn. "Go on," urged Mark.

She sniffed. She had her hands in her lap, held very still as if she was concentrating very hard on keeping them there. The skin on her knuckles was flaking. Had it been like that before?

"I've been disloyal to the British state," she whispered.

Mark leaned towards her. "A bit louder please."

She cleared her throat. "I confess that I've been disloyal to the British state," she said.

Mark smiled at her. Jennifer tried not to stare, but what else was there to look at? She glanced at Sally, now opposite her. Sally looked back at her, her face hard. Jennifer turned to Bel.

"What did you do?" asked Mark.

"I supported a terrorist organisation," Bel said, her voice low again.

Sally grunted and made to stand up. Mark pushed her back into her seat with his eyes.

He turned back to Bel. "Can you go on?" Bel nodded. "Good. This one's easy," he told her. "Go on."

Bel looked up from her hands and faced the group, looking over Jennifer's head to the empty space behind her. "I accept the support of my counsellor." She squeezed her eyes shut. "I accept the support of my group."

Mark stood up, his hand on Bel's shoulder. He looked relieved. "Let's congratulate Bel," he said. Reluctantly they all stood up and went to her, clapping. Each woman in turn gave Bel her own congratulations.

Finally they were all back in place.

"Well done, everyone. That's all for today," said Mark.

Paula cleared her throat. "I'm at Step Four. I want to rehearse."

"Not today. Next time."

"But I need the group's help. I've already accepted it, so I need to use it. Let me work through my steps."

Mark looked at his watch. "Alright. But make it quick."

Paula looked around the group and took a deep breath. "I confess that I've been disloyal to the British state. I've—"

"Straight to Step Four, please," interrupted Mark. He sounded bored.

"OK. I harmed the people in my family and my workplace. I harmed everyone who I recruited to my organisation. I will make amends by telling as many of them as possible that they need to leave it, like I have."

Jennifer stared at her, wondering what organisation she referred to. Was this what Samir would have to admit to? She doubted his ability to be as calm as Paula, then wondered if Paula was really speaking her mind, or if she was lying too.

But they weren't finished. Sally had stood up and was in the process of dragging her chair back.

"Sally, what are you doing?" Mark asked.

"What does it look like?"

"It looks like you're trying to leave the group."

She barked out a laugh. "Yes. Well done. How can I accept the support of this lot? You're scum, the lot of you." She pointed at Paula. "Her, and her bloody lefty organisation." Then she moved her finger to Bel. "Her, fucking terrorist. And this one," she was staring at Maryam now, "who hid her little terrorist friends. You should be ashamed of yourselves."

"Now then, Sally," urged Mark, approaching her. "Let's not—"

"Oh, fuck off," she said. "I don't want any part of this. Put me in with my own kind."

Jennifer saw Mark swallowing. "Come back, Sally. Rejoin the group. That's not a request."

She sneered at him. "How are you going to make me?"

He headed towards the door. A panic button had been installed since Rita's outburst; if he hit it, the orderlies would appear, ready for challenge.

"Alright!" Sally shouted. "I'll be a good girl."

Jennifer smiled. Sally was all talk.

"Good," said Mark. Sally had left her chair to approach him at the door and so he nipped around her and grabbed it, placing it back with the group. This time, it was where it should be: between Maryam and the empty chair for Rita.

"Well done, everyone," said Mark. "That's it for today. Let's move all the chairs back to the centre for the next group before we leave."

He walked out, Sally staring after him with incredulity. She stormed out behind him, not moving any chairs.

CHAPTER THIRTY-TWO

THE ROOM WAS DAMP, AND SMELT OF STALE URINE. Rita slept on a thin bed wedged into a corner next to a sink that was stained with years of water deposits. On the other side of the room, just inches from the foot of her bed, was a toilet. She guessed this had been a bathroom once. Now it was a cell. The floors and walls were covered in black and white tiles that made her voice echo when she shouted out and her fists smart when she drummed them against the cold porcelain.

From time to time she heard movement outside the door. She huddled into herself whenever someone passed, hugging her knees to her chest as she sat on the bed. Waiting. But four times out of five the footsteps would pass and she'd be left alone.

At first the orderlies had come frequently, sometimes to bring her food, sometimes to punish her. Her arms ached from being yanked from the bed. Her ribs bruised from the punches that Tim had landed on her.

"You're like a feral animal," he'd told her. "It would be kinder to put you down."

His words made her tremble. No-one knew she was here. She wondered what her group thought of her being taken away like that. If they were relieved to be rid of her, or if they were asking where she was. She doubted it. They were better off without her.

The only people who came were the four orderlies. Sometimes it was Tim and Roy, but sometimes – thank God – it was Leroy and Mary. She'd been startled to see a female orderly, and wondered how she felt about keeping all these women in order. But Mary had been businesslike. Making it clear that she'd go easy on Rita if she cooperated.

And cooperate she did. Terrified of more beatings, she'd behaved like a meek child every time the door had opened. Shivering on her bed, she'd wait until she knew what they were here for, then do just as they asked. She hated herself for it. But her body couldn't take any more punishment.

Right now she was lying on the bed, trying to sleep. The room was dimly lit twenty-four hours a day, making it difficult to judge night and day. Sleep eluded her; it was hard to relax when that door could open at any moment. She clenched her eyes shut, willing herself to sleep. She needed it; her body needed to repair itself, and her mind needed a route out of the torment.

There was a sound beyond the door. She lifted her head from the thin pillow, torn between fear and fatigue. There it was again, the sound of a foot moving on the floor outside. Its owner was standing still, not walking, but shuffling, as if waiting to come in.

She sprang upwards and backed towards the corner, pulling her knees up. Her clothes felt damp and grubby and her hair fell in greasy shards in front of her face. She tried to tuck it into her collar.

The door opened and she held her breath, hoping it wouldn't be Tim. She was sure he enjoyed hurting her.

It wasn't Tim. It was Dr Clarke. She let relief wash over her, immediately replaced by anger.

"Why have you put me here?" she said. She'd been trying to shout but her voice was hoarse and dull. She gulped in air and then gagged; this room stank.

He wrinkled his nose, glancing at the toilet.

"I've come to see how you are," he said. He closed the door behind him and kept a hand on the doorknob.

"I'm not going to attack you, if that's what you're thinking," she muttered.

He didn't move. "How are you, Rita?"

"How do you think I am? Your thugs have been beating me up and I've been shut in here for goodness knows how long. And you want to know how I am."

He sighed. "You look terrible."

"Of course I bloody look terrible."

There was a pale patch over the sink where a mirror had once been, but it had long since been ripped off the wall, the only evidence the spots where the plaster had come away. But she didn't need a mirror to know how she looked. Sleep deprived, unwashed and miserable.

"Have you been behaving yourself?"

She gulped. "Yes." It was true. Or at least, it had been for the last few visits.

He arched an eyebrow. "I've heard otherwise."

She shrugged. "I've seen the error of my ways. Ask Leroy. He's been in here the last few times. I've been good. Done as he said."

"And what has he said?"

She frowned. Didn't he know? "I dunno. Stay there,

don't move. Eat this. Use the toilet. The sink. There's no water supply, you know."

He nodded, his nose wrinkling. "I'll see if I can get that fixed."

"Wouldn't it be easier just to let me out?"

She willed herself to stay calm. Angry outbursts hadn't helped so far; maybe reason would. But she couldn't bring herself to roll over and do everything this man said.

He stepped towards her, his eyes on her hands. She tucked them under her legs and pulled closer in to the wall. The tiles were cold, with a thin layer of mould. If she hadn't already got pneumonia, she would soon.

"Take a seat," she said, nodding towards the end of the bed. He hesitated then perched on it, brushing his hands on his trousers.

"Ask the orderlies," she said. "I admit I fought them when I got here – no more than they fought me, mind. A lot less. But now I'm being a good girl."

"Your tone won't work with me, Rita."

"This is as good as I can do."

"I know. That's what bothers me."

She reached deep inside herself. Did she have the capacity to become a meek creature for him? Could she play that game? And if she did, would it work? She thought of Jennifer, playing along, doing everything he asked her. Calling him *Mark*. Look where that had got her.

She shook her head. "Sorry."

He stood up, looking more sad than angry.

"I need to see more evidence of good behaviour. I need you to sort out your attitude towards me. Then maybe we can go back to having a couple of one-to-one sessions. See how you get on."

"I need to get out of here. Can't you see what they're doing to me? Those dogs you call orderlies?"

He didn't look at her.

"Prove yourself to me, Rita."

He didn't wait for her answer. Instead, he made for the door, not looking back while he closed and locked it. She stared at it, wishing she knew what to do.

CHAPTER THIRTY-THREE

Their little table was like an island of stillness surrounded by the motion of other inmates shifting around the dining room. Women came and went, picking up their breakfast, eating and then heading out again.

But Jennifer, Maryam, Bel and Paula stayed put, huddled at a table against a wall. It was set slightly apart from the others, in an alcove. The enclosed space still smelt of institutional cooking, as did the whole room.

Sally had taken a seat with another group across the room from them, refusing even to return their stares. That was fine with Jennifer, and she imagined the rest of the group felt the same.

Finally the room was empty. Members of the kitchen team emerged from behind the closed hatches, wiping down tables and sweeping floors. From time to time a puzzled glance would be sent in their direction, but nobody asked them to move. Even the sole remaining orderly stood quietly at the door. She was new; Jennifer hadn't spotted her before and guessed she didn't want to make trouble on her first day.

"What are we going to do?" asked Maryam. "We have to find her somehow."

Paula nodded. "Maybe we can search the building. She has to be somewhere."

Bel was sitting quietly next to Jennifer. She hadn't said much during breakfast and only spoke when directly addressed. Her eyes had regained some clarity but the repetitive movements were beginning to return. She kept raising her hand to her forehead and scratching it, putting it down on the table, then doing it all over again a few seconds later.

Paula turned to her. "Bel, where did they put you, when you were in the infirmary? Was it an infirmary?" She blushed. "Sorry."

Bel shrugged. "We don't mean to pry," said Maryam. "But if you can help us find out where Rita is, that would be a big help."

Bel shrugged. "It was a kind of hospital ward. Smaller. Just two beds."

Jennifer swallowed. She'd seen this room. But she waited for Bel to finish speaking.

"There was a nurse. She was nice. Gave me medicine." Bel scratched her forehead again and slumped back against the wall. The bench seat shuddered.

Jennifer nodded. "I've seen it. It's on the first floor, near the back." She eyed her companions. "Are any of you on that corridor? Right at the back, looking out over the bushes behind the kitchens."

She and Paula were on the left side of the house. All Jennifer could see was an expanse of lawn bordered by a long hedge. No paths or shrubberies, just an expanse of green.

"Me," said Maryam. "My room's in the far right corner, at the back."

Jennifer considered. Maybe Maryam would be able to sneak out of her room at night, make another check on the infirmary? She thought of the room when she had stumbled upon it, the empty bed and the nurse who had raised an eyebrow when she saw Jennifer open the door. She had shooed her away like a naughty child.

"I don't think she'll be in there, but it's worth another look. Do you think you can get out of your room at night?"

Maryam shrugged. "Depends on my roommates. I wouldn't want them hearing me, raising the alarm."

"How many do you have?"

"Three. We're in bunks. Aren't you the same?"

Jennifer blushed and glanced at Paula. "No. I'm with Paula and Mandy. We've got three single beds, squashed in together."

"Oh. OK, I can try to get out, take a look. The orderlies come past every two hours in the night. I can listen out for them, then count the minutes till it's safe."

Jennifer squeezed her arm. "Don't take any risks."

Maryam twirled her hair between her fingers, a casual gesture that Jennifer hadn't seen before. "I won't."

Paula was frowning. "I can't see the point. If you've already been up there and checked, and she's not there, then why should she be now?"

Jennifer shrugged. "I don't know. But surely we have to try something. I'm not leaving this place until we find her."

Paula snorted. "I don't think they're in any hurry to let you go."

Jennifer felt her cheeks redden. "Maybe, maybe not."

"Lying isn't going to get you through Celebration a second time, you know."

Jennifer changed the subject. "Look. She could be in the basement. The only times I go down there are for my one-to-ones. What about you?"

The others shrugged. "Same," said Maryam. "And the door to the stairway gets locked in the evening."

Jennifer sighed. Rita would most likely be somewhere in that basement – if she was still in the building – but how would they ever get to her?

"Our only alternative is to badger Mark until he lets something slip."

Paula snorted again. "Fine chance of that."

"I wouldn't be so sure. I think I can work on him."

Maryam stiffened and Paula raised an eyebrow. Bel added a murmur to her routine of scratching her forehead. Jennifer looked at her, wishing she could help pull her back from wherever she was.

"How's that?" asked Paula, her voice sharp.

Jennifer surveyed the group. How much could she tell them? Maryam had smoothed her hair down and Paula was looking over Jennifer's shoulder towards the door. Eager to find Mandy, no doubt.

These women were her friends now, her allies. Step three of the programme mandated that they should accept each other's support, but she hadn't known what that meant. Until now.

"OK." She licked her lips. "He offered to help me."

Paula scoffed. "Of course he bloody did. That's his job."

"No. I mean help me cheat Celebration." She hesitated. "At least, that's what I think he was saying."

Paula's eyes were on her, hard and untrusting. "He's lying to you."

She shrugged. "Probably. But at least it means I've been

able to talk to him. He opened up to me about himself. Told me about his son."

Paula shook her head. "You mean Olivier, the one in Canada?"

She blushed. "Yes."

"Yeah. He uses that one on all of us. Thinks that by telling us how sad he is without his *little boy*," – she said this in a mocking tone – "we'll tell him all our secrets."

Jennifer felt like a burst balloon. "Oh." She thought about the visit from Catherine. Had Mark arranged that? Had he been trying to help her? Or had it all been Catherine's doing, or a coincidence?

Somehow getting to Catherine, getting her help, felt like the answer. But then she remembered Catherine's tone when she visited. *I can't do it again*, she had said. If she wasn't prepared to stick her neck out for Jennifer, then she certainly wouldn't for Rita.

And she wasn't ready to talk about Catherine with her new friends. Not yet. She was too confused, too curious to know what was happening with Catherine, how Jennifer's own arrest had impacted on her. They had agreed to work together, to attack Trask. But then Samir had been arrested, mobiles buzzing in the Commons Chamber, and it had all gone sour.

"Come on, ladies. Out now."

The new orderly was behind them, her hand resting lightly on Paula's chair. She shifted her weight between her feet and didn't look them in the eye. Jennifer looked at her and then caught Maryam's eye; maybe this new orderly could be a way in?

But not yet, when she was so new, and had no information. Give her a day or two – long enough to know where

Rita was but not long enough to lose that greenness – and they could ask.

They shuffled to their feet. They didn't need to clear their trays; one of the kitchen staff had whisked them away already, cleaning the table top while the four of them watched in silence. They gave each other pats and light touches on the arm, small gestures of reassurance. Of hope.

Jennifer sighed and headed for the stairs.

"It's my one-to-one in a bit," she told the others. "I'll try asking him, see what he'll tell me. You never know."

Paula shook her head and Maryam gave her an encouraging smile. Bel was already at the door, her back to Jennifer. Her feet scraped along the floor, the sound echoing in the empty dining room.

She turned towards the basement stairwell and settled in on the plastic chair outside Mark's office. She was early today and would have to wait for the woman ahead of her to come out and give her the nod that meant she could go in. She had the same contact with this woman twice a week, a pale-skinned, waif-like woman whose long grey hair was tinged with white streaks. They never spoke or asked each other's names; the only communication was that nod.

The woman emerged, nodding as usual. Jennifer smiled at her.

"Hello," she said.

The woman's eyes widened. This wasn't the way it was done. "Er, hello," she replied, and scurried off towards the staircase.

Jennifer shrugged. At least she'd made the effort.

She went in to find Mark standing under the window, looking up and out. The day was dull and his office was bathed in a patchy grey light that made its position underground even more stark than usual.

He turned at the sound of the door opening. "Good morning. How are you today?"

She stood with her back to the door, not taking her seat. "Still worried about Rita."

He rolled his eyes. "That again. Look, I promise you I'm doing all I can. You have to be patient. Just bear with me."

He moved to his desk and picked up a copy of the programme booklet. "Now, let's work on Step Three."

"What's the point?"

"Well, I rather think that the point is that if you can work through the steps and complete the programme, you'll be able to leave here."

"Don't give me that." She stepped towards him, looking down on his head which was bent over the desk. He didn't look up, but she could see the muscles in the back of his neck tensing. "You've already told me that you'll help me get out. I've told you that I won't accept your help until Rita is back with us. What have you done with her?"

He unbent, bringing himself up to eye level. He glanced over her shoulder. "Of course I've offered you my help," he said loudly. "I'm your counsellor. That's my job. And the help and support of your group is important too. You will all be reunited very soon, I promise you. Please, give us time to get Rita ready."

She gritted her teeth. She'd get nowhere with that camera upon them. Was he imagining Yonda Hughes in her office, watching them now?

"What do you mean, ready?"

He shook his head. "I mean better. That's what I mean, and you know it."

"She's not in the infirmary, is she?"

He frowned, and flicked his gaze up to the camera then back to her. "Why would you say that?"

"Because I looked."

"That's impossible."

"Nope. I searched the building, found it. She's not there."

He glared at her. "We have more than one infirmary."

"So where's the other one, then?" It certainly wasn't on any of the above ground floors; she'd searched them all. She tried to remember the outside of the house from when she'd arrived. Was there a separate annex, beyond the hedges to its right?

"Is it outside? In that other building?"

He smiled. "Well done, Jennifer. That's exactly where it is. It's a quiet, peaceful spot away from the noise of the main house. Perfect for convalescing. She's being well looked after there."

He grabbed her wrist and sat down, pulling her down with him. She landed heavily on her chair, tugging at her arm and scowling at him. He let go but pinned her to the chair with his eyes.

He leaned in and lowered his voice.

"You want to get out of here. You told me you were desperate to be reunited with your family. Surely by getting out of here you can help Rita more?"

"I've thought about that. How public is this place? What do people know about it?"

He shrugged.

"You see," she continued. "I think that as soon as I said anything I'd be leaned on, encouraged to keep quiet. I'm not an MP anymore."

"I know that. But I encourage you to consider it."

It was tempting. By getting out of here, maybe she could find a way to influence Catherine, to expose what was happening here. There had to be something. Even as a disgraced MP, she still had a voice. And then there was Yusuf. He was at home; she could be with him.

He watched her, tapping his chin with a smooth finger. "Your family, Jennifer. Think about your family."

"Stop it!" she snapped. "Stop telling me what to think." She stood up, feeling dizzy. "You're trying to get inside my head, and it won't work."

He stood to face her. "I'm only trying to help you—"

"No you're not. You don't give a damn about me, or Rita, or anyone. How can I believe that you'll help me anyway, even if I do say yes?"

"Please."

She shook her head. "No. You lied to me about Yusuf. You lied to me about Rita. I'm having none of it."

She threw her booklet onto his desk and stumbled to the door, throwing herself into the quiet corridor outside.

CHAPTER THIRTY-FOUR

turned out the light.

At first it was a welcome relief from the twenty four hour glare of the bare bulb. She'd finally closed her eyes to find blackness behind her eyelids instead of orangey redness. She'd even managed to sleep. But waking up to total darkness was a different matter.

How long had she been asleep? It could be hours, it could be minutes. It was long enough for her bladder to be full. She fumbled her way out of bed, feeling for the edges of the metal bed frame, peeling paint and dents rough to her blind fingers. The sink was next to her, she knew – she'd bumped her hip on it, making her cry out in pain. And the toilet was at the end of the bed, facing it. She edged to the foot of the bed, flailing with her hands in the blackness, until her fingers landed on the cistern. She breathed with relief.

Now she was back on the bed, which felt like the only safe place in the darkness. Sounds had become amplified. The tap over the sink was dripping, and there was a regular tap-tap sound coming from somewhere through the wall behind her. She turned to it, knocking gently then waiting for a response. Nothing.

When the door opened it felt like an assault on her eyes. She threw an arm up to shield her face, curling into herself on the bed. The corridor outside had seemed dark and cold on her way here, shrouded in dim light from the small windows that lined the pathway outside at ground level. But thrown in relief against the pitch darkness she had been sandwiched in, it was like a searchlight on her face.

A shadow fell over her. She looked up, blinking, trying to make out its shape. It was too slim to be Tim and didn't smell like Roy. She let her breathing slow. At least she wasn't due a beating.

"Come with me," said a voice. Her counsellor?

He held out a hand and waited for her to take it. She hesitated, focusing. He was stooping over her, his face registering concern. Not the anger she had seen last time.

She looked at the hand then decided anything was better than this. Or at least, she hoped it was. She slipped her own hand into it and let him take her weight as she pushed herself up from the bed. Her back screamed as she moved, and her legs were sore from the last beating. There would be bruises the size of melons on her abdomen when she was at last allowed to look.

He smiled as she pulled herself upright, allowing her a few moments to regain her balance.

"Good," he said, and let go of her hand. He turned to the door.

She shuffled after him, squinting against the light in the corridor. It was dull outside; she could hear raindrops against the glass of the high windows. But still, the light hurt.

They turned a few corners – two or three, she wasn't sure – and stopped at the door to his office. The corridor was empty, the only sound that of distant kitchen noises. She wondered where everyone was. But at least she knew where she was now.

She followed him into his office. It hadn't changed; the same desk shoved against the wall, the same two plastic chairs, the same view of feet and car tyres from the window. The gonks. She wondered how he, as a senior member of staff, hadn't been able to get himself a nicer office. Meena's had been larger than this. But then, Meena's hadn't had a window.

"Please, take a seat," he said. Formal, polite. She obeyed, glad to rest her aching limbs. She looked down at herself. Her arms were patched with red marks and her feet were bleeding. The counsellor looked at her face, ignoring the injuries.

He opened a cupboard and brought out a sweatshirt and a pair of jeans. "Put these on," he said.

She stared at him. "Here?"

"I'll turn my back."

He walked to the window and raised his hands to the sill, intent on the limited view. She looked at him furtively then grabbed the clothes. The gown she had been wearing clung to her, blood, snot and sweat plastering the rough fabric to her skin. She peeled it off, glad to let it drop to the floor, and threw the new clothes on as fast as she could manage with her sore limbs. It hurt, but that didn't stop her racing against the moment that he turned around.

She sat down. "Ready."

He turned and smiled. "That's better."

She grunted, brushing her hair behind her ear. It felt heavy and damp.

"Are you letting me out of there?" she asked. Her voice was hoarse.

Another smile. "That depends on you."

"Doesn't it always?"

He shook his head. "You don't change, do you Rita? Whatever we do to you, you're still fighting."

She shrugged, pulling the sweatshirt farther down over her stomach. She could feel her ribs. "Dunno." She hesitated. "You do know what they did to me down there, don't you?"

He took the chair opposite her, at a diagonal. The table was empty today; no booklets, no files. He laid his hands on it.

"You've got a chance to prove yourself," he said. "I brought you here because I want to help you get past the problems you've been having."

"Aren't you going to answer my question?" She narrowed her eyes. "Did you *tell them* to hurt me?"

He sighed. "You were behaving violently. They just restrained you, that's all."

She was about to pull her sweatshirt up, show him her bruised stomach, then thought better of it. Instead she pulled up a trouser leg. It hurt to bend down, pain attacking her hips and back.

"What about this?" she asked, looking at the red marks on the back of her legs.

He glanced at her legs then looked away. "Please, Rita. We need to discuss your problems."

"What problems?"

"I think you know what I'm talking about. Your insubordination and uncooperativeness, for a start."

She shrugged her shoulders, thinking of all the chats she'd had with Darius Williams. He was a bright kid, but bored easily. They were just chats, though. The sort of treatment that was meted out here had been long since banned in schools. She wondered what he'd make of this place, then shuddered at the thought of any child in here.

"Not saying anything, then. That's fine." Dr Clarke leaned back, putting his hands behind his head. Below the table his feet touched hers. She jerked them away. "I'm going to ask you to run through the programme for me. Right here, today. All six steps. If you do it correctly – and honestly – you'll be allowed back up to your room."

"How am I supposed to do that?"

"What do you mean?"

"You've seen me try before. You were there for my Celebration. The idea of me doing the six steps, and of you believing me, is absurd."

"I don't agree with you."

"Then you're an idiot as well as a bully."

"I really don't appreciate those sort of accusations."

She raised an eyebrow. How did that hurt, too?

He sighed, leaning back towards her. "Two days ago you were desperate for my help. You told me you were being a good girl. That you were scared of the orderlies."

She leaned back, saying nothing.

"Don't you want to get out of that room? Or are you happy for me to take you back there? To call Tim?"

She felt her heart skip a beat. She looked up at him. "Alright."

He smiled. "Good. OK, let's start with step one." He leaned back, pushing his chair away from the desk.

He nodded for her to start. She sniffed, trying to remember. Her mind felt dull and clogged. Had they hit her on the head? She was pretty sure they hadn't, but if they had, would she remember it?

"I confess that I have been disloyal to the British state. I failed to recite the British Values Oath with the children in my class."

That was easy enough. Step One was just the facts. If it got her out of that cell, she could deal with the facts.

"Very good," he said. "Now, can we move on to Step Two. Do you accept the sovereignty of the British state?"

There was a knock on the door. He leapt up from his chair, glancing at the high camera before moving towards the door. He cleared his throat, his expression uneasy. "I'm in the middle of a one-to-one. Who is it?"

The door opened. "It's me. I've come to see how you're getting on."

Rita turned to see the governor standing in the doorway, filling it with her bulk. She wasn't fat, not really exactly, more well-built. And the heels meant that the top of her immaculate hairdo scraped the top of the doorframe.

She sensed Mark go taut next to her. "Ah, Yonda, come in."

The governor stepped inside, peering around the room as if she'd never been in quite such a dismal space before.

"Thank you, Mark. Hello Rita." She gave the camera a meaningful look. "I thought I'd come and sit in."

Rita looked up at the camera. Was someone else watching them? Or had Yonda been watching all this time? It hardly mattered to her now.

"Very well," Mark said, putting a hand on his chair. "Please, take a seat."

She shook her head and approached Rita. "I'm fine standing, thank you."

There was a moment's awkwardness as Mark decided whether to sit again. Finally he opted for remaining upright so that the two of them flanked Rita in her chair. She stayed where she was, feeling cornered.

Mark pulled at his shirt sleeve. It was frayed at the cuff. "We were working on the six steps. Step Two, precisely."

Yonda gave Rita a look that made her think of school inspectors. "I know. Go on, then."

Rita could remember the second step; she'd done it a few times, in group. "I accept the sovereignty of the British state."

Yonda rolled her eyes. "Give it some feeling, girl. From the heart." Her voice rose on the last sentence, making Rita cower. Yonda's cheeks were glowing and her hair was loosening.

Rita sniffed. She could do this. "I love this country. I'm lucky to be a citizen of it."

She clenched her knees together. That was no lie. She *did* love her country. Just not the way it was being governed right now.

Yonda laughed. "You're not a citizen, you stupid woman. Jesus, who do they employ for teachers these days? You're a *subject*. Of Her Majesty the Queen. How do you feel about that?"

Rita shrugged. "Fine. It doesn't make much difference."

She felt movement on the back of her chair and looked down to see Yonda's hand on it. Her knuckles were pale.

"You're lying."

She shook her head, her eyes wide. "No. Honest. I love this country just as much as anyone."

Yonda pulled on the chair, turning it so Rita was almost facing her. "Not that bit. Try again."

Rita tried to remember what she'd said; why was it so hard to recall your own lies?

"I don't know what you want me to say."

Yonda gave a satisfied nod. "Exactly. You'll never get out of here with that attitude."

"I don't understand. I'm trying my hardest—" She flung her head back towards Mark. "Please, help me try. Help me get through the steps. I can do it. I know I can."

Mark gave Yonda a wary look then crouched down to Rita. "I know. You just need to try a bit harder. I can't help you unless you help yourself, can I?"

His eyes were full of kindness but his words were no better than Yonda's. She shrugged.

The chair moved again, almost tipping her backwards. Yonda leaned over her, her hands on its back either side of Rita's head. Rita drew her shoulders forward, the proximity of Yonda's skin feeling like an insect about to bite.

"Go on then," Yonda said. "Show us what you can do. Step Four."

"What about Step Three?"

"That one's easy. Everyone gets that one." She looked past Rita to Mark. "Especially when they have a counsellor like Mark. Who wouldn't accept this man's support?"

Rita clenched her teeth. Did Yonda know what Mark had got his orderlies to do?

The chair shifted again. "Go on then. We'll take Step Three as read. Accept the support of the counsellor and the group, blah blah. Now give me Four."

Rita could feel her heart rate accelerating. She couldn't remember Step Four. The only time she'd done it was in Celebration, and that was a blur.

"Sorry," she murmured. "Can you remind me..."

Mark answered her. "Tell us who you harmed. And how you'll atone for what you did. Please."

"OK. I harmed the children in my class."

"How?"

"Sorry?"

"How exactly did you harm them?"

"I don't have to say that. It's not in the programme."

Yonda shook her head. "Rita, if you're to get through these steps, you have to convince us. We have to believe that it's coming from your heart. That's why we ask follow up questions." She paused, eyeing her. "Have you ever had a job interview?"

"Of course." *I'm a teacher, you idiot*, she thought. She'd had plenty of them, moving from school to school as budgets were cut.

"Well, think of these as the probing questions. The ones the interviewers pop in after the politically correct standard questions. The bit where they get to the meat, if you will."

She wrinkled her nose. "OK."

"So, how did you harm those children?"

She considered. As far as she was concerned, she'd done quite the opposite. How could refusing to brainwash a class of kids bring them to harm? But she'd heard the mantra, she'd been to the teacher training sessions. She'd barely listened, but enough had gone in.

"By not reciting the oath, those children will be more likely to commit acts of disloyalty. They're at greater risk of radicalisation, or of taking an interest in proscribed groups and activities."

"Mm-hmm. All very textbook. But how do you believe *you* harmed those children? How you *really* harmed them. Tell me how it makes you feel."

Rita closed her eyes, turning her face towards the wall. What did they expect her to say? What would get her though this?

"Those children deserve to become productive members of society," she said, searching through her memory for what they'd told her at school. "They deserve to love this country as much as I do. I didn't help them do that."

"I'm not buying it," said Yonda, her voice hard. "But let's move on. How will you make amends to those children?"

Rita's mind was blank. She had no idea what this question meant. Her limbs ached from the constant movement of the chair and her head felt heavy. She wanted to sleep.

"I don't understand."

Yonda kicked the chair leg, narrowly missing Rita's shin. Rita pulled her legs in underneath her.

"It's not rocket science, girl. Tell us how you'll fix what you did. Then you can go back to your room, and your lovely group."

Rita blushed. She was desperate to get out of that cell, to see daylight again. She let herself look up at Mark's high window, to imagine what might be outside. If she pushed past Yonda, could she make it to the window and shout something? Would anyone hear her?

Mark put his hand on her shoulder as if sensing what she was thinking. The touch was gentle, but sent a tremor through her. She thought of Jennifer and Maryam, sitting in breakfast, discussing her Celebration with her. Trying to help her. Would they be missing her? Or would they just have assumed she'd been released, or sent to a different centre?

She had to get back to them. The only way was to convince her captors that she'd changed heart, that she was loyal. But how?

She closed her eyes, drilling into her mind.

She opened her eyes again, to find Yonda closer to her.

She could smell the woman's heavy perfume, mixed with a faint layer of sweat.

"I will go back to my school. I will talk to the children about the oath, and why it's important. I will apologise to them."

Yonda shrugged. "Sounds convincing. But will it convince us if you repeat it at Celebration?"

Rita didn't move. She suspected Yonda knew the answer to that as well as she did.

Mark took his hand off her shoulder. "Let's try Step Six, eh? Your pledge."

"My pledge? The oath, you mean?" She wasn't even sure if she could remember that, the way her head was pounding now. She felt like she was going to be sick.

At least she could aim for Yonda's expensive heels. She allowed herself a smile.

Yonda slapped Rita's knee with the flat of her hand. "Behave yourself."

Rita stifled a moan. "Sorry."

"Do it, then. Give us your pledge."

Rita tried to remember; had she heard any of the other women do this? There had only been Jennifer, in Celebration. What had she said? It was a blur. She had been so focused on her realisation of what was in that glass, that she'd barely listened. She closed her eyes. Focus. Concentrate.

She had it. Something about spreading a message. Encouraging others.

"When I leave this place, I'll spread the message." She paused, begging her screaming muscles to calm down, and her mind to stay sharp. "I will encourage people to love this country as much as I do."

"What message, Rita?" asked Yonda. "What's this message you're so *keen* on spreading?"

Rita felt herself slump in the chair. This wasn't working. Try again.

"The message of... of loyalty. Of love for the state. Of not being rebellious. Or difficult."

"Ha!" Yonda's laugh was surprisingly sonorous. "I'm not buying it."

"Why not?"

"Because you're lying. Of course you are. You want to go back to your friends. But this isn't you, and we both know it."

Mark shuffled towards Yonda. "Maybe if we try again—"

Yonda waved a dismissive hand at him. "There's no point. Take her back."

"No! Please!" Rita almost fell off her chair, trying to clutch Yonda's hand as she headed for the door. "Don't take me back there. I'll be good. I'll do the programme. I promise."

Yonda looked back, shaking her head. "Oh, Rita. Stop lying to me. It won't get you anywhere."

CHAPTER THIRTY-FIVE

Mark opened the door to his office and gazed at the empty space. It had felt so full just ten minutes earlier, with both Rita and Yonda in there. This was the first time Yonda had been here, and her presence threw the dim, damp space into harsh relief. Not to mention the way she'd treated Rita.

He knew what this place was – he wasn't naive – and he'd supported it. He was a fervent loyalist, a believer in the benevolence of the state. For him it went along with his socialism, his belief in big government. There would be no health service without it. And the rise of extremist groups at both ends of the political spectrum – especially the far right – had convinced him that places like this were justified. That helping these women to understand how they'd gone wrong and to help them see sense was a noble thing. It was certainly better than prison, if that was the alternative.

But that had been when he'd believed the centre to be humane. The hippocratic oath was just as vivid for him now as it had been on the day he'd qualified, and he knew he was violating it. He'd managed to convince himself that he was acting in the cause of a greater good, that sacrifices had to be made, tough decisions taken. He grimaced. *I sound like a politician*, he thought, wondering how many times thoughts just like these had gone through Jennifer's mind. But then, she was the woman who'd made the truly tough decision, who'd chosen her conscience over her government. She wasn't to know what it would lead to. And he secretly admired her for it.

Rita had sobbed all the way back to her cell – he refused to think of it as anything other than that, now he'd seen her reaction to it. She'd walked next to him, her head low and her greasy hair hanging in front of her face. Her hand had repeatedly gone up to her eyes, to wipe away tears or catch a sniffle. But once they'd rounded the first corner, she'd given up on the pretence. She openly wept as she walked back to that awful, stinking room. As he took her back to it.

He'd let her in and watched her shuffle to the bed and lie down on it, curling up into a ball. She looked small and vulnerable, like Olivier when he had hurt his head as a toddler.

He shook his head. He mustn't compare his son to these women, mustn't even think of him in the same context as his work here. He was tempted to throw in this job, to catch the next plane to Canada and seek out his ex-wife and son. But Canada was vast, and he needed stable employment if he was ever to regain custody. Something that would be lost to him, now and in the future, if he resigned this post. Yonda had her claws in too many pies for that.

He closed the door and ran through the day's schedule. Sally was next for her one-to-one. He despised Sally and knew she felt the same way about him. But his professionalism had to overshadow his decency. Somehow he had to support her, to help her find her own way through this system. Maybe if he tried hard, she really would repent, would change her outlook. But she was showing no sign of it.

His mobile rang in his trouser pocket. He fumbled for it, frowning. He didn't feel like being disturbed.

It was Yonda.

He lifted it to his ear and stretched his face into a smile. "Yonda. What can I do for you?"

"Come to my office, please."

She hung up. He glared at the phone, almost hurling it across the room, then regained control of himself. He had to take it easy. Rita would never get out of here under her own steam. She wouldn't get anywhere by being difficult, as she'd already learned. And now she was learning, as had Jennifer, that lies wouldn't work either.

Her only hope was Jennifer. If he could help Jennifer get out of here, then she had the influence to help her friend. She'd do something, surely.

He paused. It wasn't just up to Jennifer. If she got out of here, he had to help her. He had to give up this job and work with her.

He shuddered, thinking about Olivier, about the custody hearing and the terms that had been laid down. A man without a job would stand no chance. But maybe if he did go to Canada, once things had boiled over...

His phone pinged. *Where are you?*

He pulled a face at the phone and plunged it back into his pocket, heading for the door.

Outside Yonda's office, he paused. He had passed three orderlies on the way, all of whom had given him respectful glances. He wondered what they thought about what happened here. Was it just Tim and Roy who meted out physical punishment, or were there others? And how did he not know the answer to that question? Why hadn't he asked?

He smoothed his hair down with a hand and put the other one to the dark wood of Yonda's door, hesitating before knocking twice.

"Come in!"

He pushed open the door, half expecting to see Catherine Moore again. But Yonda was alone, all but obscured by that tank-like desk.

"Hello, Yonda," he said, and walked towards the desk, ignoring the low chairs. He stood opposite her, his hands fingering the wood. Her laptop was closed on the desk, and the porcelain dog had been joined by another, almost identical.

She gave him an insincere smile. "Hello. Take a seat, please."

He smiled, remembering her response to the same invitation in his own office. "I'm fine, thanks."

Would she pull rank and insist that he sat? It seemed not. She frowned but let it pass.

"You're being too soft on them," she said.

"Pardon?"

"Your group. The troublemakers. They need a firm hand. The way you treated Rita this morning—"

"That's not true. With all due respect, Yonda, I'm an experienced clinical psychologist. I know the best way to proceed with women like these."

She narrowed her eyes and leaned forwards, raising herself up a little. It looked uncomfortable. "And I'm experienced with criminals and I understand that they need a firm hand."

He shook his head. "This is different." His heart was thumping. He had to stop letting her walk all over him.

Yonda rose slowly, patting down her bright pink blouse which had ridden up around her neck. "Tell me. If I hadn't been there, what would have been the outcome of that cosy little session you had going on with Rita?"

"I have no idea."

She raised an eyebrow. "Really? None at all?"

"No. Who's to say how a clinical session will pan out?"

"I think you're being naive."

She turned her back on him, meandering towards the window. She paused at the curtains and pulled one further aside, taking in the view. It was sunny today, but chilly. He wondered if any of the women in the infirmary had been allowed out.

"I don't agree," he said, trying to project confidence. He had to be careful. He hated the idea of Yonda belittling him, of her challenging everything he knew as a psychologist. But he couldn't afford to anger her. "In my experience, working with women as disturbed and confused as Rita can rarely have predefined outcomes."

She waved a hand. "*Predefined outcomes*. Don't talk shit. If I hadn't been there, you'd have fudged it. She'd be sitting pretty up there in her cosy bedroom, thumbing her nose at us."

"I hardly think her room is—"

She span round. "Do you think I give a shit what their rooms are like? My job is to rehabilitate these women. To ensure that they believe in the goodness of the state, body and soul. To make them repent their crimes and promise to make retribution. Your job is to assist in that." She folded her arms across her chest. "Understand?"

"Absolutely. That's what I want to achieve too."

She raised an eyebrow. "Lately, I haven't been so sure."

"That's unfair. I've been faced with particularly trying

circumstances in recent weeks. Two failed Celebrations, and Rita's behaviour—"

"You say you've been faced with all this. Have you considered it could be your fault?"

He clenched his teeth. "Absolutely not. Do you think Rita would be any further forward if she still had Meena as her counsellor?"

He looked down, ashamed of himself. Yonda gave him a satisfied smile. "Criticising your colleagues. Not all that professional."

"Sorry. I spoke out of turn."

She approached the desk again, sighing. "Look. Rita is trouble. Women like her are bad for our statistics. She's gone beyond anything you can do for her."

His mind raced. "What do you mean?"

"Not your concern. Let me worry about Rita. Now, I need to talk to you about another member of your lovely little group."

"Who?"

He knew the answer. "Jennifer Sinclair."

He nodded. "What about her?"

"She has to fail another Celebration."

"What? Another one? But no-one's—"

"I know, I know. But Jennifer will be an exception."

"That won't look very good for your statistics."

"*Our* statistics, Mark. We all bear responsibility. This one will be an exception. She won't be included."

"You can't do that." He'd been present for their inspections, knew how closely their data was scrutinised. Admissions, Celebrations, releases. It was all monitored.

"I can. This time."

He realised this would be something to do with Catherine Moore. "So why have things changed? I thought

I had to make sure she didn't have another Celebration? Can she be allowed out, now?"

Yonda sighed. "You didn't hear me. I said she had to fail another Celebration."

"But no-one has ever failed a second time."

"I know."

"So what will happen to her?"

"I imagine she'll go back to prison." She shrugged. "It won't be our concern."

He felt his chest fill. How could she be so callous, so uncaring? Jennifer had been traumatised in prison. She'd told him in her one-to-ones, before she'd decided not to trust him. As an MP she was the inevitable victim of prison bullying. And she wasn't the type to handle that well.

"I don't think that's a good idea," he said.

Yonda raised her eyebrows. "And since when was that your call?"

"I'm her doctor."

"Ha. Glorified doctor. You know what your role is."

He stepped towards her, feeling a momentary urge to grab her stupid pink collar and shake some sense into this woman who he'd tolerated – even enjoyed – working with for the past year. How had he not seen what she was really like?

He paused, listening to his own breathing. If he stayed here, would he become like her?

An idea hit him.

"Alright," he said.

"Sorry?"

"Alright. I'll persuade Jennifer to apply for Celebration."

"I don't think that's necessary."

"No. I want to do it right. By the book. I'll work on her. She'll think she's ready."

She smiled. "Good. Glad you're seeing sense."

"But there's one thing."

The smile dropped. "What?"

"It has to be fair. According to the regulations."

"Regulations?"

"If she fails, she goes back to prison. Or wherever they want to send her."

"Yes."

"But if she passes, she's released. As per the regulations."

"Seriously? This is what you're asking for?"

He nodded.

"Fine. She's never going to pass, so what do I care."

He nodded again, trying not to smile.

CHAPTER THIRTY-SIX

The sitting room was busy today. Women sat in pairs, small huddles or singly, almost all the chairs taken.

Jennifer looked past the whispering women towards the view beyond the faded chairs and sofas. Rain poured down the window, turning the lawns behind into a dim green blur. The panes rattled occasionally, drafts piercing the thick air of the room and making the hairs on her neck rise to attention.

She surveyed the chairs, debating whether to stay here or go up to her room. But Paula and Mandy were up there, and she didn't want to disturb them. Her resentment of their relationship and her feelings of isolation at being left alone with them had transformed into something different now that she had got to know Paula. Mandy was taciturn but friendly enough. She responded to Paula's wordless encouragement to be sociable with muttered hellos and shy smiles. For someone like Jennifer, used to the dishonest smiles of politicians, it was enough. The calm of the friendships that grew here, the empty time that allowed them to unfold without the pressure of constant activity and changes in hierarchies and connections made it feel easier to get to know her fellow inmates than it had her former colleagues.

But she mustn't allow herself to get too comfortable. There was Yusuf to think about, waiting for her at home – where would he think she was? Could he have applied for a visitor's pass at Bronzefield and been denied? She wondered too what Edward had been told, why he hadn't been allowed here. She couldn't believe he wouldn't have attempted it. In prison, she knew that visits from lawyers were a regular occurrence, even if she hadn't had her own. But here, she'd seen no evidence of the women receiving visits from anyone, lawyer, friend or family. How did they deal with that?

Maybe that was why the women became so dependent on each other. Maybe it was why so many were able to embrace the programme, to shift their thought patterns. Take them away from the outside world and all its influences, and anything seemed sensible. Even the six steps. Anything to get out.

A woman sitting alone in a high-backed chair opposite the window stood up, heading for her one-to-one no doubt. Jennifer took her place. She settled into the chair, trying to ignore the rasp of its fabric against the back of her neck. She'd brought a book with her, needing the distraction. *Anne of Green Gables*. She picked it up and started to read.

Just a few pages in, she noticed that the room had gone quiet. She glanced up to see Mark standing at the door. She looked around the women. It wasn't her day for a one-to-one, so who was he summoning? And why hadn't he sent an orderly?

But he was looking at her.

"Jennifer, can you come with me please?"

She pointed to her chest – *Me?* – and then put down her book to ease herself out of her chair. She felt the eyes of the other women on her as she passed through them to the door. There would be muttering when they were safely out of earshot. She cursed him for doing this.

As she approached, he gestured with his head and turned for the corridor. She sighed, not wanting the ordeal of a one-to-one today. She'd been looking forward to a quiet day of reading and maybe a snooze, if she could calm her mind and keep it away from her anxiety about Rita.

She followed, expecting him to turn right, towards the basement. But instead he turned left. She frowned and followed, scurrying to keep up.

As they came to a door she hadn't ever seen open, he glanced up and down the hallway and then opened it, bundling her inside. She flinched, grumbling at him.

"Shh," he whispered. "Trust me."

She frowned, feeling her flesh go cold. Then she regained her footing and managed to get into the room without falling. He peered out of the door again and closed it. He leaned against it, breathing heavily.

She looked around the room. It was large, but not as large as the grand space they used for group meetings and Celebration, and not as impressive as Yonda's office. On the far side was a window, draped in heavy curtains that blocked the light and trailed on the floor. She could see dust in the folds of fabric. In front of those was what looked like a painting draped in a sheet. Next to that, two chairs, also covered with sheets, and a low mahogany table.

"What's this?" she asked, her pulse rising. "Why have you brought me here?"

He unbent himself, pulling his palms off his thighs, and

swept a hand through his thick hair. "I'm sorry," he said. "But I need to talk to you."

She gritted her teeth. "What's wrong with your office?"

"You know what's wrong with my office."

He took his eyes off her and started to examine the walls. She joined him, scanning for cameras. There was no sign of one. This room was unused, she guessed. It would have made a far more suitable office for him than that dingy space below ground.

"What's going on?" she asked. Surely she'd made herself clear last time; she didn't trust him, and wasn't about to let him attempt to fix Celebration for her.

He gulped down a few heavy breaths, gaining control of himself. She wondered what he'd been doing before he came for her. Surely their bungled rush along the hall hadn't made him like this?

"I asked you what's going on," she repeated, her teeth gritted. She pushed past him and put a hand on the door. It was solid and heavy, with woodworm trails running across it.

He put a hand on her arm. "Don't. Please."

She yanked her hand away. "Don't touch me."

"I'm your counsellor, Jennifer. You don't get to talk to me like that."

She said nothing.

"OK," he breathed. He looked at his watch then grimaced. "I've got Sally in ten minutes. We need to be quick."

"Quick with what?"

He stepped towards the draped chairs, throwing himself into one. Dust billowed up around him and he coughed. Then he looked up at her, his face red. "I haven't been entirely honest with you."

"No."

"I'm sorry. We're only supposed to tell you what you need to know to help you get through the programme. We're certainly not supposed to share details of what's happening to one patient with another."

She tapped her foot and folded her arms across her chest. He wasn't guarding the door now; she could easily leave. She decided to give him ten minutes.

He breathed in. "Rita's in solitary confinement. In the basement."

Jennifer's eyes widened. "I knew you were hurting her. What have you done to her? How is she?"

"Don't worry." He paled. "She's going to be OK."

He drew his hand through his hair again and closed his eyes. "No. I'm lying again. She's not going to be OK. Tim and Roy – the orderlies. The ones who took her out of group."

Jennifer nodded.

"They've been pretty rough on her."

"In what way?"

He wiped an eye, blinking. The dust was still settling around him. "Use your imagination."

She approached him, clenching and unclenching her fists, digging her thumbnail into her palm. "What have you done to her?"

He shook his head. "Not me. The orderlies."

"Don't give me that. You're their superior. They wouldn't do it without your say-so."

He opened his mouth to speak then thought better of it. "I'm sorry."

The sound of voices approached behind the door, two women, their tone lightening as they approached. Jennifer stiffened and stared at Mark, whose hand went to the arm of his chair. Which of them would be in the most trouble, if they were found here?

They waited in silence, Mark's breathing ragged in the quiet and Jennifer's heart thumping. At last the voices receded.

Jennifer approached him. "Where is she now? Is she still there? Are you going to get her out?"

"I can't." He stood and met her gaze. His face was pale and blotchy. He looked genuinely worried. But what for: Rita's welfare, or his job? Was he supposed to order beatings of inmates, or had he stepped over a line?

"Of course you can, you shit," she said.

He closed his eyes. "I'm not what you think I am."

"Course you bloody well are. Look, I don't give a damn about you. What about Rita? Where is she? Can I get to her?"

"No. You already know that. The orderlies guard her. Their office is before you get to her – her cell."

She shivered, thinking of prison. At least the cells there had been above ground. At least people had known where they were.

"Jennifer," he muttered. "I need to be quick. Sally—"

"Yes, yes. Spit it out then."

"I need your help. I think you're the only person who can help Rita now."

"And how do you propose I do that? You've already told me I can't get to her cell."

"No. Celebration. If you get out of here, you can tell people what's happening here. She shouldn't be treated like this. It's not in the legislation. Yonda has over—"

"Don't blame your boss. This is your doing."

"I know. And I want to help you."

"You've already told me that. You want to help me get through Celebration."

"Not just that."

She raised an eyebrow.

"Afterwards," he said. "Once you're out. I'll join you. I'll back you up."

"And how can I know you'll do that? You've lied to me plenty of times."

He grabbed her hand. She stiffened but didn't pull it away. His hand was hot, fiery around her own.

"I'll resign," he said. 'I'll quit my job and help you expose Yonda."

"I've already told you—"

"I'll own up to what I've done too."

She shook her head. "No. That would be counterproductive."

He smiled. "So you're considering it?"

She felt her shoulders slump.

"Your family," he whispered. "Think of how happy Yusuf will be to have you back."

"Don't. Just don't use that tactic on me. My family is my concern. Alright?"

"Sorry."

She considered what he had told her. He was right about Rita; Jennifer was most likely her only hope. And if she delayed, things could only get worse for her friend. But how could she trust Mark to deliver on his promise? If she failed Celebration again...

"What happens if I fail Celebration twice?"

"You won't."

"Just tell me what happens."

He blushed and let go of her hand. "You'd go back to prison. I think. No-one's ever—"

She screwed up her eyes. Could she face prison again? Was the chance of being with Yusuf again, of helping Rita, worth that risk?

"How will you do it? How will you get me through Celebration?"

He shrugged. "I'm your counsellor. I'll be right there with you. I'm the one who gives you the drug. I'll just switch it for something else."

She imagined Rita, alone in the basement, in some windowless room. Of Tim, large and cruel, being allowed free rein on her. Rita was young, and slight. Her health had been deteriorating since she'd joined the group. It could kill her.

She opened her eyes again. "Alright."

CHAPTER THIRTY-SEVEN

THE LIGHT HAD BEEN ON FOR A FEW HOURS NOW. AT least it felt like a few hours.

Rita had almost wept with relief when it blinked out the previous night – if it had been night. She hoped they were being kinder, but they could be doing the opposite. Despite her horror of the darkness before, the light had become an attacker, slicing into her eyes with its harsh yellow glow.

In the dark, she didn't have to see this room. The mould climbing up the wall next to the sink. The droppings of some unseen creature in the corner behind the toilet. And the toilet itself, its brown-green stains and cracked seat.

In the dark, her imagination filled it all in. Twice she had woken, certain she could hear a scurrying sound near her left ear. She batted it away, jerking up from the bed. The mattress had groaned under the weight of the movement. She closed her eyes, trying not to think of the mattress stains. One of them was large and rusty, creeping across a corner of the bed towards the metal frame.

But at least she had slept. It felt like three or four hours maybe; enough to get some refreshment, sufficient to keep her mind from feeling as if it was about to tear in two.

She had attempted to wash herself at the sink. The tap was faulty, dripping incessantly, refusing to give her a proper flow of water. She'd pulled at it as hard as she could in her weakened state, gritting her teeth. But all she'd got was those drips. She attempted to gather them in her palm and wipe her face, her lips. Her mouth felt furry and acrid, her lips dry and her teeth as if they were coated in bacteria. Her body felt wrong under the clean clothes, slimy. She tried to ignore the itching that had broken out on her feet.

She was sitting on the bed, staring at the wall opposite, tracing a crack in the tiles with her eyes. Counting the tiles gave her something to do. She had scanned the room for some kind of writing implement, something she could use to track time. But then she remembered what had happened to the marks behind the bed in her attic room, and gave up. Instead, she stared at the wall, her vision blurred.

She heard noises outside and turned to the door, her breath shallow. She swallowed and stared at it, hoping it would be Mark.

It wasn't.

Tim shoved the door open, letting it slam into the wall, and grinned at her.

"We've got a treat for you."

A wave of cold sickness rose up from her stomach. She stared at him, transfixed.

"Come on, then. Get up."

She couldn't move. Her hands felt as if they were stuck to the mattress and her neck was fixed in place, stiff.

He heaved his bulk towards her and grabbed her wrist. She looked down at it. How had he moved it? It wouldn't move. If she couldn't move it, how could he?

She watched his face as he yanked her upwards, knowing he wouldn't be able to move her. Her body was like marble. Her mind felt cold and still.

But she was wrong. He dragged her towards the door, her feet skittering on the cold floor. She summoned all her willpower and managed to regain control of her feet, placing them instead of letting them be dragged.

"Where are you taking me?" she whispered.

"You'll see. Now shut up and come with me."

Roy was outside. She stared at him, uncomprehending. Normally they would come in together and close the door. Any beatings were done quietly, professionally. They had stuffed a dusty rag into her mouth so no-one would hear her scream. If she did, they would just hurt her more.

Where could they be taking her? Back to her room?

She felt her muscles relax, and was horrified to realise that she'd wet herself.

Roy sniffed the air. "Jesus Christ, woman. That's disgusting."

She blushed but said nothing. *Your fault*, she thought, staring at the back of his neck. There was a mole in the centre of it, with one long coarse hair sprouting from it. His skin was taut and ruddy, unlike the folds of skin that adorned the back of Tim's neck. She could see the sweat between them, pale and viscous. It made her stomach turn.

At the end of the corridor they pushed her into another room. An office, with a desk and two chairs but no other adornments. Like Meena's office from her arrival here. Or had she imagined that? This one had no window, and the furniture was thrown into stark relief by the single flush light in the centre of the ceiling.

In a neat pile on one of the chairs were more clean

clothes. Next to them, on the floor, was a bucket. She baulked. Was this going to be her cell now? At least that had a functioning toilet.

Roy nodded towards the pile of clothes. On top was a stiff looking flannel. "Clean yourself up. Get changed," he barked. Tim stepped back into the corridor, taking up a sentry position outside. Roy closed the door and sat on the other chair, staring at his nails. They were clean and long.

"What, here?" she asked. "With you watching?"

He looked up at her, his eyes betraying sympathy for a fleeting moment. "Nothing I haven't seen before," he said, then returned his gaze back to his fingers.

She took a tentative step towards the chair. She'd been leaning against the wall, where Tim had deposited her, and hardly dared trust her legs. Her body dipped as she crossed the room. Everything swayed in front of her.

Roy looked up. "Alright?" he said, not moving from his chair. It was on the opposite side of the desk, arranged like Meena's office, not like Mark's where the desk had been pushed to one side. She could remember. Both offices were clear in her mind, which meant she wasn't going mad. Didn't it?

She nodded, forcing her legs to behave themselves, and knelt as carefully as she could in front of the pile of clothes. It was her own clothes, the trousers and blouse she had been wearing in the classroom when they'd arrested her.

"Am I being released?"

Roy laughed. "You'd like that, wouldn't you?"

"But these clothes. They're mine."

"We promised you a treat, didn't we?" He looked at his watch. "Now hurry up. We haven't got much time."

She nodded and threw off the clothes Mark had given

her. Had that been yesterday, or earlier today? Or maybe two days ago?

She picked up the blouse and sniffed it; it smelt of washing powder. Unwilling to soil it, she grabbed the flannel from where it had slid on the floor and dunked it into the bucket, starting to wash herself; face, armpits, breasts. It felt good.

She looked at the flannel; it was a darker shade of grey now. Satisfied, she slipped on the bra that had been beneath the blouse, and then the blouse itself. It whispered over her skin, feeling luxurious. It was only a cheap thing from Top Shop but it felt like the most expensive silk.

She stood up, examining the trousers. Tucked between their folds were her knickers. She grabbed them and the trousers and turned her back to Roy, checking that he wasn't watching. She hunched over like an embarrassed bather in a swimming pool changing room, and slid the underwear on as fast as she could. Then she paused to drag the flannel over her bruised legs and push it inside her pants, knowing that it would make her feel damp but preferring that over the urine that was drying on her skin. She pulled on the trousers.

She stood up, the clothes giving her the confidence to breathe deeply and hold herself upright. "Ready."

He looked up. "Good."

"Are there any shoes?"

He shook his head. "Sorry. We can't have you using them as a weapon."

How could she use the flat burgundy pumps she'd been wearing as a weapon?

He passed her and opened the door, muttering with Tim, who poked his head round the door.

"Lovely," he said. A shiver ran across her flesh under the thin clothes. "Now come on. We're taking you upstairs."

Upstairs! Then maybe she was being let out. And at the very least she could be going back to her room. Surely the clothes meant release, though? She couldn't see why else they would take the trouble to launder them and bring them to her.

She nodded and followed them along a second corridor to the stairs leading to the first floor. The silence in her cell had sharpened her hearing and she could hear voices upstairs, the hubbub of the dining room. It was a mealtime. But which?

"I'm hungry," she said. Her stomach growled obligingly.

"Time for that later," said Tim, and started up the stairs. She lifted her head high, desperate to see what was up there, to make contact with her group again.

Upstairs, the corridor was empty. Her heart sank. She could still hear voices, but they were distant; the dining room was at the other end of this hallway. No-one passed them as they turned a corner, heading for the back of the building. She hadn't been this way before.

Then, suddenly, there was a woman in front of them, heading right for them. She stopped, startled. Rita stared at her. Maryam!

Tim leaned towards Rita, his lips almost touching her ear. "Keep quiet." She widened her eyes, desperate to communicate with her friend.

"Rita!" Maryam cried. "Where have you been?" She looked Rita up and down, puzzled by her attire. "Where are they taking you?"

Rita opened her mouth to speak then felt Tim's hand on her back, his finger boring into her spine. She shook her head.

Maryam looked at her, seeming to understand. "I'll tell the others."

"Shouldn't you be going somewhere?" snapped Roy.

Maryam stared at him. "Er, yes. I'm on my way to breakfast."

Rita let out a shaking breath. It was morning.

"Well, get a move on," replied Tim. Maryam nodded and hurried past them. Rita didn't look round, aware that Tim's finger was twisting further into her spine.

"Move," he muttered into her ear, and pushed her forwards.

Finally they came to a heavy wooden door. Tim paused, smoothing his shirt, then lifted his fist to knock.

"Come in," came a voice, before his knuckle had hit the wood. He flinched then pushed the door open.

He held the door, gesturing for her to go in. She passed the two orderlies, torn between curiosity and dread.

The room was generously sized, with a tall, full height window to her right and a massive desk in front of it. The desk was strewn with papers and files, all surrounding two single porcelain statuettes of dogs, the kind of thing her grandmother liked. Behind the desk, her fingers steepled in front of her chin and her face glowing with an insincere smile, was Yonda Hughes.

Rita licked her lips and stood still, waiting. Yonda looked at Tim and beckoned. He followed Rita inside, looking nervous.

"Sit down," Yonda told him. "This won't take long."

He glanced back at Roy, who was hovering by the door. Yonda nodded and he stepped out, closing it.

Tim lowered himself into one of easy chairs, smoothing his hands on his trousers. He looked huge in the low seat, his pale, heavy bulk incongruous in this space.

Yonda ignored him and leaned back in her chair, surveying her prey. "You clean up nicely," she said.

Rita ignored the compliment. "Are you letting me out?"

Yonda shook her head. "You do like your questions, don't you? Just speak when I ask you to, please."

Rita said nothing. Yonda raised her eyebrows, clearly unsure whether this was an act of obedience or rebellion.

"Hmm," she said. "Look, Rita. I respect you. Really I do. I understand what motivates you, why you're clinging to your principles. But because of that respect, I want to help you."

She leaned over the desk, looking up at Rita. Rita's bare feet squirmed on the soft rug. She gritted her teeth, pushing down the impulse to speak.

"I don't believe that this is the best place for you," she continued. "I think you would prosper more in a different setting."

Rita balled her fists. *Setting.* What was this, a pupil progress meeting? This was a prison, not a *setting.* She held her jaw firm and said nothing.

"But first I want you to see something."

"Something?"

Yonda chuckled. "Please, resist your constant urge to talk. We don't have long." She let out a theatrical sigh. "I do regret that you weren't able to convince me you'd changed the other day. It would have made life so much easier for both of us."

The other day. "What day is it? How long have I been in that cell?"

Yonda gave her an admonishing look. "It's not a cell, Rita. We don't have cells here. This is a psychiatric facility, designed to help people get better."

Rita felt as if a thousand ants were crawling up her

spine. This place was as far from being a medical facility as she could imagine. She wondered how much people knew about these centres, about what happened here.

"But I don't want to be cruel," Yonda continued. "You've been away from us for four days now. It was only yesterday that we met in your counsellor's office."

Rita nodded; that made sense. So the lighting had been in sync with the time, at least to some extent.

"Anyway," said Yonda. "I brought you here to bid you farewell. You won't be seeing me again. Or your counsellor. You're going to watch your friend's Celebration, and then you'll be leaving us."

"Whose Celebration? Where? Where are you taking me?"

Were there worse places than this, higher security places for 'difficult' prisoners like her? She closed her eyes, wishing she'd been able to find it in herself to be more cooperative. She wanted to see her group.

"Will I see my group again?"

"You'll see them at Celebration."

Rita smiled, relief washing over her. She felt her legs weaken.

"But you won't be able to talk to them."

She almost collapsed in frustration. "What's the point then!" she cried.

"Please. That isn't going to help. I want to help you, honestly." Yonda glanced up at the ceiling. Rita followed her gaze. What was up there? A camera?

Yonda shuffled, her jacket rustling against the scarlet blouse beneath. She stood and rounded her desk, approaching Rita. Her eyes were only inches away and her musky perfume overwhelmed Rita's senses. Rita leaned back, her nostrils flaring. Behind them, Tim shifted in his chair. She could hear him breathing through his mouth.

"This isn't my decision," Yonda muttered, her eyes wide. "I've been told to move you."

Rita shrugged. Even if she did believe her, what difference did it make? She said nothing, but stared back at the governor, defiant still.

Yonda glanced over her shoulder towards Tim then leaned in to embrace Rita. Rita stiffened, horrified. Was this an opportunity for Yonda to say something more? Were they being watched? And if not by the governor of this place, then who by?

Yonda pulled away and gave Rita a smile. The crows' feet that flanked her heavily but skilfully made-up eyes deepened.

"I am truly sorry we haven't been able to help you, Rita. I hope you can get better at your next placement."

Placement? She wasn't a supply teacher, being shifted between schools. Rita clenched her fists, feeling sweat drip down from her wrists.

"Please," she croaked. "I'll cooperate. I'll do better this time. Just take me back to my group."

She thought of the other women. Jennifer and her insistence that lying would get them out; Maryam and her protectiveness towards her group-mates, her shock on seeing Rita in the corridor. Even Sally would be a welcome relief. She wondered if Maryam had found the others, if they were discussing her now.

"Please," she whispered.

Yonda put a heavy hand on her shoulder. "I'm sorry. I wish you luck."

Rita blinked back tears as Tim approached her, the smell of his sweat joining that of Yonda's perfume. She sniffed and drew herself up, determined not to let them see the effect they were having on her. She looked past the governor, towards the window. Then she remembered the other thing Yonda had told her.

"Whose Celebration is it?"

Yonda smiled. "Good question. It's Jennifer's."

CHAPTER THIRTY-EIGHT

Jennifer had been here before.

She sat in the room where prisoners were prepared for Celebration, her mind racing. She was no closer to being the person they wanted her to be last time, to saying what they wanted her to say and meaning it.

This room was cramped, like a smaller version of the room Mark had dragged her into yesterday. There was the same smell of dust and neglect and the same two chairs near the window, both covered with drapes. One chair had been uncovered this time and moved to the centre of the space. She waited here. Again she wondered why they didn't make use of these rooms; this was larger than Mark's office downstairs and would have been far preferable for one-to-one sessions.

Maybe the view, or the promise of it behind those drapes, distracted the prisoners, kept them from focusing on what they had to do to work their way out of here.

She so wanted to believe what Mark had told her yesterday, hidden in that dusty store room, but wasn't confident. He'd lied to her about Yusuf. He'd taken Rita away from them. Maryam had spotted her during breakfast, flanked by two orderlies. She'd been pale and drawn, Maryam said, like a woman starved of food and light. It had been four days since they'd carried her out of the group session, screaming at the orderlies. And everything Mark had told her, or rather the gaps where he'd refused to answer her questions, informed her that she was being mistreated. That she was in danger.

The door opened and her breath caught in her throat. Would Mark run through it again? Would he give her the details of what he was going to do, how he would cheat Celebration for her?

She lifted up from her seat, ready with questions. But it wasn't Mark. Instead, a petite woman wearing a bright purple headscarf edged her way into the room, blinking nervously.

Jennifer frowned at her. "Hello," she ventured, feeling cold run down her back.

The woman brushed an invisible speck off her cheek. "Hello."

"Who are you?"

A tentative smile. "I'm your counsellor."

"No you're not. Mark's my counsellor. Mark Clarke."

The woman blushed so hard that Jennifer thought she would start to steam. "I'm sorry. He's indisposed."

Without Mark, she would fail.

"You've got it wrong," she said. "I'm waiting for my counsellor. Mark. He needs to take me into Celebration." She paused, eyeing the woman. The image of that photo flashed in front of her eyes. She ground her thumbnail into her palm. *Stay calm.*

The woman took a deep breath, the colour in her cheeks

dissipating. "Mark can't be here today." She shrugged. "You've got me instead."

Jennifer shook her head and stepped towards the woman, who drew back. "No. That's wrong. No."

She squeezed her fists, digging her nails into her flesh. *Breathe*, she told herself. *Think. Ignore who she is. Don't let on that you know her.*

She stepped back, lowering herself into the chair. "It's OK," she said. "I think if you go and fetch Mark, then everything will be OK. I need my counsellor with me for Celebration." She struggled for an argument to strengthen her case. "Step Three," she said, relieved. "In Step Three I accepted the support of my counsellor and my group. That's why the celebrant's group sits at the front. For support. That's why you can only do Celebration with your own counsellor."

Was this true? She had only witnessed one Celebration, Rita's, and that had been far from ordinary. Her own first one was a haze of jumbled memories. Maybe it wasn't normally done like that?

The woman smiled. "It's implicit that you accept the help of everyone here. All of the staff and all of the women."

"All of the staff?" Jennifer raised an eyebrow. "Even those thugs of orderlies?"

The woman blushed again. "Please," she said. Her voice was gentle, and betrayed her youth. How old was she? Twenty, maybe? Young enough to be Jennifer's daughter. "Please don't make a fuss. I can help you get through this. I know it's hard. I really do."

Jennifer shrugged. *No you don't*, she thought, remembering her last Celebration, the way she had felt when she woke up knowing she had failed. It was all about to happen again.

"In that case, I'd like to delay it," she replied.

"Delay it?"

"Yes. I can do it some other time, when Mark's here." Her heart was pounding still. A second failure would mean prison, and no Yusuf. "Please."

The woman shook her head. "I'm sorry. I can't do that. They're ready for you in there."

Jennifer glanced at the door. Would one of the orderlies be outside, ready to pounce if she put up a struggle? Would they sedate her, wheel her in on a trolley like they had Rita?

"Mark understands me," she said. "We've worked through this together. I don't think I should do it without him."

The woman approached her, glancing back at the door. When she was standing right in front of Jennnifer's chair, she bent over her.

"Do you know who I am?" she whispered.

Jennifer met her gaze, not betraying the emotions that whirled in her head. "Are you a prisoner?" She looked at the woman's hijab and thought of Maryam winding her uncovered hair round and round her neck whenever Mark was present.

The woman smiled. "My name is Meena Ashgar. I hoped you'd recognise me."

Jennifer sighed. "I know who you are. I know what you did to my son. I don't know how you've got the nerve to come in—"

"I loved him. I still do. I've been looking for him."

Jennifer's eyes widened, taking in this young woman, not more than a girl. She was pretty, with large, dark eyes and soft lips. She could tell what Samir had seen in her.

"I don't believe you," she hissed. "If it wasn't for you, he wouldn't have been arrested. Did you think of that, when you – when you seduced him?"

She raised a hand, then thought better of it and drew it back down to her side. Her breath was coming in short sharp bursts. She had to stay calm, for her Celebration. But there was so much she wanted to say to this girl – this woman.

Meena glanced at the door. "Shush," she said. "Please. I don't think they know the connection."

"Why on earth wouldn't they?"

Meena paled. "No-one's said anything."

Jennifer raised an eyebrow. "Of course they know. That's why I haven't seen you before."

"But you have. At Rita's celebration."

She thought back to Rita's Celebration. Rita, poor Rita, failing so spectacularly. She'd called out Meena's name as she was wheeled into the room. Had Rita known about Meena and Samir?

"Why are you here?" she growled. "Why are you pretending to be a counsellor?" She hesitated. "Did Mark send you?"

Meena frowned. "Why would he do that?"

Jennifer said nothing, calculating what this woman might know about her, what she might be expecting. Was there a possibility she was in on it with Mark, that he'd sent her as a way of removing suspicion from himself?

Or was this something bigger than what Mark was up to, something else?

She shook her head. She wasn't ready to trust this woman. She stood up, towering over Meena by almost a foot. "Where is Samir?"

Meena paled. "I don't know. I've been trying to find out myself. I'm really sorry, Mrs Hussain."

"I'm not Mrs Hussain. I'm Ms Sinclair. But how come you're a counsellor? Were you working for the government?" She took a step forward. "Did you entrap my son?"

Meena shuffled backwards. "No. Honestly. I came here as a prisoner, like you. Some months before you. They arrested me long before Samir. I went through the programme. I had my own Celebration." Her voice grew low. "I passed."

"That doesn't answer my question. You should have been released."

Meena shrugged. "They rewarded me by giving me a job. I guess I'm a nice token for them. Nice Muslim girl in a hijab. A success story."

"Why do you put up with it?"

"That's none of your business. I needed a job."

There was a knock at the door. They both jumped and glared at it.

"We can't stay here," said Meena. "I want to help you. I'll go easy on you, in the Celebration. I won't push too hard. But you'll be OK, won't you? Mark wouldn't have put you forward for a second Celebration so soon if you weren't."

Jennifer frowned. "So you'll be giving me the truth drug?"

"Yes."

Jennifer closed her eyes. Maybe Mark had already switched it. Maybe not.

"I'm not ready," she said. "If you do want to help me, then tell them to put this off."

There was another knock at the door. This time, the knuckle stayed resting against the obscured glass window, the skin pale.

"I can't do that," said Meena. She blinked. "I don't have the authority."

They stared at each other for a few moments. Jennifer tried to imagine what had gone through Samir's head when he had looked at this girl, how his feelings for her had made him risk so much. She pinched her lip, focusing on her breathing.

"Do you need me to fetch an orderly?" said Meena, her voice hardening. "If you don't cooperate we'll need to sedate you."

Jennifer's eyes widened. "No."

"Good. Let's go."

CHAPTER THIRTY-NINE

The room was empty except for Rita, Tim and about a hundred chairs arranged in semi circular rows facing the door.

Tim led Rita to a seat at the end of the front row and pushed her lightly on the chest. She sat down.

"Wait there," he said, and crossed to the door, peering out. She looked around the room, so familiar yet so alien after four days. The curtains were open. She could see heavy clouds outside plunging the world into shadow. She was at the far end of the room so the gardens were invisible, sloping downhill from the window. But she could imagine the lawns sunk into gloom, the trees looking sinister.

"Take this." Tim had returned with Roy, who was holding out a small plastic cup. In it was single white tablet. Rita stared at it, her chest hollowing out.

In his other hand was a glass of water. He gestured at her with it, slopping water onto the floor between them. "I said take it."

She reached out for the cup and played with the pill for a moment, pushing it around with the tip of her finger.

Tim sighed and moved to stand facing her at the end of the row. His knees touched her chair. He drew himself up to his full height; she resisted the urge to look up at him.

"Take it," he said. "Or we'll have to force it down you."

She screwed up her eyes and tossed the pill into her mouth, tipping her head back to swig down the water. It went down first time. Only once it was gone did she think to hide it under her tongue.

"Stick your tongue out," said Roy. She did. He pulled a pen from his lapel pocket and lifted her tongue with it. It was sharp, pushing at her skin.

"Good," he said, then wiped the pen on his sleeve and replaced it. "Now sit there and wait. You keep quiet for the whole thing, OK?"

She nodded.

The two orderlies walked away from her, pacing around the furniture that had been arranged at the front; two chairs and a low table with a tray, ready for the syringe. Rita wondered what had happened to Jennifer, to make her ready so quickly. Surely she hadn't changed so much in four days. But then she had said something about a plan.

Tim and Roy were becoming blurred shapes across the room, diminishing in intensity. She blinked a few times then felt her pulse. It had slowed. She felt a sharp pain in her chest. What had they given her?

She groaned. What would happen if she fell ill here, if she collapsed? They'd just drag her out and take her back to that cell. Or to her room? She couldn't remember.

She balled her fists and drilled them into her thighs, trying to pull herself back into wakefulness. The room had stabilised now, the blurriness equivalent to about three pints of beer. She could cope with this, as long as she didn't stand up too quickly.

"What have you given me?" she shouted. Her voice was husky.

She flinched to find Tim back at her side. How had he got here?

"I told you to be quiet." He sighed. "Alright, then."

He sat in the empty chair next to her. She looked past him at the row of chairs. It seemed to go on for ever, alternately advancing and receding. She screwed up her eyes then opened them again and the chairs stilled.

Her wrist felt cold. She looked down to see she had been handcuffed. The other cuff was attached to Tim's wrist. She tugged at it, angry. "I don't need this," she hissed, spitting on the side of his face.

He wiped it. "Can't be too sure."

She looked back to the front of the room. Roy had disappeared; she was alone with Tim. She shivered, sending a jolt through her that tore at the handcuff. It hurt.

"Stay still," Tim muttered.

The doors opened. She stared at the advancing women as they poured in, voices high and excited. Those that passed near her turned to stare. She frowned back at them, trying to focus on the faces, to find her group. But they swam in front of her eyes as if waving in an artificial breeze.

Someone cried out. "Rita!" She squinted to see a woman staring at her, her mouth wide. Rita opened her own mouth to mimic her, then clamped it shut again. Who was it? She tried to focus. The woman had long dark hair, a blur against her brown skin. It was like a balaclava framing her face.

She gasped. Maryam. The pain at her wrist intensified.

"I told you to behave."

Maryam waved to her and started to run, but she was pushed back by a blurred figure wearing a white coat; an orderly. Rita lifted her hand to wave back but Tim's grasp was too strong, she couldn't pull against it. He grabbed her hand and plunged it down into the space between them, squeezing the fingers. She lifted the other hand but it wouldn't move. She looked down to see it too was handcuffed, but this time to her chair leg.

She slumped back into her chair, resigned. Waiting for Jennifer to appear.

At least she had seen Maryam. She had a sense of deja vu but then shook it away, unable to work out where it came from. The rest of the group would be with her, they would have seen her too. They knew she was still here. Just knowing that they were aware of that gave her a sudden glow of satisfaction, almost joy. She giggled.

"Shush," hissed Tim. "You're making a fool of yourself."

She bit her lip, feeling blood spurt between her teeth. "Sorry."

The room was full now. She could sense all the women behind her, waiting. They were noisy, talking amongst themselves, letting out whoops of anticipation. She grinned; this was fun. There was a shushing sound from around the room and the voices dropped. She tried to crane her neck, wondering who had shushed them all. For a moment she was back in school assembly, listening to the teachers quieting the children. She gasped and let out her own 'shush.' Bad of her not to calm her own class too.

There was a titter behind her. Tim pulled her hand up and pushed it onto her lap, bringing her back to the present. She grunted, wishing she was back in assembly. She'd recite the oath, next time.

The double doors opened, clattering loudly. Rita grinned, expecting Jennifer and Mark. She remembered Jennifer's plan now, or thought she did. It involved Mark, didn't it? He was going to help her get out. And she was going to be here to witness it. How exciting.

But instead of Jennifer and Mark, a large yellow shape came through the door. Rita didn't need to focus to know who it was. She shrank back in her chair, thinking about what Yonda had said in her office. Had she really pulled close to her and whispered that she wanted to help her, or was Rita imagining things?

Yonda clapped her hands and Rita frowned, her ears ringing.

"Welcome everybody," she said, her voice deafening. Rita looked past Tim at the woman beyond him. She kept giving Tim sidelong glances, and had sat as far as she possibly could from him without falling off the other side of her chair. Rita snorted and did the same, shuffling along in her own chair. Then she remembered the handcuffs.

The bright yellow woman at the front was saying something indistinct. Rita hunched up her shoulders, trying to cover her ears. The words assaulted her senses. She wanted to sleep.

Finally she stopped, and the booming tones were replaced by shouts and the sound of feet pounding on the floor. Oh, this was fun! Rita could join in with this. She lifted her feet one at a time, slowly thunking them on the floor. Tim's hand clenched her thigh but she ignored it, laughing breathlessly.

She felt his breath on her ear. "Will you stop it. You're making a spectacle of yourself."

She laughed. The yellow person came closer, resolving into the recognisable form of Yonda Hughes. Rita curled up her nose.

She put her hand on Rita's shoulder. Rita shrugged it off.

"Be quiet, girl," she said, and glared at Tim. He grasped Rita's hand again and put it on his own knee.

Then Yonda receded, blurring into something more like that bird off the children's programme from the seventies; what was it, Big Bird? Yes. Big Bird. She felt her shoulders shake but kept the laugh in.

The doors opened with a thud and she turned her head sharply to look at them. Two people entered, one tall and the other short. She frowned. Weren't Mark and Jennifer the same height? She squinted, staring at the two forms. The taller one, she was sure, was Jennifer. The shoulder length mousy hair and shapeless clothes were unmistakable, and Jennifer was probably the tallest inmate here. But who was the other person?

She gasped. Meena!

She rose up in her seat, overcome by excitement. Tim yanked at the handcuffs, muttering under his breath. She felt something sharp attack her wrist, and looked down to see him withdraw a syringe.

He shifted and blurred in front of her, and then became as dark as the rest of the room.

CHAPTER FORTY

The double doors opened. Jennifer stepped inside, matching Meena's pace. Somehow it was important that she didn't trail behind.

Inside was a familiar scene; rows of women facing her, voices raised in anticipation. The floor shook with the sound of a hundred feet pounding against the wood.

Jennifer scanned the faces, looking for her group. Paula was waving at her, in between whistling through two fingers. Bel was smiling nervously, standing next to Paula. Even Sally was clapping, although there was no smile brightening her face. And Maryam was waving madly, pointing sideways.

Jennifer frowned and shrugged at her friend, a question. Maryam mouthed something Jennifer couldn't make out and carried on pointing, jabbing her finger sideways.

Jennifer looked along the front row, following Maryam's finger. At the very end of the row, between the wall and Tim the orderly, was Rita. She looked delirious. Her face was damp and her hair clung to her skin. She wore a smart blouse and trousers as if at a meeting.

Jennifer frowned.

Rita was staring at Meena. Jennifer remembered the way she'd reacted to Meena at her own Celebration. What was the connection between the two of them? And why did her appearance make Rita so agitated?

She looked back from Meena to Rita, to find Tim blocking her view, standing over Rita. He stood unevenly, one arm drawn down towards Rita. The other was at her wrist. Jennifer gasped as she saw him pocket a syringe. Rita convulsed once in her seat and then relaxed, her head falling back so that her face was towards the ceiling.

Jennifer stepped forward, desperate to help her friend. But Yonda was in her way. She opened her mouth in a grin; there was lipstick on her teeth.

"No," she said. "Don't worry about your group now. Think about yourself. Your Celebration."

Jennifer tried to push her away. With Yonda wearing her platforms, she was a little taller than Jennifer, and weighed significantly more. She didn't budge.

"I wouldn't do that. You don't want to be accused of assaulting the governor, do you?"

"What have you done to her?"

Yonda shook her head. She raised her voice to be heard. "Turn round. Go with your counsellor."

"She's not my—"

Yonda put a finger on Jennifer's lips. Jennifer was so shocked she didn't push it away.

"She is now."

Meena was waiting in one of the two chairs at the front. She smiled as Jennifer approached.

"Relax," she said. "It'll be fine."

Jennifer nodded at her.

Meena stood. "Are you ready?"

The bed was ready, clean sheets and restraints. Jennifer looked at it and swallowed, phlegm thick and rancid in her throat.

"Ready as I ever will be."

"Good." Meena offered a hand and Jennifer took it as she lifted herself onto the mattress, pulling her legs around. Meena helped ease her head back to the pillow and then gave her cheek a stroke. Jennifer flinched.

She settled into a tilted position on the bed, looking up towards the ceiling. The noise had abated now, hoots and stamping replaced by murmurs and whispers. She sniffed and tried to compose herself. She closed her eyes, imagining Yusuf smiling at her. She pictured his dimpled chin, the way his hair curled on just one side, and the soft touch of his palm when he held her hand. She wiped away a tear.

Meena leaned in. "Are you OK?"

She nodded. "Fine." She looked at her, wondering if she had thoughts about Samir, if she missed him. Or had she set him up?

Her stomach tensed as if ice had been dropped onto her skin.

Yonda was at the edge of her vision, waving for the women to calm down. "Get a move on please, Miss Ashgar," she said.

"Sorry." Meena turned to Jennifer. "Drink this."

Jennifer held out her hand. Meena handed her a glass. The liquid was clear and tasted bitter again, although less so than last time. She squeezed her eyes shut. Her children were in front of her now. Samir, so angry sometimes but sincere and loving when he wanted to be. Hassan, weeping over his cat when it died.

She had to focus now. She opened her eyes. The ceiling was clear.

"Feeling OK?" Meena 's voice was clear in her ear. She felt her stomach flutter. It was working. Meena had given her a placebo.

She bit her lip, trying to conceal her joy. "Ready," she said. How long had it been before Rita had lost consciousness? Five minutes, was it, that Mark had given her? She needed to remember, to pretend.

No. No, no, no. Her mind was becoming hazy, as if she had drunk a bottle of wine. She groaned. She was wrong. This was no placebo. It was the same humiliating experience all over again.

"Let's start with Step One," said Meena. Jennifer blinked.

"Speak up, will you," said Yonda, her voice faint. The women were quiet now.

"Sorry. Let's start with Step One," Meena all but shouted. Jennifer winced.

"Sorry," said Meena, and pulled her chair a little way back. She took a deep breath. "Please tell me what you did."

Jennifer took a deep breath. She could do this. She drilled into her memories, thinking of John, and Michael. Of Catherine, and Leonard Trask. Of the look of glee in the face of Maggie, her fellow rebel, as she had made that speech denouncing her own government.

She swallowed. Her throat was dry.

"I need water."

"Err..."

There was a flurry of movement to one side and a fresh glass was passed to her. She lifted her head to drink; it felt soft and heavy.

"Be quick," said Meena. "You'll lose consciousness in a few minutes."

She gulped it down. "I confess that I have been disloyal

to the British state," she said, allowing herself a frisson of self congratulation.

"Thank you," said Meena, her voice becoming distant. "Tell me what you did."

"I hid my son. He was suspected of belonging to a proscribed organisation."

Her mind was feeling loose, and she had that urge to tell the truth again. It was all she could do to keep control over her lips, to stick to what was expected.

"Very good," said Meena. "Don't worry," she whispered. But this was up to Jennifer now.

"So," Meena continued. "Do you accept the sovereignty of the state?"

Jennifer sent her mind back to her first induction as an MP, clamping her lips shut as she tried to remember the words. She pictured the Commons chamber, the dispatch box in front of her as she placed a hand on a bible and took the oath. Such a momentous day it had been, even though she was one of hundreds being sworn in. "I promise to serve," she said. "I swear that I will be faithful and bear allegiance to the Queen, her heirs and successors."

Meena put a hand on Jennifer's arm. "That's good. Now do you accept my support, and that of your group?"

Jennifer imagined her group watching her, holding their breath. Was Rita still unconscious?

"I accept the support of my group," she croaked.

"And your counsellor?"

She thought of Mark, dragging her into that storeroom. Insisting that he only wanted to help her. Where was he? Had Yonda known what he was doing?

"I accept the support of my counsellor," she said.

She brushed away a tear that had worked its way into her hair. Meena was smiling at her. When she saw Jennifer looking back at her, she blushed. Jennifer almost laughed at the thought of how they might have met. *Mum, meet my girlfriend.*

Then she clenched her fists. Why hadn't he told her? She wiped away another tear.

She was feeling woozy now. "Want to sleep."

"Oh," gasped Meena. "We need to hurry. Who did you harm? How will you make amends?"

"I harmed my son. Both of them."

She sensed Meena tense at the mention of Samir. "Is that all?"

Jennifer sent her mind back to the day of that vote, to the crowds of people who had stood in Parliament Square, marching in her support. They had hated Michael Stuart even more than Maggie had. "I harmed the population of this country. I put them at risk."

Meena's breathing levelled. She was on the home straight now. She spotted movement from the corner of her eye, a flash of yellow. *No,* she thought. *Don't interrupt. Don't challenge it.*

"How will you make amends?" asked Meena.

Jennifer's mind was blank. What was she going to do when she got out of here, except work to get the place closed down? Her first priority was to find Yusuf, and to work on Samir's appeal. Then to get Rita released. But that wasn't what Meena wanted to hear.

She allowed her mind to empty, feeling as if she was free falling through space. Her eyelids were a deep red; the clouds had thickened and the room must be dark. Why hadn't they turned the lights on?

She pinged her eyes open. "I will use my influence and authority as a politician to undo the wrongs I have done. To make everyone in this country safer."

She clenched her fists. She'd done it. Had she?

Meena drew a breath. Jennifer felt her eyelids grow heavier. She heard Yonda's voice but couldn't make out what she was saying.

"I need you to hurry now please, Jennifer," Meena said. She sounded worried. Jennifer tried to nod her head but it wouldn't move. She smiled. It felt like she was drifting, buoyed up by this bed.

"OK, I think you've already done Step Five, told me how you'll change. Let's move on to Step Six."

Jennifer waited.

"Can you pledge allegiance and tell me how you will spread the message please."

Again Jennifer reached back to her early days as an MP. This was easy. "I will serve my Queen and country in every way I can. I will do everything in my power to improve the lives of the citizens of this country. I will work to ensure greater security and freedom for all."

As she drifted off to sleep she spotted Meena's frown turn to a smile as Yonda whispered something in her ear.

CHAPTER FORTY-ONE

Rita woke in an unfamiliar space. She blinked a
few times, passing her mind over her body. Legs, stomach,
arms, head. Had Tim beaten her again?

The only pain was the dullness from before.

She pulled her head up to look around. She was on a
bed with just a white top sheet. She moved to check what
she was wearing, but was restrained by straps attached to
the bed, tight around her hands and ankles. She was still
wearing her blouse. Something she couldn't see was
covering her legs, and she could only assume that it was the
same pair of trousers Roy had given her earlier.

She took a few heavy breaths, trying to still her dancing
heart. Where was she? Was this the centre, or had she
already been transferred? Would she ever see her group
again? Would she ever see the outside world again?

She looked around as best she could. Beyond her feet
was a high window, at ceiling level. Outside were some
scrappy looking shrubs. Below that the wall was bare, paint
peeling around patches of damp. She was back in the
basement.

She made herself lie still, listening as best she could, twitching her nose to test for familiar smells. The faint aroma of institutional cooking meant she was near the kitchens. She closed her eyes, trying to remember the layout. If she hadn't been transferred, then she was at the same end of the house as Mark's office.

She could hear clattering from far off; the kitchens? The sound passed her door then receded. She shivered as she listened. It was cold in here.

Then she heard voices through the door. A man and a woman. The man's voice she recognised; Tim. Her heart sank. *Please don't come in*, she thought.

She closed her eyes, listening to the woman. Yonda? But no, the voice was too low, too gentle. Meena?

The door behind her opened. She twisted her head as best she could. The person entering appeared to be upside down. It *was* Meena. She felt her breathing slow.

Meena approached the bed and gave Rita a tentative smile. "Hello again."

"Where am I?"

"You're in the basement. A few doors along from my office."

She'd been wrong. Meena's office was in the centre of the building, nowhere near Mark's room. But the smell of the kitchens was real enough.

"Are you real?" she asked. 'Or am I imagining you?"

Meena shook her head. "I'm real enough. Do you want me to prove it?"

Rita nodded.

Meena smoothed her hand over Rita's hair. Rita closed her eyes, luxuriating in the gentle touch. It seemed like months since anyone had touched her like that.

"Are you going to be my counsellor now?"

"I'm sorry. I'm here to help you with your transfer." A smile. "You've got me instead of Tim. Hope that's OK?"

Rita allowed herself a laugh. "It's more than OK." Then she felt her stomach churn. "Transfer?"

A wrinkle appeared in the centre of Meena's smooth forehead. "I'm sorry for the way you've been treated." Her eyes darted up to the ceiling, where the camera would be. She blushed and grabbed Rita's hand, giving it a quick squeeze and then dropping it.

Rita thought back to her first session with Meena. If she'd gone along with her, done what she asked...

"I can change," she said. "I can prove myself. Don't let them transfer me."

"I can't do that. I'm sorry." There was a moment's silence. "Please, don't make me fetch Tim."

Rita frowned. "Why would you do that?"

A sigh. "Just, I thought you were about to... nothing. It's alright."

"Can you get Mark? If I can convince him, he'll be able to talk to the governor. He'll make sure I don't get transferred."

She held her breath. Would he? The man who had ordered her imprisonment in that stinking cell, and her repeated beatings?

"Mark isn't available right now," said Meena. "Come on, let's get you up. It's good that you're already wearing your own clothes. I've got your shoes and then you'll be all set to go to your new home."

"Home?"

Meena blushed. "Your new centre. I'm sure it'll be fine. You'll make new friends there."

"I don't want new friends. I want to see my group. I want to talk to Jennifer."

Rita gulped down tears. Meena had released the restraints, watching her warily as she did so. But she was still lying down, not having found the energy to sit up yet.

"Did Jennifer pass?" she asked.

"Sorry?"

"Her Celebration? You know what I'm talking about. You were there. I saw you." She thought of Tim, the sharp pain in her wrist. She sat up, suddenly alive.

"Tell me what happened. Tell me if she passed." Her hands were on Meena's upper arms. Meena pulled away, her eyes wide.

She let go. "Sorry. But please. Tell me."

Meena rubbed her eyes, giving Rita a sidelong glance. "I can't tell you."

"Can't, or won't?"

Meena put her hands on her hips. "A minute ago you were telling me you'd do anything to be allowed to stay. That you'd be compliant, that you'd do as we asked. Now look at you. You haven't changed a bit."

"I have. Really. I have."

"How?"

"I understand now. I understand how what I do has consequences." She sounded like a naughty child, trying to convince her, the teacher, that they'd seen the error of their ways.

She leaned forwards, twisting her fists into her thighs. Had she really learned anything? Or was she about to go through it all again? At a centre that could only be worse than this one, or else why would they be sending her?

"Get Mark," she said. "Let me do the steps with him."

"No," said Meena. She held Rita's shoes out to her.

"Why not?"

Meena closed her eyes for a split second. Something passed across her face, something different. She looked sideways, as if suddenly aware of the camera behind her. "Mark can't help you now," she muttered.

CHAPTER FORTY-TWO

JENNIFER WAS SHAKING. SHE STARED AT YONDA'S office door. Roy was beside her. It made her think of John Hunter's office in the House of Commons, the times she'd barged in there without knocking.

Roy shifted his weight and lifted his fist again, hesitating. He gave her a sheepish look then pulled his hand down to his side. Jennifer thought about knocking herself.

"Come in!"

Jennifer allowed herself a sigh of relief, quickly replaced by a tightening of her chest. She hadn't been brought to Yonda last time. Mark had told her that if she failed twice, she would be going back to prison. A tremor jolted through her.

Roy pushed the door open and Jennifer pulled her shoulders back. If Mark was in there, she would know her fate as soon as she saw his face.

Yonda sat at the grand desk, today's pink blouse garish in the sunlight from the window behind her. Opposite her, in one of the low chairs, was Meena. Meena looked up at

Jennifer and gave her a nervous smile. Jennifer felt her pulse quicken.

"Come in, Jennifer. Please, take a seat." Jennifer did as she was told. "That will be all, Roy."

Yonda closed her laptop. She rubbed the bridge of her nose, pulling her lips into unattractive shapes. *Hurry up,* thought Jennifer.

There was a movement next to her; Meena's hand reaching across the gap between their chairs. She wasn't looking at Jennifer, but had her eyes firmly on the governor.

Jennifer decided to break the silence. "I was expecting Dr Clarke to be here."

Yonda frowned. "Your counsellor is here with you," she said, nodding towards Meena, who blushed and fingered her hijab.

Yonda stood up, putting her hands on the desk. "Don't you want to know if you passed?"

Jennifer swallowed. "Of course."

Yonda scratched her nose and straightened up, licking her lips. Then her face broke into an unconvincing smile. "Congratulations," she said. "You passed."

Jennifer felt her muscles loosen. She turned to Meena, who was all but crying. Jennifer's cheeks were stiff from tension and her chest hurt.

"I passed?" she said, searching Meena's face.

"Yes. Well done."

Yonda grunted. "Personally I think Miss Ashgar made it easy on you." She scratched her nose. "I would have been more inquisitive."

Meena's blush deepened and she looked away from Jennifer towards the governor. "I only had limited time," she muttered.

"I suppose so," replied Yonda. She gave a deep sigh.

"And the rules are clear. Jennifer, you answered the questions truthfully – you had no choice – and you answered them satisfactorily. I have no choice but to let you go."

Tears were streaming down Jennifer's face. She wiped her eyes, thinking of Yusuf.

Yonda wiped her hands on her skirt and then rounded the desk, holding out a hand. Jennifer stared at it. Yonda wiggled her fingers and Jennifer realised she was supposed to shake it.

She stood up and shook the governor's hand. Her handshake was loose.

"I'm going home?" Jennifer breathed.

Yonda nodded. "I made a promise, and I have to keep it."

"A promise?" Jennifer thought of Catherine, sitting in this very office. *You have to stay here*, she had said. What had changed? What promise had Catherine extracted from Yonda?

She looked back at Meena. "Thank you," she whispered. Meena smiled and shrugged.

She turned back to Yonda, who had perched on the desk, her legs crossed at the ankles.

"I hope you will do what you promised in Celebration," she said.

Jennifer blinked. "I – I don't remember."

A smirk. "Of course not. You promised to spread the word, of course. Your love for the state."

Jennifer detected a sarcastic tone.

"And," continued Yonda, "I'd be grateful if you could tell your parliamentary colleagues – former colleagues – how fairly you've been treated here."

"Fairly?"

Yonda's eyes narrowed. "Yes."

Images swam in Jennifer's head: Bel, muttering and moaning in her chair; Rita, sedated in Celebration; Maryam, robbed of her headscarf. And of Roy and Tim dragging Rita out of the group session, screaming. She opened her mouth to speak, but then stopped herself. There would be plenty of time once she was safely out.

"Do I get to say goodbye to my group?" she asked.

"Of course not."

"Do I get to speak to my counsellor before I leave? I'd like to get Meena's advice."

"Advice? What advice could you possibly want from Meena now?"

Meena coughed. "I don't mind."

Yonda glared at her. "No. Don't be ridiculous. Roy is waiting outside. He'll take you to your room, where you'll be given your clothes and belongings. We'll call you a taxi, give you a train voucher. You'll be home in no time."

Home. Jennifer thought of her house in Birmingham. Would they have to move, after everything that had happened? She wasn't sure she could face the neighbours.

Yonda waved a hand and returned to her chair. "You're dismissed. Good luck."

CHAPTER FORTY-THREE

The swaying of the van made Rita feel sick. She braced herself against the side wall, cursing the handcuffs. She took deep breaths, willing her stomach to stay calm.

The driver looked into the rearview mirror. She was new, not someone Rita had seen in the centre. She wore a white coat, like the orderlies. The van itself had been unmarked, an anonymous white van like so many others. There had been two of them parked outside the back of the centre, this one in front.

"Keep quiet back there," she said, looking as if she didn't want to be doing this drive one little bit. "And we'll have a smooth journey."

Rita nodded and instantly regretted it. She turned to the window behind her, craning her neck. Maybe a glimpse of the outside world would quell the nausea. They were making their way up the long driveway at the front of the house, heading away. She thought of the last time she'd driven along here, the two policemen. They'd seemed such amateurs compared to the orderlies here. Never again would she complain about police brutality.

She swallowed, gulping in the stale air of the van. It smelt of diesel mixed with antifreeze. She clamped her lips together and screwed her eyes shut.

The van paused and she opened her eyes again. She felt woozy from the sedative they'd given her before leaving. *Don't throw up over your only decent clothes*, she told herself. Maybe if she closed her eyes again she could sleep.

The van started up and her eyes jolted open. The trees outside were bright green, the seasons passing without her. Had the Easter holidays arrived yet? Would her parents be told where she was, or would they wait for her habitual visit home? A tear slid down her cheek and into the corner of her mouth. She blinked, wishing she could wipe her face.

Outside the window was a high hedge, hiding the centre from the road. Did passers-by know what was in there, what they did to people? She shuddered, feeling the handcuffs tug on sore wrists.

They passed a car parked at the side of the road; a taxi with a sign on the roof. She squinted to look at the woman getting in. She was tall and blonde, wearing a suit that looked a couple of sizes too large.

Rita's eyes widened. Jennifer!

She shifted her weight and started knocking on the window with her forehead, shouting Jennifer's name.

"Quiet!" shouted the driver. Rita ignored her.

But Jennifer was oblivious. She slid into the taxi and closed the door. She had nothing with her; no bag or coat. Rita looked back as the van sped up. Sadness filled her body.

"Do that again, and I'll have to knock you out," grunted the driver. Rita nodded vigorously and slumped onto the floor.

CHAPTER FORTY-FOUR

This room was familiar. Mark had sometimes used it to interview patients, when he wanted privacy. Three doors down from his own office, it was bare and cool, never heated.

He had no idea how long he'd been in here. An orderly – a new woman, whose name he didn't know – had appeared from time to time with food. At first he'd refused it, demanding to be taken to Yonda. But the orderly had only shrugged at him, refusing to speak. After the first three untouched meals his stomach had overtaken his willpower. He'd eaten greedily, glad to fill his groaning stomach.

The light had gone off and come on again four times now. He could only hope that they were giving him the same light cycle as he would have if he were in a room with windows. He thought of Rita and the way he'd subjected her to twenty-four-hour darkness followed by twenty-four-hour light.

What had come over him, to make him so cruel?

Thoughts of Rita led him to Jennifer. He had requested her Celebration just hours before being brought here, and knew that Yonda would ensure it went ahead. Roy had found him in the medicine store, switching the drugs. It was a simple as that; no camera evidence, no eavesdropping on their one-to-ones. Just bad luck.

He'd tried pulling weight – *I've prescribed a different drug, a new one* – but it wasn't enough. He'd been summoned to Yonda's office, but instead they'd brought him here. Tim and Roy, pulling him along the corridors like a recalcitrant child.

Maybe he deserved it. But Jennifer didn't.

Without him, she was doomed. She would never get through those questions, never say what was expected if unable to lie. Maybe she was already back in prison.

The door opened. The orderly peered in. He fought the urge to shrink back, afraid of the same treatment he'd allowed them to inflict on Rita.

"Who are you?" he demanded. "Do you know who I am?"

She shrugged. "I've been told to take you upstairs."

"About bloody time. You'll be punished for this, you know. Does the governor know you're keeping me down here?"

She frowned. "It was Ms Hughes who told me to come and fetch you."

A shudder ran through him. "She wants to see me?"

"No. I'm taking you for transportation. To another centre."

CHAPTER FORTY-FIVE

THE STATION WAS EMPTY. NO-ONE THERE TO recognise her, or question why she was catching a train this late in the afternoon with no bag or coat. She gathered her arms around her and shivered. The suit she'd been wearing on the day of her arrest was thin and loose, and she had to clutch at the skirt for fear it might slip down.

She turned the train voucher over in her hand. One way to Birmingham New Street. She remembered the last time she had been here, standing on this very platform. It had been a Sunday evening, after a conference at Burcot Park. She'd caught the only train coming for hours. But that time she had been waiting for a direct train to London. She wasn't sure how she'd get to Birmingham. If her ticket would let her on the Tube.

She looked along the platform. A short, pale man looked up from his perch in the ticket booth. She shook her head. No point asking him. He would guess where she'd come from.

She heard the rumble of an approaching train and stepped forwards, lifting her face to feel the wind.

It stopped and she climbed on. She didn't look back at the station.

The carriage was quiet, just a woman and her teenage daughter at one table and a solitary man in a suit at another. He was reading a newspaper, a free sheet he would have picked up at a station. She wished she'd taken the time to look for one.

He glanced at her over it and she felt her heart skip a beat, waiting for the frown of recognition. It didn't come.

She lowered herself into a seat further along, where she could surreptitiously read the headlines of his paper. *MPs debate terror laws in wake of more unrest.* So nothing had changed.

She gazed out of the window. Countryside raced past; green fields, ramshackle farm buildings, the occasional field of cows. A church steeple flashed by in the distance. She leaned her forehead against the glass, taking it all in.

The train entered a tunnel and she pulled back. The window was cold and felt clammy. She looked at the woman and her teenager. They were each engrossed in their phones. Separate but together. She thought of Samir. Samir in his room sitting alone night after night. He'd told them he was doing homework. Yusuf had reassured her that he was being a normal teenager.

But he wasn't.

He was being radicalised.

Yusuf would know where he was, surely. Would he have been allowed to visit?

Would he have made any progress on his promise to her, as she'd been led away at the magistrates' court? Was it even possible for him to get their son back?

Now they could do it together. She had contacts still,

and she was damn well going to use them. Never mind Catherine's behaviour in Yonda's office. She owed her.

She leaned back in her seat and closed her eyes. It was almost like a normal train journey, back when she'd been an MP. Letting the miles slough off the stresses of the parliamentary week, and preparing for the weekend's work in the constituency.

She had plenty to prepare for, but she was ready. She knew how they were going to get Samir back, and she knew who she had to speak to.

She opened her eyes. The woman, the mum, was looking at her. Her daughter leaned against her, poking at her phone.

Jennifer swallowed. *Don't worry*, she told herself. Even if she was recognised, it didn't matter. It was a good thing.

The woman gave her a tentative smile. She smiled back.

It was going to be OK.

To read the opening chapters of the next two books in advance, plus a series of short stories featuring the characters from the books, join my book club at rachelmclean.-com/bookclub.

You'll get weekly emails with stories, character notes, musings on my research and lots more. And if they ever manage to work out a way to send cake by email, that may be on the cards...

Happy reading!
Rachel.

9 781999 878276